WHITE LINES

A JOHN TYLER ACTION THRILLER (#2)

TOM FOWLER

Cover design by 100 Covers.

Editing by Chase Nottingham.

Published by Widening Gyre Media.

1

John Tyler walked outside to find his daughter Lexi unplugging the Tesla Model X from the charger. After they came into dubious possession of the vehicle following its prior owner's well-deserved demise, Tyler paid for the charging port installation. Lexi promised to pay him back when she got a job. She now drove the electric vehicle more often than the Honda Accord coupe she and Tyler spent weeks restoring. "Where are you off to?"

"Picking up the new laptop for school," she said.

Tyler remembered their conversation about it. Lexi bemoaned her computer being all of three years old—apparently ancient in the technology kingdom—and talked Tyler into buying her a new one even though she was still in the middle of her first college semester. She used terms like solid state drive and graphics card which he'd heard before but didn't really understand, so he simply nodded and let her pick the model she wanted within a set budget. "I hope this one lasts for a while."

"I'm sure it will." She sighed. "I need to choose my classes when I get back."

"You're going to commute again?" Tyler said. Lexi bobbed her head. "You'll be tired of me soon."

Lexi grinned. "I've been tired of you since I moved in, Dad." He chuckled. "Love you, old man."

"Yeah, yeah."

Lexi left in the silent Tesla. She returned about an hour later and carried the laptop box up to her room. While she unpacked everything, Tyler ordered a pizza for lunch. It arrived before Lexi walked back downstairs. She smiled when she saw it on the counter. After snagging a couple slices, Lexi joined her dad in the living room.

"New computer's great," she said. "Thanks."

"Sure. Glad you like it."

She munched on a few bites before talking again. "At least I'll be on campus this semester. You won't get tired of me as quickly."

Tyler smiled. "Probably not more than once a day." Lexi stuck her tongue out at him. "I sometimes wish I could work from home."

"I'm not sure the neighbors would want people dropping off their old cars in the driveway," Lexi said.

"Probably not." Work at Smitty's Classic Car Repair had been slow, but Tyler maintained his regular hours. After recovering from a bullet wound to his arm—and dealing with Smitty's occasional barbs of how he was "milking it"—Tyler had been back to full duty for about a month.

"Speaking of work, don't you need to go in?"

Tyler glanced at his watch. "I guess I should."

"You all right, Dad?"

"Sure." Tyler grew a little bored of the job, but he didn't need to tell Lexi. After a long career in the army and private security, he finally got to work as a classic car mechanic a few months ago. Maybe the years he'd spent building up the job made the reality bland by comparison. For every gearhead who knew their vehicle inside and out, two idiots who bought a car because it looked or sounded cool sauntered in. Tyler figured dealing with stupid people was part of any job where the public could walk through your door.

He climbed the stairs, changed into work clothes, and came back to the first floor. Lexi had eaten another piece of pizza while he was gone. Tyler grabbed one, put it on a napkin, and pointed at the remainder as he left. "Can you put it away when you're done?" Lexi's reply around a mouthful of food sounded affirmative.

In the driveway, Tyler fired up his vintage Oldsmobile 442. The V8 rumbled as he pressed the accelerator. Tyler set his pizza on the passenger's seat, backed out onto the street, and headed to the shop.

TYLER TOOK the Mustang for a test drive.

It was a mid-'eighties GT with the five-liter V8. Great engine, wrong timeframe. Today's pony cars made a lot of power. Thirty-odd years ago, however, automakers were still used to making puny motors thanks to the oil crisis of the 'seventies and a focus on fuel economy. No one who bought a Mustang GT gave a whit about miles per gallon. The V8 sounded loud, and it growled in response to throttle input, but it lacked the punch it needed.

Still, Tyler could make do. He'd spent yesterday afternoon and this morning replacing the clutch. Judging by the mileage, it was probably the car's third—unless the owner drove like an asshole. Plenty of people who could barely handle two pedals insisted on a third for the street cachet, and they gave real enthusiasts a bad name. The wear and tear on Tyler's knees compelled him to drive an automatic every day, but he still relished a good manual when the opportunity presented itself.

Traffic near the shop was unusually light, which allowed him to drive faster than normal. He got to row through the gears and see how the clutch responded to heel-toe downshifts. Everything operated as he expected. After going a little more than a mile up Belair Road, he turned around in a parking lot and headed back to the shop.

The Mustang's owner arrived a short while later. Tyler went over everything with him and handed him the keys after he paid Smitty. "Good work," the boss said when the man drove away. Smitty was probably about sixty, giving him ten years on Tyler. His graying hair and lined face added some character to his appearance. He wiped a hand on his persistently dirty shirt.

"It was a clutch job," Tyler said. "Not exactly splitting the atom."

"Fine. You suck. Now, go be a lousy mechanic on the next car."

Tyler grinned and surveyed the lot to see what other work awaited. The shop had gotten busy over the last couple months, about half of which he spent with his arm in a cast or a sling, relegating him to simple jobs he could do with only his right hand. Smitty's son Jake, who also worked at the garage part-time, picked up some slack, but he returned to an erratic schedule once Tyler got off light duty. Ever since, he'd pulled more hours than either he or Smitty anticipated.

Four cars waited. The phone rang, and Smitty answered it while Tyler checked the book to see what each needed. A few hours remained on his shift, and he preferred to knock out a job in its entirety rather than come back and finish it another day. He picked a thirty-year-old Jeep in desperate need of new brakes and eased it into an available bay.

Through the window into the office, Tyler could see Smitty remained on the phone. He had a knack for dealing with the public—something Tyler lacked—so he answered calls whenever he could. He rarely stayed on the line long, however. After Tyler lifted the Jeep to check out the work he would need to do, Smitty still held the receiver to his ear.

A few minutes later, Tyler finished taking the front two tires off. Smitty walked into the service area. "Who was on the phone?" Tyler asked.

Smitty waved a hand. "Nobody."

Tyler didn't push it. He didn't want to think anything untoward might be happening. However, Smitty neglected to mention his son Jake was in trouble when Tyler started, though the two enforcers who knocked the boss around made it obvious. Tyler liked working here, but Smitty didn't enjoy the best reputation for transparency. Whoever it was, he didn't seem troubled by the conversation. Smitty steered an old Trans Am into the bay and got to work beside his hired man.

TYLER AND SMITTY finished their jobs around the same time. "Coffee?" the boss asked.

"I'll never say no to a cup."

They walked back into the office. Smitty dumped whatever inky sludge remained in the pot and brewed a fresh one. The aroma spread, and Tyler closed his eyes to inhale it. It smelled far better than the motor oil and linoleum scents which usually dominated the shop. When the machine finished, Smitty poured a cup for himself and Tyler. Both men took their coffee black, though an array of powdered sweeteners and creamers made many of the customers happy.

A few minutes later, Tyler heard an unfamiliar engine pull into the lot. A pair of headlights sat low. Probably a sports car. They winked out as the motor cut off. A moment later, the shop door swung open, and a beautiful redhead walked in. Her green eyes took in the two men drinking java on the job. She wore tight jeans, a T-shirt with a low enough neckline to show some terrific cleavage, and a denim jacket. Tyler stepped to the counter, and he hoped the young woman didn't notice Smitty gaping at her. "Can we help you?"

"I hope so," she said in a voice carrying a faint French accent. "I recently got a car, and I'd like to make sure it's going to keep running. It's pretty old." She chuckled. "Older than I am."

"What year?"

"Ninety-seven."

"A little newer than we normally see around here," Tyler said. "What make and model?"

"A Porsche Boxster."

"Damn German cars," Smitty said. "More trouble than they're worth."

"He's probably never driven one," Tyler said to the potential customer, who smiled.

"Nope. American all the way."

"Have you driven a German auto?" the woman asked Tyler.

"Sure. Even spent a couple days behind the wheel of a Nine-eleven." Her eyes widened. Tyler shrugged. "It was a while ago. I was stationed in Stuttgart. The place is lousy with Porsches."

"Perhaps you could work on my car, then?"

Smitty looked like he'd spent the afternoon sucking a lemon, but Tyler nodded. "I'm not sure we're the best place for something like this, but we can at least see what's going on. Why don't you drive it around? If we can't fix it, I'll tell you."

The young woman smiled again. "Thank you." She walked back to her car, and both Smitty and Tyler watched her leave.

Once the door closed behind her, Smitty said, "You ever work on a Porsche before?"

"No."

"You know the engine ain't in the front, right?"

Tyler rolled his eyes. "Yes. In fact, for the Boxster, it's in the middle."

"You think we can fix this thing?"

"We won't know until we look at it. The car could be in good shape."

"The girl driving it certainly is," Smitty said with a grin.

"I wasn't sure you noticed."

"I might be old, but I ain't dead." The Boxster's headlights shone through the long window to the service bays. "Hell, we might as well take a look." Smitty clapped Tyler on the shoulder. "What's the worst that can happen?"

The new laptop worked great. Lexi snagged a killer sale and got a lot of computing bang for her buck. Her dad's buck, really. She'd chosen classes for the next semester, and her schedule would be ready in a few days. One of these times, she would need to pick a major. Her mother's more interesting life choices steered Lexi toward criminal justice. She was still in her first term, though. Plenty of time for that later. For now, she took as many required classes as she could.

She was three pages into writing a paper for American History 101 when she took a break. A granola bar and fresh bottle of water later, Lexi sat back down at her desk. She popped over to her browser and noticed a new message in her Gmail inbox. Her eyes narrowed when she read the sender's ID. *Maryland State Correctional System.*

"Great," she said to her empty bedroom. Lexi leaned back in her chair and blew out a deep breath. Since her mother's imprisonment over a year ago, they'd traded a couple of quick, terse emails, but silence prevailed for the last nine months. Lexi was thirteen when she realized her mother swindled people. Rachel spent the next four years lying about it until her crimes caught up with her. Lexi never lived with her dad before then, but she was beyond ready to get out of her mother's house.

So why the message now? What did Rachel want? What was her angle? She always had an angle. Always a trick to play. These thoughts sounded like her father's. He was honest with Lexi about who her mother was and what she did, though he never tried to color her opinion. Maybe he didn't need to. Living with a responsible person who cared about other people did it anyway.

Lexi rolled her eyes and opened the message.

ALEXIS,

I know we haven't talked in months. It's my fault. Adjusting to life here has been harder than I thought.

While I hoped you would write or visit me, I don't know if I was in a good place. Things are better now. I have a new cellmate, and I'm in a regular group therapy session.

I haven't seen you since the night I got hauled away. It would be great if you could come and visit me. Other people here see their children and loved ones pretty regularly. You have to call ahead or go online, but I can have visitors any weekday. I know you're in college now—at least, I hope you are—but if you could find an hour to stop by, it would be great to see you.

LOVE,
    Mom

LEXI FROWNED at the email when she finished it. "Way to go, Mom. Accept the blame, then hit me with a couple guilt trips and take a subtle shot at Dad." She shook her head. It made her realize how much she'd wanted to leave her mom's house when she lived there. Lexi considered going across the country for college. Then, she went to live with her dad and stayed local. Stability was great, and she never before realized how much she craved it.

"Why now?" she whispered. Lexi glanced at her phone. She'd wasted enough time on her mother's message. Lexi closed the Gmail tab and went back to her assignment.

~

TYLER NAVIGATED the Boxster onto the lift. The car was a plain shade of gray, and its two-seat interior was solid black. It looked like an older version of the 911 he drove while in Germany. Tyler remembered people at the time being upset at the Boxster and 911 sharing parts. Now, every automaker employed the practice up and down their lineups.

He walked under the chassis once it sat about six feet off the bay floor. Rust pockmarked the exhaust pipes. If they were original, they'd been in service for almost a quarter century. Some wear and tear would be expected. Considering the age of the vehicle—and its unknown maintenance history—Tyler thought the undercarriage was in good shape. The young woman stepped under the vehicle, too. "How does it look?"

"Pretty good, Miss . . .?"

"Alice," she said. "Alice Simard." She extended her hand, and Tyler shook it.

"John Tyler. I go by Tyler."

"You think it looks all right, Mister Tyler?"

"For its age, sure," he said. Smitty joined them, standing under the front wheels. "After twenty-four years, you're bound to need some work. Do you have the maintenance history?"

Alice shook her head, and her fiery ponytail wagged behind her. "No. I just got it recently. I don't know much about what happened before."

"You know much about these cars in particular?" Smitty said.

"A little," Alice said.

"How many miles?"

"A hundred and twenty thousand."

"We'll need to get parts," Smitty said, scratching the top of his head. "Ain't really ordered parts for a German car before. We get a lot of American models in here."

"I'm sure we can find what it needs," Tyler added. "You should know foreign cars can be expensive to maintain, though."

"I understand," Alice said.

"We'll definitely need to replace the exhaust. Should be pretty easy to get. How's she run?"

"Good. Sounds normal."

Tyler nodded. "All right. What about the clutch?"

"Feels a little . . ." Alice moved her hand in a so-so motion. ". . . off. Not bad. I can drive it fine, but the car probably needs a new one. Do you know about the IMS bearing?" Tyler shook his head. "It's an issue on Porsches from this period. I don't know if it's been replaced or not. They recommend doing it along with the clutch. Can you see?"

"We'll figure it out," Tyler said. Smitty frowned but didn't say anything. "We'll need to look her over and see what we can do. If you want to bring it back, it's fine."

"It's all right," Alice said. "I can get a ride home." She and the boss adjourned to the office. Tyler followed a moment later after walking around the Boxster's underside one more time. Smitty signed an estimate, tore off the bottom copy, and handed it to the young woman, who took it with a warm smile. "Thank you."

She walked back out through the door. "I hope we can get the parts and do all the work," Smitty said as Tyler strode up beside him. "I'd hate to disappoint your new girlfriend."

Tyler rolled his eyes. "We don't get a lot of enthusiasts who happen to be women in here."

"Even fewer who look like her."

"True," Tyler said.

"You more in love with her or the car?"

Tyler grinned. "The car." He looked at his watch. "I'm going to get some lunch. Want anything?"

The owner shook his head. "I'll look this thing over while you're gone. If we can get the parts and do the work, this is your project."

"Only fair," Tyler said. "I don't want another man working on my new girlfriend's car."

~

TYLER GAVE his hands a thorough washing and changed his shirt before venturing out. The shop stood a short distance across the county line from the city of Baltimore, and restaurant options were plentiful in both directions. Tyler went into the city last time, so today, he made a right out of the parking lot. An Asian fusion place greeted him at the top of the hill, but he kept going and turned into the McDonald's lot, parked the 442, and walked inside.

Despite arriving an hour after the lunch rush commonly ended, Tyler found the place moderately crowded. He ordered his meal, picked it up, and surveyed the tables. There were entrance doors on either side of the restaurant. A kids' playhouse —currently empty—took up the rear. He sat at a spot around the middle which allowed him to keep both doors in view and unwrapped the first of his two Quarter Pounders before taking a large bite.

Tyler appreciated McDonald's. It was consistent. He'd been to many in this country and several overseas. The meals were always about the same in terms of quality. Maybe they wouldn't pack a display case with awards, but the food was solid and predictable. He liked things he could rely on. A couple bites later, the door on Tyler's left swung open.

Alice Simard walked in. She glanced to her right, saw Tyler, and smiled. So did he. Alice ordered her meal and carried a tray toward the table. "Mister Tyler. Do you mind if I join you?"

Tyler gestured toward the available chair. "Help yourself."

"Thank you." She slid onto the seat. Her tray held a grilled chicken sandwich, a smaller box of fries than Tyler got, and a cup of what looked like iced tea—a much healthier lunch. "I'm glad you'll be able to work on my car."

"As long as we can get the parts," Tyler said.

"You seem more eager to work on my car than your boss is."

"You remind me of someone I knew in the army. She was a young enlisted soldier who was big into cars. Even got to drive a few Porsches when we were both in Germany."

"Did you work with her?" Alice said.

Tyler waffled his hand. "Sort of. She took a class I did on Jeep repairs. Wanted to apply what she learned to her own cars someday."

"Did she?"

"I don't know," Tyler said. "We lost touch. It was years before social media." He didn't tell Alice the truth. PFC Kate O'Shea died from a roadside IED before she got the chance to use anything Tyler taught her. He lapsed into silence at the memory.

She inclined her head over Tyler's shoulder. "Do you drive the green car out there?"

Tyler nodded. "Loud and American. Kind of like me."

Alice grinned. She looked very pretty when she was happy. "What do you call them? Muscle cars?"

"Yes. There are cars today with more power, but the driving experience isn't the same."

"It is how I feel about my car, too." She took a delicate bite of her sandwich. "What year is yours?"

"'Seventy-two," Tyler said. "It's almost as old as I am."

"You wear your years as well as the car."

"Thanks." Tyler knew the 442 looked better than he did, but he wouldn't turn down the compliment.

"Mine is the second year Porsche made the car. I could have gotten a later model, but I liked the idea of driving one of the early ones . . . before they made some improvements."

Tyler polished off the remainder of his first burger. "Sounds like you wanted it specifically."

"I wanted a good first-generation Boxster. They came out with the S a few years later, but they were pricier. I guess it costs more for the extra power."

"Always does," Tyler said.

"My boyfriend bought the car," Alice said. "He tried to tell me it was for him, but I knew he got it for me."

"Mighty nice of him."

"It was." Tyler noticed she didn't smile. "He's an immigrant, too . . . from Mexico. We both came to the US around the same time. We have a shared experience."

Tyler thought they probably walked very different roads as immigrants, but he didn't want to ruin Alice's mood. "You mentioned getting a ride home from here. You live far away?"

"Not too far. Near Bel Air."

He knew the area. Bel Air served as the county seat of Harford County, the next one north in Maryland. It extended all the way to Pennsylvania at its northern tip. Many cities were pockets of strip malls and expensive houses nestled amid acres of farmland. Depending on where exactly Alice lived, she could have driven at least a half-hour to get here. "I'm sure there must have been a closer shop. Isn't there some kind of German specialty place up there?"

She nodded. "In Aberdeen. My boyfriend has a mechanic he uses a few miles from here. I don't think he does great work, though, so I looked for a new place. Your boss's shop is well reviewed."

It seemed a little odd. Aberdeen was closer to Bel Air than Overlea. It had been years since Tyler was on the proving ground up there, but he remembered it being a pretty straight shot. A dedicated German repair center would be a much more logical place to take a twenty-four-year-old Porsche than a general shop like Smitty's. "Are you all right, Mister Tyler?"

"Fine." He offered a small, automatic grin to cover his usual skeptical nature. "Have you always been into cars?"

Now, Alice beamed. "Since I was a girl in Quebec. My father had a Mustang . . . one of the 'eighties models. I could drive a clutch by the time I was eight. My dad was always under the hood trying to get more power out of it. I don't know how to do much of that, but I've always enjoyed driving sporty autos."

"Me, too," Tyler said. They chatted about cars for a while longer. Tyler finished his lunch, and Alice eventually did, too. He offered her a lift back to the shop, but she said she'd wait at the McDonald's for a ride. She didn't seem happy about it. "You sure?"

Alice looked at her phone. "I guess it doesn't matter. Sure, I'll ride back with you."

Tyler held the door for her as they walked outside. A feeling nagged at him. Something struck him as unusual about Alice bringing the Boxster here. Was she angry at her boyfriend? She never smiled when talking about him, even when mentioning he bought her a car. It seemed like an odd situation. Tyler held up his keys as they approached the 442. "Want to drive?"

A bright smile took over Alice's face. "Very much, yes." Tyler climbed into the passenger's seat. She backed the car out of the spot and pulled onto Belair Road with screeching tires and a determined grin.

3

Throttle open, the 442's classic V8 growled. The car surged down Belair Road at speeds well above the suggestions on road signs. "I like this engine," Alice said as she blew through a yellow light.

"Having eight cylinders helps," Tyler said. "There's no replacement for displacement."

"You don't like turbos?"

Tyler spread his hands. "I like the immediate shove, but it's not predictable. Give me a big engine like this. Good linear power."

Alice kept going past Smitty's shop. Tyler made no effort to get her to turn in. Let her enjoy a turn behind the wheel of a true classic. Most people never got to pilot a car like this. Modern vehicles needed to comply with standards from many countries. Manufacturers downsized engines and bolted on turbochargers to meet fuel and emissions standards. Tyler liked some autos made today, but he found many of them boring. Too few cylinders, too little excitement, too much front-wheel drive.

"I only wish it didn't have an automatic." Alice glanced sidelong at Tyler as she spoke.

"Me, too," he said. "Too much wear and tear on my legs to drive a stick every day. I get to take them for a spin when they turn up for service, though."

"Will you test drive my Boxster once you finish it?"

"Sure." He grinned. "I'll even open her up an extra ten percent just for you."

At a red light, Alice swung around and headed back toward Overlea. "Thanks for letting me drive."

"No problem." Tyler realized no one else had been behind the wheel since he bought the car and made it roadworthy again. It was a little over five years. He'd done all the work himself, so there was never a need for any mechanic to take the 442 for a spin. Smitty and Son appeared at the bottom of a hill. Alice piloted the large coupe onto the lot, stopping near the door. Tyler noticed Smitty staring at them and knew he'd get an earful about this little joyride later.

Tyler held the door for Alice as they walked into the shop. Smitty tapped on the keyboard. "I think we'll be able to get all the parts we need," he said. "They can't all get here at once, though. You want to bring the car back in a day or two?"

"No need to do that," Alice said. "You can keep it here. I have a ride coming."

"All right. We'll let you know when she's ready."

Alice grinned. "Thank you." She waved at Tyler, and he swore the wattage on her smile increased. "I like your wheels, Mister Tyler."

"Thanks," he said. "I think we both have good taste."

She nodded her concurrence and walked back out. "Jesus Christ," Smitty said. "Tell me she's not your new girlfriend, now."

"Way too young for me. She just wanted to drive the 442. Can you blame her?"

"Guess not." Smitty eyed the young woman. "With an ass like hers, I can't blame you, either."

"She's a nice girl," Tyler said.

"I'm sure she is. Being a knockout don't hurt, though."

"It never has."

Another car pulled up. A Honda Civic at least a decade old. It sported a clearly modified exhaust—both by looks and sound—and a ridiculous wing on the back. Tinted windows prevented Tyler from seeing inside. Alice got into it, and it drove away.

THE CIVIC DROVE AWAY, and Alice walked up the flagstoned path to the front door. The grass and bushes as usual were well manicured, though the approach of winter meant they no longer needed regular maintenance. Still, living with a boyfriend who happened to be the community landscaper had its perks. Alice unlocked the door and entered the house.

It was the smallest in the posh community, but it also happened to be the nicest place she'd ever lived. The tiled foyer yielded to a living room covered in lush carpet. Rodolfo sat on the couch and stared at her. Alice smiled. He didn't. She frowned as his glare remained in place. "What's going on?"

"Where's the Boxster?" he said.

"We knew it needed work when we bought it."

"You mean when *I* bought it."

Alice noticed four beer bottles on the coffee table. The TV was off. By now, Rodolfo usually held a Playstation controller. Today, it looked like he'd started early on the booze. "Fine . . . when you bought it. I took it somewhere to get it looked at."

"You know we have a guy we can take the cars to," he said.

"I don't like him." She crossed her arms. "He's always staring at me. It's creepy."

"Where did you take it?"

"A place near Perry Hall. It's well-reviewed."

Rodolfo stood. As he stepped closer, Alice could see the effects of the alcohol in his eyes. He wasn't slurring his words yet, but another bottle would guarantee it. She hated when he drank too much. The saving grace was he rarely did. Usually only when his cousin hassled him about business. He stopped a foot away, close enough for her to smell the beer on his breath. "You should have talked to me first."

"It's my car," Alice said.

"I bought it for you," Rodolfo said. He backhanded her across the face. Alice's head snapped to the side, and she stumbled but stayed on her feet. "Never forget. I bought it for you."

She rubbed her stinging cheek. "How can I forget when you remind me all the time?" He'd only hit her once before, and in the aftermath, he swore he'd never do it again. Maybe she could calm him down by changing the subject. Something about the Boxster clearly had him worked up. "I got to see a really cool classic car today." She stopped before mentioning her turn behind the wheel. It would do nothing to improve her boyfriend's mood.

Rodolfo narrowed his eyes. "I don't care. You know who I bought the Porsche from?" She shook her head. "My cousin put me onto him. He knew I was looking."

So much for changing the subject. Alice blew out a breath and resigned herself to finishing the conversation. She wouldn't tolerate him hitting her again, though. "And?"

"There was product in it." When she didn't say anything, he continued. "We got it all out first, as far as I know. This is why we take cars to the same place all the time. They don't ask any questions if they find a baggy or a little residue." He moved into her space again, and she took an involuntary step back. "I doubt your shop is so . . . discreet."

"I'm sure they won't find anything," she said. If whoever unloaded it did his job right, that would be the case.

"They won't. I'm going to get the car back. Tell me where you took it."

"It's a shop called Smitty's. They're very nice. I'm sure they don't want any trouble."

"You should've thought about it this morning." Rodolfo took a stride forward and punched Alice in the stomach. All the breath left her body, and she folded in half. Her midsection blazed with pain. Before she could draw in more oxygen, Rodolfo decked her in the face, and she spiraled to the floor.

Mercifully, he walked out of the room. Alice would leave him. The hell with the car. No vehicle was worth this. Ever since Rodolfo got tangled up with his cousin in this damned community, he'd changed. He stopped being a landscaper and tried to moonlight as some kind of commando. It didn't suit him, but she never wanted to hear it. Alice made it back to all fours when Rodolfo strode back into the room. She put a hand up. "Please."

To her horror, he held an aluminum baseball bat. "You should have told me first," he said as his arms went back.

RODOLFO STARED at the body of Alice. He'd beaten her into unconsciousness quickly, and then added a few more blows to be sure. Once the reality of the situation set in, her eyes looked confused and hurt. She didn't understand. She never understood. Alice saw him as the sweet boy she fell in love with two years ago. Rodolfo was a man now. He'd still ply his trade as a landscaper, but the real money came in working for his cousin.

He needed to call Héctor and let him know what happened. The argument and beating hadn't been too loud. Houses here were far enough apart for privacy. No one in the community would have heard it. They might wonder what happened to Alice. Everyone knew her. Especially the men. Rodolfo simmered at the thought. They all were eager to smile and wave at the pretty young redhead. In turn, she sported low-cut tops and smiled freely. Did the men at this repair shop agree to fix the car because of her looks?

No matter. He would get the Boxster back.

Rodolfo dialed his cousin, who picked up on the fourth ring. "I have a problem, Héctor."

A long sigh was the only response for a while. Then, Héctor said, "Tell me what happened."

"Alice. She's dead."

"What?"

"I had to," Rodolfo said. "She took the Porsche to some shop to get it looked at."

"You didn't tell her it came with a full shipment of product in it?" Héctor asked. The edge to his voice could cut glass.

"I didn't think I needed to. We just argued about it. She put the whole operation at risk." Héctor remained silent. "I did what I had to."

"And what do you want from me?"

"We need to clean this up," Rodolfo said.

"We? Did I murder your girlfriend?"

"No, but—"

"Listen, cousin. You're young. Brash. You do things without thinking. I've told you before it would hold you back, haven't I?"

"Yes," Rodolfo said in a small voice.

"I'll find someone to take care of the mess," Héctor said. "You can't do this again, though. I know we're in an ugly business, but we have to keep it out of our houses. Alice didn't need to die."

"I'm sorry, Héctor."

"Don't be sorry. Be better." He paused. "And get the goddamn Porsche back."

Rodolfo was about to answer when the line went dead.

4

T yler put the finishing touches on dinner. He opened the oven door long enough to peek at the baked potatoes. The skins looked crisp thanks to the olive oil and salt Tyler applied before putting them in. He'd never been enthusiastic about cooking, but most of the guys he served with held similar views, so Tyler learned how to improve in the kitchen. When he lived alone, he didn't put much effort in, but he enjoyed cooking for Lexi.

His daughter, of course, considered herself a foodie. It seemed like a requirement among her generation. She took frequent pictures of her meals—"for the 'gram," as Tyler soon learned— no matter who cooked them. With the help of Google, he learned on his own she meant Instagram. Asking her would have proven too embarrassing.

The steaks finished searing in the cast-iron skillet. Tyler turned the heat off and moved the pan to an unused burner. He put a slab of meat, a potato, and a few asparagus spears on Lexi's plate and then texted her with the news. He considered sending her a photo, but she'd just take her own. Lexi's footsteps raced down the stairs a moment later, and she bounded into the kitchen with a wide smile on her face. "It smells really good, Dad. Thanks for cooking."

"Sure thing, kiddo. I'll leave you to ruin your potato."

She stuck her tongue out at him. Tyler only added butter, salt, and pepper to his spuds. By contrast, Lexi used them as a vessel for a slew of toppings. She added sour cream, bacon bits, diced green onions, and two different kinds of cheese. Tyler set all she needed on the counter. It took him far less time to prepare his, but he waited for her at the kitchen table. He cut into his steak when she sat across from him. A perfect medium.

Before she could eat, Lexi had to snap a picture of her dinner. She held the camera above her plate and took a few different photos. "I'll pick the best one after I eat," she said.

"Don't let me get in the way of your social media popularity."

"You should try it sometime."

"I have enough friends," Tyler said, "and I've actually met them."

They both dug into their steaks. Lexi normally talked more at dinner, especially when she liked what Tyler cooked. He was about two-thirds through his New York Strip when he raised the subject with her. "You're quiet."

"Just enjoying dinner," Lexi said. Her grin looked automatic. Tyler stared at her. "What?"

"Is something wrong?" he asked.

Lexi shook her head. "Can't a girl enjoy a steak her father cooked?"

"Sure. It's merely unusual when the girl hasn't said a couple hundred words by the time her father takes his third bite."

Lexi's fork rattled off the plate as she set it down. She stared across the table at Tyler. He didn't say anything. He learned years ago Lexi was far too headstrong to be coaxed. She'd talk on her own if given the space. It fit in with Tyler's general philosophy on the merits of being silent. "Fine," she said after a moment. "I heard from Mom today."

Tyler stopped chewing for a few seconds. When he finished the bite, he said, "She called you?"

"No." Lexi shook her head, and her auburn ponytail wagged back and forth. "Email."

"From prison?"

"You making sure she's still in?"

"What if I am?"

"Yes, Dad. From prison."

"What did she want?"

"According to her email, to catch up," Lexi said. "It seemed more like a guilt trip to me. 'Why haven't you come to see me?'" She affected a catty voice. "'I hope you're in college.' Who does she think she is? Like you'd let me just skip out on it?"

"She probably didn't want me to lead you toward the military," Tyler said. "If she knew you better of course, she'd realize there's nothing to worry about there."

Lexi speared a piece of steak and chewed it angrily. "It's been months since she reached out. Why now?"

"I gave up trying to figure out why your mother does anything years ago."

"She blamed you for leaving us for a long time."

"I know," Tyler said. "She's never enjoyed a close relationship with the facts."

"What should I do?" Lexi asked.

"You're an adult. Make your own decision."

"You won't be mad if I see her?"

"Of course not," Tyler said. "I know she's a . . . difficult person, and it's not easy to see her now. She's still your mother. I'd never be mad at you for wanting to maintain a relationship with her."

Lexi nodded slowly. Tyler figured she knew his answer already and simply wanted the reassurance of him saying it out loud. He was happy to provide it. The timing struck him as unusual, though. Lexi was wise to wonder why now. Rachel had been in jail over a year and still had quite a while to go on her sentence. Lexi could be married with kids of her own by the time her mother breathed outside air again. What did she want?

Whatever it was, Tyler trusted his daughter to see through it. She'd wised up a lot where her mom was concerned even before the woman went to jail. This would be yet another lesson.

SMITTY ARRIVED at his shop not long after sunrise. It was a Sunday, so he wanted to get in early and be done in time to drive home and catch most of the Ravens game. He unlocked the door, turned the alarm off, and set a half-pot of coffee to brew. All three bays were full. He tried to keep as few cars outside as possible, both to minimize exposure to the elements and chances for theft.

An old Mustang, an Oldsmobile Starfire, and the Boxster occupied the slots. Two boring early-'eighties commuter cars sat in the lot. No one would want to steal one of them. Smitty was surprised the owners cared enough to keep the jalopies on the road. The fuel-sipping Chevette would not mark a high point in the history of Chevrolet.

Business had picked up over the last few months, which was good. Smitty considered himself a mechanic first and foremost, so he liked putting cars on the lifts and getting his hands dirty. Both his son Jake and Tyler worked part-time and rarely together, so Smitty never lacked for something to do. It forced the management aspects of the job to the weekends, however. He always stayed after the shop's limited Saturday hours, and trips in on Sunday became more frequent.

Still, he wouldn't complain. It beat retirement, even though he wouldn't even be eligible to collect all the benefits for a few more years. Jake didn't share Smitty's passion for cars, but the two fared well together, and it provided an easy excuse to see his son. Tyler made a big difference since Smitty hired him several months ago. In addition to rescuing Jake from some rogue soldiers he'd served with, the man possessed a strong work ethic. Even during his stint on light duty, Tyler did more than Smitty thought he would.

One of the things Tyler insisted on was a better security system. The shop took a beating from the men looking for Jake, and Smitty agreed he didn't want to see a repeat of it. Cameras now covered the full exterior of the building, its parking lot, and the street running alongside it. A fancy new monitor sat on Smitty's desk, and he could check any of the feeds whenever he wanted. Video footage got sent to the cloud for backup. It sounded like a good thing. Tyler nodded like he understood the term, so Smitty had followed suit. Between the pair of them, maybe they could figure it out one day.

Armed with a fresh cup of steaming java, he dove into some paperwork. The parade of bills—both inbound and outbound—never stopped. One of these years, he would need to hire a part-time person to cover the accounts payable and receivable. Neither Jake nor Tyler had a head for this stuff, so Smitty kept doing it. He never seemed to get any better at it, but no one from the state told him to close his doors, so he must have done all right.

A couple hours—and a second cup of coffee—into his Sunday work, a car drove onto the lot. Smitty changed the camera to one which would show it better. His old system displayed grainy images. This new one clearly showed a black Subaru WRX with gold aftermarket wheels and an obnoxious spoiler the manufacturer would never install. Smitty used the zoom—another new feature—to see two Latino men sitting in the front seats.

The sedan idled but sat in place. The men made no move to get out. Were they with the woman who dropped off the Porsche? Did they expect anyone to be working on Sunday? Maybe they were just casing the place. Smitty opened his desk drawer and took out the gun Tyler gave him. The man's hyper-vigilance rubbed off. Smitty held the pistol in his lap as he watched the monitor. All remained quiet except for the WRX's idle.

Five minutes passed. Ten. The two men inside chatted with one another, but the system didn't record audio. If they spoke Spanish, Smitty wouldn't have understood much, anyway. Fifteen minutes. The semiautomatic felt heavy resting on Smitty's legs. Then, the WRX's engine barked, and the car sped away. He kept watching the monitor, but it never returned.

When the Subaru had been gone a half-hour, Smitty finally put the gun away.

HÉCTOR ESPINOZA OPENED his door and let Rodolfo enter. The younger man barged in and plopped down in a living room chair. Héctor closed the door, sighed, and followed his cousin. "Something wrong? Did the cleaner not do a good job?"

"What? No . . . it's fine."

Not for the first time, Héctor considered the wisdom of bringing Rodolfo into the cartel activities. Setting him up as the community landscaper proved to be the easy part. Rodolfo was still only twenty-two, and he acted his age far too often for Héctor's tastes—and for his continued business interests. "Something is bothering you." Héctor sat on the plush sofa opposite his impetuous relative.

"You told me to get the Porsche back," Rodolfo said.

It was Sunday. Most repair shops would be closed. Retrieving a car under the circumstances would be loud and messy. Too many missteps, and Mexico would pull the plug on their nascent operations in the area. The business of the cartel came first. "I did," he said after a couple calming breaths. "Tell me you didn't make a scene."

Rodolfo had the gall to look offended. "I asked a couple guys to check the place out. The Boxster was inside, and someone was there."

"They were open?"

"I don't think so. It sounded like the owner catching up on some stuff. I heard he stayed behind a desk the whole time."

"The men drove away?" Héctor asked.

"Yeah." Rodolfo nodded.

Héctor folded his hands in his lap. "Had someone not been in the shop, what would have happened?"

"I don't know," Rodolfo said. "I probably would've told the guys to get the car back."

"You know they work for me, right?" Héctor heard the edge in his own voice, and Rodolfo's recoil in the chair meant he did, too. "These men you sent aren't yours to command."

"I know." Rodolfo fidgeted under Héctor's glare. "I asked them to do me a favor."

"And it would have extended to breaking into a business and stealing a car."

"It's my car!"

"No one walking or driving by would think so." Héctor slapped the couch cushion. "Alice shouldn't have taken it to a shop we don't know. Fine. I don't think anything got left behind from its transit here. Even so, a mechanic doesn't have drug-sniffing dogs." He paused, and Rodolfo wouldn't meet his eyes. "You know who does?"

"The cops," his cousin said in a small voice.

"Yes. Do you know who people would call if they saw two men breaking into the place?"

"The cops."

"Precisely," Héctor said. "Your name is on the registration, yes?" Rodolfo nodded glumly. "Let's suppose some residue remained . . . enough for the dogs to pick it up. Their next stop is your house. Our entire operation is threatened."

"It didn't happen," Héctor said. "They left."

"You should thank Jesus in your prayers tonight."

Rodolfo spent a moment staring at the floor before he spoke. "What are we going to do about the Porsche?"

"Tomorrow is Monday," Héctor said. "The shop will probably be open. The car's in your name. Go get it . . . the right way."

"What if they don't want to give it back?"

"They will." A scowl darkened Rodolfo's youthful features. "Relax, cousin. It's your vehicle. They have to give it back to you."

"They'd better," Rodolfo said.

Héctor let his comment hang in the air unanswered. If Rodolfo caused too much of a problem, Héctor would need to deal with him. The business of the cartel came first.

5

Tyler arrived at the shop shortly after eight on Monday morning. Smitty was already there—and probably had been for hours—talking to a short, paunchy customer with curly hair. Tyler listened as he poured a cup of coffee. The man drove a late-'eighties Daytona and needed an oil change and tune-up. Smitty tried to explain tune-ups weren't really things anymore, and they agreed on a set of services to be performed. Tyler figured he would be stuck with them. The boss didn't like to work on anything made after 1980 if he could help it.

When the customer left, Smitty asked Tyler, "Ever work on a Daytona?"

Tyler shook his head. "I don't think I've seen one on the road in fifteen years."

Smitty pointed at the car. "Technically, you still haven't. It's in the parking lot."

Tyler grinned in spite of the lame joke. "So it is. How are the parts for the Boxster coming along?"

"Don't want to disappoint your new girlfriend?"

"I like to keep them around for a month or so before I let them down," Tyler said.

"We're supposed to hear something today." Smitty shrugged. "Stuff isn't as hard to come by as I thought it would be. Has to travel farther to get here is all."

"*Den ganzen weg von Deutschland?*"

"What?" Smitty frowned.

"All the way from Germany?" Tyler asked in English. "I was stationed there for a while. It helps to be able to do more than order sausage and ask for the bathroom."

"No. Some place out west. Local suppliers were sold out." He pointed to the middle bay. "Before you work on your ladyfriend's car, how about a brake job on the Starfire?"

"Sure." Tyler admired the car as he approached it. It featured the redesigned styling of the 1965 models. The body was a beautiful light blue topped by a white convertible roof. The coupe version of the Starfire bore a passing resemblance to Tyler's own 442. They both shared the 425 cubic inch Rocket V8. Tyler raised the car on the lift and got busy.

When he'd finished, he walked out of the bays and back into the front part of the shop. Smitty had his head under the hood of an old Mustang, so Tyler checked the computer. The order of Porsche parts showed a potential delivery date three days out. Nothing displayed as back ordered or out of stock. Alice's Boxster needed some work, and it would get it all. She'd be thrilled, and Tyler would be glad to see it. Enthusiasts should be encouraged. He looked at her phone number on the estimate and called from the landline.

Straight to voicemail.

Tyler frowned and hung up without leaving a message. He backed the Starfire out and brought the Daytona into the bays. Then, he tried Alice again. Same result. He listened to her entire voicemail greeting and left a message. "Hi, this is Tyler from Smitty and Son. We're able to get all the parts for your Boxster. They'll take three days to get here, so there's a chance we could be finished Friday or

Saturday. Smitty or I will keep you in the loop. Thanks . . . bye."

He set the receiver back in the cradle. Maybe Alice was busy, or perhaps she didn't answer calls from numbers she didn't know. Tyler had operated this way since he first got a cell phone. Something nagged at him. Alice mentioned her boyfriend bought the car but never seemed happy about the fellow in any other context. She only smiled when talking about cars—or driving them in the case of the 442.

Tyler realized he couldn't worry about every young woman within a few years of his daughter's age—no matter how much they reminded him of women he served with. He got back on the job before Smitty had a chance to walk inside and tell him to stop loitering behind the counter.

A COUPLE HOURS LATER, Tyler watched a black Subaru WRX pull into the lot. The bright gold rims and crazy aftermarket wing on the back caught his eye. At least the car had a turbocharged engine. Modifying it to make more power—and perhaps justify the monstrosity over the trunk—was easy. Tyler never understood why people put enormous spoilers on vehicles like Honda Civic sedans. A fine car, but definitely not a racer without an awful lot of work.

Two men got out. The driver was a Latino man of average height and build. The passenger unfolded himself to climb from his side. The man must have stood at least six-seven and weighed close to 300 pounds. Even from afar, the hulk gave off a menacing vibe. Tyler's hand confirmed the presence of the shotgun stashed under the counter. Smitty emerged from the shop. "Same car was here yesterday," he said.

"Was Andre the Giant inside?"

"Hard to tell, but I doubt it." Smitty paused. "I think this is about the Boxster. I don't like it."

"Me, either," Tyler said as the smaller man opened the door. He looked down his nose at Tyler and Smitty. The guy's mouth probably couldn't write a check the massive fellow trailing him couldn't cash.

"You have my car," he said in a lightly-accented voice. This painted him as the boyfriend Alice didn't seem thrilled about. He put his hands on the counter and flashed a smug grin. Overhead lights glinted off the two gold chains around his neck. The extra-large enforcer lingered a couple steps back, crossing his massive arms. Tyler had chopped down smaller trees.

"Got a few here," Smitty said.

The man jabbed his finger toward the center bay. "The Boxster. I want it back."

"A young lady dropped it off for service. We just ordered the parts."

"Sounds like your problem, old man."

"It could use some work," Tyler added. "Whoever owned it before didn't keep up with the maintenance."

The Latino stared at him. "Did I ask your opinion?"

"Maybe you should before you drive it out of here."

"Just give me the damn car."

"I'll need to see some ID," Smitty said. "Anyone can come in and say something is theirs."

"Fine." The guy fished a wad of cash out of his pocket. A rubber band held it together. In the center were a few cards including a driver's license. Tyler and Smitty both looked at the name. Rodolfo Espinoza. "We good?"

"I'll check the registration," Smitty said. "Wait here."

Rodolfo glared as Smitty walked away but didn't say anything. His huge friend remained vigilant and silent. Tyler wondered how many cows died to make the leather jacket he wore. Rodolfo drummed his fingers on the counter. Smitty returned a moment later. "Looks like the car's yours. Sure you don't want the work done?"

"I just want the car." He held his hand out for the keys Smitty carried.

"I'll back it out for you."

"I can handle it."

"No customers in the service bays," Smitty said.

"Excuse me?" Rodolfo narrowed his eyes and stared. He was a man used to getting his way. Tyler wondered how often he did it without the help of the giant behind him. Rodolfo didn't possess a lot of charm or personality. Intimidation would be the tactic of choice then, and his stature didn't lend itself to inducing fear.

"I'll bring it around. Only be a minute." Smitty moved back through the door.

"Your boss is kind of a prick," Rodolfo said without a hint of self-awareness.

"Alice made some good choices about the work she wanted done," Tyler said. "She's smart about cars."

"I wish she were smarter about where to take them. We have a shop we like."

"I guess she didn't get the memo."

Rodolfo leaned across the counter. "You got a problem?"

Tyler wanted to clobber him. He deserved it. The giant would get involved then, and Tyler didn't have a good solution for him other than the shotgun under the counter. Too messy. He would be diplomatic for now. If this young asshole took a swing at him, all bets were off. "It's just unusual for someone to pick a car up before we do any work on it."

"Life ain't always usual."

A horn honked outside. Smitty pulled the Boxster alongside the building. He walked in via the front door and handed Rodolfo the keys, which he snatched rather than politely accepting. "Good luck with the car."

"Piss off," Rodolfo said. He deliberately bumped into Smitty as he went past him. The large enforcer exited without word or contact. He compacted himself behind the wheel of the Subaru while Rodolfo got into the Porsche. They both drove away, but not before Rodolfo stalled the Boxster the first time.

"I hope we don't see them again," Smitty said as he moved behind the counter.

Tyler nodded. "Me, too." Having met Alice's boyfriend, he wondered again what happened to the young woman.

6

S ara Morrison walked back to her office in the Pentagon. The final meeting in a day full of them finally wrapped up. She looked at the nameplate on her door. Assistant Secretary of Defense for Special Operations and Low-Intensity Conflict. *For now, at least,* she thought. November meant a new regime regardless of who won the White House. Sara heard whispers of her bosses wanting to promote her to a more "valuable" role.

She liked where she was. Part of the desire to kick her upstairs, she felt, came from an obligation to protect her. A rogue former colonel threatened Sara's life a few months ago, and if she held a different position, his file never would've crossed her desk. She couldn't prove this of course, and office scuttlebutt didn't support it. Still, she'd spent enough time entrenched in the old boys' network to know how they liked to do things.

Finally free from a SCIF and its rigid measures to protect sensitive information, Sara checked her phone. She texted John Tyler earlier. He rarely replied quickly, and today proved no exception. Sara wanted to know if they were still on for dinner. She liked spending time with him, though she found fewer and fewer hours to spare over the last month. Tyler sent a couple messages while she was in her series of meetings. *Sorry, busy morning. Dinner is good. Lexi misses you.*

Sara grinned. The last part meant *he* missed her. Lexi might have, too. The girl was nice enough. She seemed focused on her freshman year of college. Sara recalled her own nearly thirty years ago and sympathized. She sat behind her desk and called Tyler. The rush of background noise when he picked up meant he was driving. "Headed home?" she asked.

"Yeah. I need to cook dinner for an important government official."

"Wow. Sounds fancy. Let me know how it goes."

"Thankfully, she puts up with my cooking," he said after a brief pause.

"You going to have any help in the kitchen?"

Another couple beats passed. "I don't know. Lexi's not an enthusiastic sous chef."

"Everything all right?" Sara said. "You seem a little distracted."

"I'm fine," he replied.

Sara frowned. Like many former soldiers, Tyler didn't talk much about his feelings. She grew used to it. Some separation from her work life in this area would've been nice, but no one was perfect. The ex-soldier saved her life a few months ago, he was a good guy, and he was trying hard as a single dad to a headstrong girl. She could give him a break. "All right. I'm going to pack up here. See you soon."

"Come hungry," Tyler said, and he hung up.

"Not a problem," Sara said to the empty office.

~

"SHOULDN'T YOU BE COOKING, DAD?" Lexi looked up from the laptop.

"It's in the oven," Tyler said. "Sara's driving from DC. We have a little while."

"All right. What was the name?"

"Rodolfo Espinoza."

"And why am I looking him up?" Lexi asked as she tapped the keys. The portable PC belonged to a company called Patriot Security, Tyler's employer before he quit and worked for Smitty. They'd never asked for it back. Designed by a bunch of cyber experts, the machine found information on people despite their attempts to hide it. Tyler didn't know a lot about computers, but his daughter had become quite adept with this one.

"I'm concerned about him. Something's . . . not right. His girlfriend dropped a car off and was really excited to get it fixed. I tried to call her today to tell her the parts were all coming, but it went right to voicemail. Today, Rodolfo shows up with a guy who could've picked up the car and carried it out of the bay." He frowned. "I don't like the situation. It makes me think Alice is in trouble."

"She was probably busy," Lexi said. "Who owns the car?"

"He does."

"Did you give it to him?" she asked.

"Smitty did. Hard not to when his name's on the registration."

Lexi turned the screen toward Tyler. "Not a lot here. He's got a Facebook page, but he doesn't do much with it. He's most active on Instagram. He seems to enjoy posting pictures of jewelry and cars and telling people he's rich."

"Sounds like a real prince," Tyler said.

"He's young. Twenty-two."

"If you bring someone like this home, I'm shooting him."

Lexi grinned. "You'd probably need to get in line. Rodolfo here seems like a jerk, but it doesn't mean something bad happened to the girlfriend."

Tyler grunted. "What about his known associates?"

Lexi clicked a button on the screen. The computer crunched a report for an instant before displaying the output. "Not a lot to go on. He lives in the same neighborhood as his cousin Héctor." Before Tyler could say anything, Lexi added, "I'm on it." A new man's picture stared back at them a second later. Héctor was older than Rodolfo, probably in his thirties, and the photo showed him in a suit.

"What's his story?" Tyler wanted to know.

"No social media presence for a couple years." She entered a few commands. "He's self-employed in imports and exports."

Tyler frowned. "Sounds like code for drugs." He hoped it wasn't. Alice didn't need to be involved in such a sordid mess.

"Just because he's Mexican?"

"You know I don't make those generalizations," Tyler said. "I served with a fair number of people whose families came from Mexico or parts of South America. They were all good soldiers. A few of them told me coke-running Colombians would come to the States and claim to work in imports. It was a front for drugs."

"It also sounds like a while ago," Lexi said.

"It was." Tyler's retirement was almost eight and a half years in the rearview. "It worked, though. Why change? I know this guy isn't from Colombia, but successful tactics spread."

"You seem awfully concerned about a girl who dropped off a car, Dad."

"We don't get a lot of young enthusiasts," Tyler said. "Most of them are guys with Youtube channels. She loves cars." He shrugged. "And she seems like a good kid."

"Don't let Sara hear you talking about her," Lexi said, giving Tyler a playful elbow in the side.

Tyler smirked. "She has nothing to worry about." He smelled the chicken, fingerling potatoes, and carrots roasting in the oven. Depending on how awful Sara's drive into Baltimore was, she might arrive around the time the food finished. Tyler walked into the kitchen and checked everything. A bottle of wine—which

Lexi suggested and picked up as part of her expertise—sat on the counter waiting to be uncorked.

"I don't see much else about these guys," she called from the living room a minute later. "They're good at staying offline for the most part."

"Let's hope we don't need to dig deeper," he said.

A couple minutes later, the doorbell rang. Tyler opened it, and Sara Morrison waited on his small front porch. She smiled when she saw him, and she owned a good one. Sara was a few years younger than him, sported a full head of black hair, and looked like a woman in her thirties. Tyler beckoned her inside, and they shared a kiss in the entryway.

"Get a room, you two," Lexi said as she entered the kitchen.

"Hello, Lexi," Sara said. She nodded to the bottle on the counter. "I presume you picked it out?"

Tyler spread his hands. "You don't think I could find a bottle of wine?"

"No," they both said in unison.

Outgunned, Tyler focused on getting dinner plated and onto the table. They enjoyed a meal of frequent and good conversation. He liked how Lexi and Sara got along. They weren't going to schedule a girls' day at the spa anytime soon, but the two women shared more than only an affection for Tyler. After dinner, Sara put the dishes in the sink, and Lexi retired upstairs. "She'll be up there the rest of the night," he said. "Teenagers." He dug a corkscrew out of the kitchen junk drawer.

"I like her," Sara said. "She's very much your daughter in a lot of ways."

"Thankfully, she gets her looks from her mother."

Sara smiled. "You're not too bad."

"I aspire for mediocrity," he said, opened the white wine, and poured them each a glass. Sara accepted it with a small nod. "The army taught me well."

They settled onto the couch. Sara shared as much about her

recent few days as she could—Tyler understood the limits of what she could tell him—and he told her about the Boxster situation. "You seem worried about the girl," Sara said.

"I'm sure you've seen intel reports from south of the border over the years. Am I out of line for thinking this guy who's supposedly in imports is really running drugs?"

"It's not a politically correct assumption . . . but I also don't think it's wrong. I've seen quite a few of the reports you mentioned. Your concern is valid."

"I don't think Lexi understood," Tyler said.

"She's young. She simply wants you to be careful." Sara paused. "So do I. You don't need to take on a drug lord, if this guy even is one."

"The whole situation bothers me." Tyler frowned. "So do the guys Lexi looked up." Tyler stopped before mentioning the giant who accompanied Rodolfo. Sara didn't need any other reasons to worry about him.

"I know what you do when things bother you," Sara said. "It's why I want you to be careful."

"I think you called me a knight-errant a few months back."

She grinned. "The label still fits."

It did. Tyler wondered about Alice and if he would soon be tilting at any windmills.

HÉCTOR ESPINOZA CALLED his superiors in Mexico. His operation in Harford County was the farthest from their base, and he always felt they took it out on him by demanding more updates than those closer. Tonight, Héctor spoke to Tomás Quintero. Héctor's distant cousin Bernardo led the cartel, but the two rarely spoke directly. Intermediaries always intervened, and Tomás proved the most frequent. He was a lawyer and some kind of lieutenant.

"We think you should be moving a little faster," Tomás said. "Your output's been steady for months. You told us you could ramp up."

"I can. I've been laying the groundwork."

"Are you ready?"

"We are," Héctor said. "Our operation is as secure as it's ever been. The men know their jobs. We've found more people who will be interested. We could use extra product."

"If we send you a larger allocation," Tomás warned, "we expect results. Both the powder and the pills."

"In this county, we can move both. I know it's taken a little longer than everyone wanted, but we're in a good spot here. Lots of bored rich people with too much money on their hands. They'll be giving it to us soon enough."

"Your money guy is solid?"

"He's been great," Héctor said. "A natural fit into the organization."

Tomás sighed, coming through the line as a hiss in Héctor's ear. "All right. Your next shipment will be larger, and we will have room to expand if you can work it."

"We will."

"Good." Tomás paused. His voice took on an amiable tone when he spoke next. "How's your cousin?"

"I have a lot of cousins," Héctor said. He wondered if Mexico somehow heard about Rodolfo killing his girlfriend and Héctor needing to clean it up.

"You know which one I mean." The friendly tone vanished as soon as it came.

"Rodolfo is fine," Héctor said. "He's young and brash, but he's loyal."

"To you."

"And through me to the cartel. He's not a problem."

"All right," Tomás said once more. Héctor heard the skepticism in his voice. "We're past the point of putting up with problems. Your cousin who matters expects you to carry your share of the load."

"We're ready," Héctor said, "and we'll prove it."

"For your sake, I hope you do." Tomás hung up before Héctor could say anything. He slammed his phone onto the couch. They were ready to move more product and make more money. Héctor built the infrastructure and seeded the desire in the county with free or cheap drugs. It was an old tactic but a good one. Rodolfo and his dead girlfriend wouldn't stop their progress.

Héctor would see to it. He could have any number of bodies cleaned up. As many as it took. The cartel's interests came first.

7

As usual, Tyler woke early the next morning. He stretched, changed into athletic attire, and stepped outside into the chilly fall air. After getting his blood moving with a short walk, the former soldier took off at a run. He bought the house about a decade ago before his final deployment with the army. One of the first things he did was map out a three-mile running course of the local streets. Tyler's final fitness test with Patriot Security showed he hadn't slowed much in a two-mile run since going on terminal leave.

About a half-hour later, he entered his house again. Lexi stood in the kitchen, pouring herself a cup of coffee. She smiled and wished him good morning before he headed upstairs to shower and get dressed. Tyler returned to the first floor a short while later, enjoyed his own mug of java, and toasted a bagel. While he waited, he brought the Patriot laptop to the table.

Lexi understood a lot more about how it worked and did better with people and their connections than he ever could, but Tyler knew how to use it for general fact-finding. He didn't grasp what happened behind the scenes—the machine seemed to go deeper than Google and simple local news—but the computer helped a lot with intelligence gathering. When his bagel popped up, Tyler slathered it in peanut butter and sat back down.

Something in his gut told him Alice was in trouble. Even if her boyfriend's cousin turned out to be a legitimate retired importer, the young man himself was trouble. He carried himself like he dared someone to get cross with him. Then, he could either shoot them or let the giant break them in half. He didn't seem happy Alice brought the Boxster to Smitty's. What might he have done to her?

Tyler entered a few search terms and let the computer do its thing. It provided some results in short order. He scrolled through them until he found a listing which made his blood run cold. *Young Woman Found Beaten to Death in Woods.* "Shit," he muttered as he clicked the link. A brief story with multiple sources opened.

EDGEWOOD, MD.—A young woman's body was discovered by a man walking his dog late last night.

The body has not been identified yet. The deceased is described as a redheaded white woman in her early 20s. The cause of death was a brutal beating, likely with a weapon such as a baseball bat.

Harford County Sheriff's deputies are investigating. No leads are reported at this time.

TYLER STARED AT THE SCREEN. He took measured breaths in and out. The body had to be Alice. Rodolfo beat her to death. In the aftermath, he probably asked his cousin to help him cover it up. If Héctor was who Tyler suspected, he could get those resources with a single phone call. The cops didn't have any leads. In the back of his head, Tyler heard Sara's voice encouraging him to turn this over to the authorities.

He would. If they refused to act, however, Tyler knew what he would do.

Lexi finished her first class and refilled her coffee cup. If she were forced to endure another tedious lecture, she'd need to brew more. Why were intro classes so boring? She liked physics, but between her professor's Schwarzenegger-like voice and the quality of his slide deck, she felt glad she opted for a different course next semester. With some time to kill, Lexi looked at her email. Her eyes landed on the message from her mother, and she sighed.

One of these days, she would need to reply. Her dad told her to do what she wanted. She'd really come to like living with him over the last year and a half. He treated her like an adult—which she now was—and it made her realize how much her mother tried to control her even as she hit her teenage years. Lexi practiced a measure of mindful breathing. If she were going to respond, doing so when angry wouldn't help.

Once she'd calmed down, she opened the message and clicked on the *Reply* icon.

Hi Mom,

It's nice to hear from you. I know we haven't talked in a while or seen each other in longer.

I'm in college online. Your daughter is a Terrapin! The classes are kind of lame right now. I haven't settled on a major yet, but there's time.

Dad's doing well. He's working as a mechanic on old cars. I know he's wanted to do it for a while. We're in a good place and getting along well.

I'll try to come and see you soon. Maybe next week. Take care. I hope you learned a few things from watching Orange is the New Black *with me.*

    Love,
    Lexi

SHE SENT THE MESSAGE. Did she really want to visit her mother in prison? Guilt clawed at her. She should've gone already. It had been long enough, and it's not like her mother was a serial killer in solitary who couldn't receive guests. Lexi looked at her class schedule. She'd find some time.

TYLER WAITED in an uncomfortable chair at the Edgewood branch of the Harford County Sheriff's Office. While he sat there, he found Alice's Facebook page and downloaded one of her better pictures. Many were of her, but others were of cars she liked and wanted to drive. Now, she'd never get to add another one—all because her boyfriend was an asshole. Tyler thanked his lucky stars Lexi had too much sense to get involved with someone who threw red flags like Rodolfo.

"Mister Tyler?" A large deputy peeked around the corner. He jerked his head, and Tyler followed him to a desk toward the rear. "I'm Deputy Parker," he said once seated. Parker looked like he stepped off a college football field last year. His round face and spiky blond hair lent him an unserious look. His massive chest and arms sent a much different message. "What can I help you with today?"

"I'm here about the young woman found in the woods," Tyler said.

Parker frowned. "We haven't released a lot of information yet. How do you know about it?"

"I'm resourceful."

"Do you have some information?"

"Do you know her name?" Tyler asked.

"It's an ongoing investigation, sir," Parker said. "I couldn't share it with you either way."

"In case you don't, it's Alice Simard. Before you ask, I didn't know her well. I work as a classic car mechanic, and she brought an old Boxster into the shop."

Parker stared at Tyler a moment before scribbling in a spiral pad. A computer sat on his desk. So did a lot of other things. A piece of paper could get lost in the cubicle jungle. Tyler wished the man would input his notes. "When was this?"

"A couple days ago." Tyler called up the picture he'd saved to his phone. "This was her before she got murdered and dumped somewhere."

"Pretty," Parker said with a nod.

"And very nice. We don't get a lot of female car enthusiasts, so she tends to stick out in my mind." Tyler slipped his phone back into his pocket.

"You seem to know a lot about her."

"We had lunch after she dropped the Porsche off," Tyler said. "She walked into the place where I was eating, and we had a nice conversation."

"Can I see the picture again?" Parker said.

Tyler narrowed his eyes. "Don't try to make something lascivious out of this. She was barely older than my daughter."

"All right." Parker put up his hands. "You think you know who she was. Who—"

"There's no *think* here. She's your dead woman. I'll bet your salary on it."

"I'm not a gambling man," Parker said with the trace of a smile. "I'll take your word for it, though. I was about to ask if you had any idea who might've put her there."

"I'm sure your people already know she wasn't killed there."

Tyler waited for a reaction, but Parker sat stone-faced. "My guess is her boyfriend killed her. Rodolfo Espinoza."

Parker abandoned the notepad and went to work on his computer. "You ever in the military, Mister Tyler?"

"Yes . . . why?"

"My old man was career Air Force," Parker said. "You got the same look about you."

"Army," Tyler said. "Twenty-four years."

"He wanted me to enlist, but I knew it wasn't for me." Parker pivoted his flatscreen monitor toward Tyler and lowered his voice. "I'll tell you this. Looks like we identified the girl early this morning. Deputies questioned Rodolfo Espinoza, but he had an alibi."

"Let me guess . . . something to do with his cousin."

"Yep." Parker returned the screen to its original position. "Confirmed by multiple witnesses."

"All of whom are likely on the cousin's payroll," Tyler said.

Parker shrugged. "This is where we are in the investigation. It's still early. I can't share any more details with you."

Tyler took a deep breath and shook his head. He knew how this would play out. Parker told him more than he expected, but the result was the same. Rodolfo enjoyed Héctor's protection in the form of an alibi, and the investigation would sputter and die from here. "Thanks for your time, Deputy." Tyler stood.

"My dad's a determined guy," Parker said. "Kind of like an old dog. He doesn't like to let go of something when he's got his teeth in it."

"I guess he and I are a lot alike, then."

"Let us do our jobs, Mister Tyler."

"It'd be nice if you'd get started," Tyler said. He turned from the desk and left the station.

yler drove back home. He didn't feel like going to work at the moment, and he texted Smitty to say he'd be in later. After leaving the 442 in the driveway, Tyler walked inside and went upstairs. He went to his spare bedroom. Years ago, a Veterans Administration therapist suggested he try painting as a means of working through his PTSD. Tyler scoffed at first, but tried it and came to like it.

He preferred watercolors, and he'd churned out some impressive works since he took the time to learn what he was doing. They stood around the room, a few on shelves, some in bins, and others stacked on the floor. He knew Lexi came in here at least once. She knew the whole story about the end of his time in the army, and he didn't mind her seeing the output of his brain processing everything. Dealing with his former commander a few months ago kicked up some unpleasant memories.

A new paper awaited. Tyler sat in the chair, closed his eyes, and took a few deep breaths. His hand shot out and closed around a thin brush. He drew the outline of a car. He waited a minute, then grabbed a thicker brush to fill in the border with silver. Wheels and tires came next, then a twisting road leading toward the top of the page. Tyler filled in the space there with a lot of brown.

He went for red again, added a few final touches, and then put his brushes down. A silver Boxster sat askew in the middle of the blacktop. A desert wasteland lay in the distance. The rear tires of the car trailed blood on the road. Tyler got up, cleaned his supplies in the nearby bathroom sink, and left his little studio the way he found it.

He grabbed his former company's laptop. Héctor Espinoza, his cousin, and their crew would pay for what they did to Alice, a girl who didn't need to die. Civilian deaths should always be prevented when possible. Only cowards reveled in needless casualties. The conversation with Deputy Parker told Tyler the Harford County SO would be slow to act if they did anything at all. Speaking for the dead fell to him.

Good thing he'd already established himself as a knight-errant.

Talbot Lakes was a swanky community in the town of Bel Air. Nestled off Route 543, it marked the end of miles of farmland and the beginning of civilization—expensive civilization. The development sprang up a couple years ago, and a bunch of rich early adopters bought the first allocation. Tyler's research before leaving the house told him all this. When he drove up to Talbot Lakes, he confirmed something he couldn't believe.

For all its glitz and glamor, the community didn't have a gate.

He drove the 442 along the main drag. Other than the occasional work van or service truck, his was probably the loudest engine to sully the air. Large single-family homes with garages lined the road and smaller side streets. The main differentiators seemed to be size, brick front, and the color of the front door and shutters. Even a million dollars couldn't buy an original design these days.

Near the end of the main street, a manmade lake sat back on the left. The smallest house in the community stood about two hundred yards before it on the right. Tyler knew this was Rodolfo's. Like the others, it had a garage, and the general aesthetic looked the same. The reduced size lent the appearance someone left a larger house in the dryer too long.

The road ended ahead and featured a wide circle for turning around like a cul-de-sac. One mini-mansion sat at the terminus, and it was the largest in the development. A long driveway and trees prevented good views from the road, but Tyler scouted it with satellite imagery. Héctor Espinoza's place was half again as large as the rest. His garages would hold four cars. A brick exterior and white columns near the front and back doors lent a general look of opulence.

Tyler turned around and headed back the way he came. He parked across from Rodolfo's and took a camera out of his bag. Hundreds of yards ahead, one woman walked a dog. The street was otherwise empty. He snapped pictures of both dwellings. He couldn't get a good shot of Héctor's, but Google could close the information gap. Lexi could probably help on the Patriot laptop, too.

All was quiet at the houses he watched. No one came in or out for a half-hour. A van drove down the road and navigated the long driveway of Héctor's home. Tyler got photos of it coming and going. Probably a harmless delivery. Nothing in the background intel he found on Héctor suggested the man was stupid. He wouldn't run a needless risk like getting a shipment of drugs at his residence.

Only fifteen minutes elapsed before the next vehicle approached. This one was a white Jeep SUV with the Talbot Lakes logo on the side. The driver steered it next to Tyler's car and lowered his window. Tyler did the same. "Can I help you find a house, sir?" Tyler couldn't see much of him, but he looked burly. His baseball cap carried the same insignia as his Jeep. It was about time security arrived. Tyler wondered who called them.

"I'm all right . . . thanks, though."

"Let me put it a different way," the man said. "Do you have business in Talbot Lakes?"

"Yes," Tyler said.

"Do you want to tell me what it is?" the guard asked after Tyler didn't elaborate.

"Not really."

The security guy scowled and rolled up his window. Tyler left his down. The fellow would need to call someone. No way he got trusted to make decisions. Sure enough, he radioed for assistance over a walkie-talkie. Tyler couldn't make out either end of the conversation. After a moment, the fellow lowered his glass again. "Follow me, please. The community president would like to speak with you."

"I'm sure he would," Tyler said.

TYLER FOLLOWED the white Renegade onto a side road. The first building on the right was the model for Talbot Lakes. He parked the 442 behind the Renegade. The security guy stepped out first. He was tall and muscular but also paunchy. His stomach hung over the belt of his Dockers. His bright red hair and goatee painted him as a young man, probably not even thirty. Tyler climbed out of the Olds, and they walked inside.

A corridor ran the length of the interior, ending in a kitchen with a slider to the deck. Another portly man sat behind the desk in what would be the living room of a normal house. Here, a desk and four chairs served as the only furnishings. A nameplate read *Todd Windholm, Developer*. Windholm looked to be about forty, and his physique suggested he spent much of his day camped behind his desk. Tyler slid onto a guest chair and turned it to the side so he could keep the front door in view. Windholm offered an insincere smile. "You interested in a house?" Like a good lackey, the guard stood near his boss.

"I have one already," Tyler said. "It's got a lot more character than anything here."

"Might I ask what you're doing sitting in your car on the street, then?"

"It's a public street, right?"

"This is an exclusive community," Windholm said.

"Is your fat ass going to get out there and fix a pothole?" Tyler asked.

"No." Windholm frowned. "We would call the county."

Tyler spread his hands. "There you go. Taxpayer funded."

Windholm crossed his arms, and the security fellow did the same. "You still haven't answered my question."

"I was taking pictures."

"You got ID?" the guard said.

"Sure," Tyler said.

The other two men looked at each other for a moment when Tyler didn't continue and made no effort to produce a card. "You gonna show us?"

"No."

The sentry glowered, and the muscles in his crossed arms flexed. "Why not?"

"Because neither of you are cops," Tyler said. "You're a glorified property manager and a poorly-trained attack dog. You do this absurd show for everyone who drives in or only the ones who stop at the far end of the street?"

Windholm focused on his very neat desk. "I'm not sure what you mean." Tyler remained silent. He was good at it. Quiet unnerved a lot of people, and they ended up filling the silence by saying too much. It didn't take long for Windholm to crack. "We value the safety of all our residents." Tyler again let the other man's words hang in the air. "You might say we're especially protective of Mister Espinoza," Windholm added after a moment.

"He must be an important man," Tyler said once the stooge took the bait.

"A community benefactor."

Tyler had an idea how Héctor and his crew benefitted the neighborhood, but he kept it to himself. Windholm was a happy Kool-Aid drinker. Tyler disparaging anyone wouldn't make a difference. "What kinds of things does he do?"

"Mister Espinoza is very involved." Windholm nodded, and the guard again mirrored him. "He even gave his cousin a job and a place to live . . . the small house across from the lake."

"He sounds like a peach," Tyler deadpanned. "Unfortunately, I'm gathering information in the murder of a young woman who lived here. In the house you just mentioned, in fact."

"I'm not sure who you mean," Windholm said. His eyes flittered from side to side under Tyler's stare. "Are you a private investigator?"

"No," Tyler said. "Even if I were, I couldn't compel you to talk to me."

Windholm leaned back in his chair. "I don't see much reason for this conversation to continue, then." A confident grin split his round face. "Glen?"

"Time to go," the rent-a-cop said.

"But I'm enjoying this thrilling chat," Tyler said.

Glen scowled and advanced, tapping his fist into his open palm. Tyler remained in the chair. Before the larger man could do anything, Tyler fired a short left into his groin. It staggered him but didn't put him down. Tyler stood, giving Glen a punch in his ample midsection and a short chop to the neck. With his foe gasping, Tyler grabbed the stunned man by his red hair and slammed his head into the desktop. Glen rebounded off the wood and hit the floor hard. He didn't move.

Tyler walked around the desk and grabbed Windholm by the tie. The panicked man flailed his arms to no effect. The knot of his tie pressed into his throat, and his pudgy face reddened. "Tell me about your alleged benefactor," Tyler said.

"Uh . . . Mister Espinoza is retired. He loves this community and wants to see it continue to prosper."

"Nice prepared speech. He probably gave you the script. What kind of career did he retire from?"

"Im . . . Imports," Windholm stammered.

Tyler let him go. He stepped over the fallen Glen, who was breathing but still didn't stir. "If I were you, I'd find a different place to manage."

Windholm straightened his rumpled tie and cleared his throat. "You should stay away from Talbot Lakes, sir."

"Who's going to keep me out?" Tyler jerked his head at the fallen guard. "This asshole?"

"We have more."

"You'd better," Tyler said. He left Glen and Windholm in the model home, got back into the 442, and left Bel Air.

9

Lexi finished her afternoon classes. She decompressed by listening to music on her phone. While she and her dad shared a few favorite bands, she still appreciated some basic pop. He could enjoy his singer-songwriters like John Hiatt. Lexi would play the new Alex Anne album and lose herself for a while in songs about love, reputation, and fame. For someone dismissed by a lot of the music press, Alex Anne wrote pretty deep songs. Lexi appreciated her more acerbic lyrics.

"I can't switch off who I am," she sang. "You knew it from the start. I think you just wanted to borrow some fame. Get lost with your broken heart." Lexi flopped onto her bed and bobbed her head to the beat. The next song came on. She played air drums until her phone buzzed a notification. The music continued while she checked. It was another email from her mother. Lexi rolled her eyes and went back to the album. She let it play in its entirety before opening the message.

ALEXIS,
I'm so happy to hear you're doing well. I hope all the upheaval in

our lives these last couple years didn't dash your dreams of traveling for college. Maryland is a great school, but I want you to go where you'd be happy.

Give your father my best. We haven't always gotten along, but we've always shared a love of our daughter. I'm sure he's good at his new job. It sounds less stressful for both of you than his old one.

I'd like you to come and see me sometime. It's been too long. Just make an appointment and show up. A lot of the women in here see their daughters every week or two. I'd like us to get to that point, and I hope you would, too.

It's not like Litchfield in here, but I wouldn't trade a minute of watching OITNB with my girl!

Love,

Mom

LEXI STARED at the missive a while after reading it. As with most things involving her mother, it was a lot to decompress. There were some sincere good wishes, a minor and a major guilt trip, and a little forced sentimentality at the end. Lexi remembered a time when she revered her mother. The more she learned about the woman's activities, the more skeptical and distrusting she became. Even if her mom's capers hadn't ended with an arrest, Lexi might have tried to live with her dad, anyway. She couldn't imagine being anywhere else the last year and a half.

The message deserved a reply, but she didn't have it in her now. With Thanksgiving coming soon, classes got busier, and instructors assigned more reading and homework. Lexi got up and sat at her desk again. Her mother could wait.

～

HÉCTOR ESPINOZA'S PHONE RANG. He could smell dinner cooking downstairs. *Carne asada* with an aggressive spice blend. Home-made refried beans. Melita, his maid, turned out to be a damned good cook. She was better in the kitchen than any other room of the house. Talking business rarely adhered to a schedule, but Héctor didn't like conversations around dinner time. He glanced at the caller ID. Todd Windholm. "Yes?" he said.

"We might have a problem, Mister Espinoza."

Héctor closed his door. "Explain." He sat on the edge of his king bed.

"Some guy came here earlier today," Windholm said. "We first saw him in his car across from Rodolfo's house. I sent Glen to see what was going on and to bring him back here."

"And?" Héctor asked when Windholm stopped talking. He hated prying information out of people unless he was torturing them. Then, he enjoyed it. The power. The pain. The tears. The blood. Talking to Americans on the phone, however, often proved excruciating.

"He came in asking questions about the community and about you. I tried to dissuade him, but then he mentioned looking into a . . . well, an unpleasant situation in the neighborhood."

No doubt Alice's murder. "Is he a cop?"

"No, sir."

"I presume you wouldn't be calling me if Glen took care of things," Héctor said.

"Unfortunately, this man took Glen out. I was surprised how fast it happened. He knew what he was doing."

"Your men also aren't very good. They're here to make the residents feel safe."

"I didn't tell him anything," Windholm said. "I did get his picture, though."

At least he did something right. If Windholm weren't so good with money, Héctor would have tried out some new torture techniques on the man. There was plenty of fat to stab, slice, and carve. "Send it to me."

"On its way, Mister Espinoza."

Héctor's phone vibrated in his hand. He pulled it away from his ear and opened the message, which consisted of a still image. A white male who looked to be of average height. Short hair. Probably kept in shape. He fit the description Rodolfo provided after he picked up the Boxster and griped about one of the shop workers giving him a hard time. Héctor squinted at the hard-set eyes. He'd seen similar ones before on killers the cartel used to take out its worst foes. This man would definitely be too much for Windholm and his mediocre security team. "You were right to send this to me." He tapped the photo and saved it to a hidden folder. "Don't worry about him."

"Are you going to handle it?" Windholm asked.

"Of course I am," Héctor snapped. He took a breath to compose himself. "We can't have a man like this sniffing around." The police wouldn't be a problem. Héctor knew how to throw them off the trail, and he could always stop investigations with money if he needed to. The stranger was a loose cannon. "Thanks for letting me know." Héctor hung up. He glanced at his watch. The shop would probably be closed now. He placed a call to one of his contacts a moment later.

"*Sí*," Patricio said.

"I need you to do something for me in the morning," Héctor told him.

"Is it the kind of work I enjoy?"

Much like Héctor, Patricio enjoyed inflicting pain. "It is. And you can take as much time as you like."

As was his habit, Smitty arrived at the shop early. He hadn't been able to sleep past six in years, and he didn't see the point of sitting at home drinking coffee when he could be doing it at his desk. After turning the machine on, the boss sat in his chair, looked into the service bays, and frowned at the papers piling up in his inbox. He was glad for the uptick in business and wondered again if he should hire someone part-time to handle a lot of the paperwork.

When Mr. Coffee beeped its completion, Smitty filled his mug. He turned on his computer along with the monitor connected to the security system. A few minutes later, he watched an older Ford Explorer creep down the narrow street running alongside the shop. It parked at the curb facing the wrong direction. The camera didn't let him zoom enough to make out many details, but he saw someone in the passenger's seat.

He kept an eye on them for a few minutes. It was a low-traffic road, and no other cars drove in either direction. Could this be related to the Boxster? The car proved to be nothing but trouble since the pretty Canadian woman drove it here. Between getting the parts, guys casing the place, and someone demanding the car back before he and Tyler could work on it, Smitty wanted to put the German car behind him. The girl's boyfriend took it. What else did they want?

Tyler arrived just after eight. He poured himself a hot mug of caffeine. "Thought you were going to come in late yesterday," Smitty said.

"Me, too. I needed the afternoon to look into some things."

"Why do I think this is about the girl with the Porsche?"

"Did you know she's dead?" Tyler asked.

Smitty's eyes widened, and he almost dropped his mug. "What the hell? How do you know?"

"I have a laptop which can gather open-source intelligence. She was beaten to death and dumped in the woods. It happened sometime in the night after she dropped off the Boxster. You're older than I am, so I'm sure you stopped believing in coincidences a long time ago."

"So when her boyfriend picked the car up . . .?"

"She was already dead," Tyler said. "Yeah. I spent yesterday at the sheriff's office and doing a little surveillance in the boyfriend's neighborhood."

"Did you happen to attract any attention?" Smitty asked.

"The neighborhood rent-a-cop noticed me." He left out the part about meeting Windholm. Smitty didn't need to know everything. "Why?"

"Take a look." Smitty pointed toward the monitor. "Can't make out a lot from here, but there are at least two guys in this Explorer. It arrived well before you did. I can't think of another reason they'd be here." He sighed. "I like you, Tyler, and I'm grateful for what you did for Jake. Sometimes, though, I think you might be more trouble than you're worth."

Before Tyler could answer, the doors on the SUV opened. "Get them into the bays if they're looking for me," he said. "Tell them I'm in the can or something." Smitty grunted as Tyler disappeared into the work area. A minute later, two wiry Latino men walked in. The first carried a shotgun. The other flipped the sign from *Open* to *Closed* and locked the front door.

10

Tyler moved two tires next to a Mustang in the bay farthest from the connecting door to the shop. He crouched and listened as best he could. "Where's the other guy?" a Spanish-accented voice demanded.

"Taking a piss," Smitty said.

"Into the shop." A moment later, the door opened. Tyler peeked under the front of the car. Three sets of shoes walked in. Someone paused to shut the connecting door. "We wait for him."

"What's this about?" Smitty asked. Tyler glanced through the car's window. The man standing closest to Smitty held a shotgun. He ducked again and held his M11 close. His boss did a good job of staying calm under the circumstances. "If he gave you some bad service, you don't need to do all this."

"Shut up, old man." A different voice. Deeper and harsher. Keeping his back to the tires, Tyler inched down the length of the classic Ford. He peered at the passenger's side mirror. No good. He needed to scoot farther down.

"Seems like a long piss to me," the first one said.

Tyler crouched at the rear quarter panel. He saw three men reflected in the small glass. The one with the twelve-gauge moved in his direction. When the footsteps got closer, Tyler scampered behind the truck. The other goon stood near the door. The other two cars in the area would help screen Tyler from his view. He hoped. The armed enforcer stopped at the door and turned around. "I don't see him. Maybe we should start with you."

He stayed in place. Tyler remained low, moved behind the gun-wielding man, and put the muzzle of the M11 in the center of his back. Before anything else could happen, Tyler pulled the trigger. Proximity to flesh dampened the report. The guy crashed forward, dead before he hit the cement floor. Tyler stood and pointed his Sig at the other one, who fumbled in his waistband. "Don't do it," Tyler said. "I just shot your friend. I have no problems adding you to the body count."

The slender man eyed Tyler warily. He looked young, probably in his early thirties, and a wispy black mustache matched his full head of hair. "You think I'm afraid of you?" his machismo demanded.

"Me?" Tyler shrugged as he stepped over the bleeding corpse. "Maybe not. The gun? Probably. I think we should have a talk."

"Nothing to say."

"Héctor send you?"

The fellow's eyes narrowed in recognition, but true to his word, he didn't respond. "Tyler, I think this has gone far enough," Smitty said.

"Depends on how much our friend here cooperates. You don't want to tell me who sent you? Fine. How about your name?"

"Patricio," the man said as he glowered.

"Good," Tyler said. "Patricio, I'm going to presume I'm correct about who sent you. Nothing else makes sense, and your boss seems like he's asshole enough to send a couple expendables. We can get past this, though. If someone comes forward and admits to killing Alice, there's no need for any more violence."

"We'll kill you."

"You're oh-for-one so far. It's still early, but I like my chances."

"Go to hell!" Patricio reached to the small of his back, and Tyler pumped three rounds into him. A pistol clattered from the dead man's hand as he sank to the floor.

"Idiot," Tyler muttered.

"Jesus Christ," Smitty said. "A few months ago, no one ever even got hurt in my shop. This is the third man you've killed in here."

"You heard him. If he didn't find me, they were going to start in on you."

Smitty sighed. "I know, I know. It's . . . just a lot to deal with."

"I'm sure it is." Tyler holstered the M11. "I'm going to get these idiots into their SUV and drive it away. Can you handle the cleanup here?"

"Sure," Smitty said. "I still have supplies from the last guy you shot."

"I knew your Costco card would pay off." He clapped his boss on the shoulder and got a weak smile for his efforts. Tyler searched both men, snagged the keys from Patricio, and gave Smitty the cash in their wallets. "For the next time you have to buy cleaner."

"Let's hope there isn't a next time," Smitty said.

TYLER SLIPPED on a pair of gloves and checked the Explorer and found nothing amiss. It was about fifteen years old and didn't feature a GPS. The only things tying the two dead guys to this location would be their cell phones. He pulled the aging SUV into the lot and backed it up to the middle bay door. Smitty opened it, and Tyler reversed the Explorer inside. As his boss closed the shop from prying eyes again, Tyler checked the dead men's mobiles. They were generic Android models. Probably burners but certainly new enough to enable location tracking.

"Where are you going to take them?" Smitty asked.

"I don't know yet." Tyler set his own phone down atop a workbench. "Someplace I can walk back from."

"There's a cemetery off Taylor Avenue."

Tyler knew the place. Lots of real estate to cover. Trees surrounding it on three sides. "Good call." He popped the liftgate. The cargo area was empty, and the space would allow for both bodies to fit so long as he stacked them. Tyler dragged the first to the back bumper and set it inside.

"You done this before?" Smitty said.

"Move bodies?" Tyler said. "Sure. Sometimes, there was a tactical reason to do it. If you mean piling dead drug runners into a Ford SUV, though . . . this is my first time."

"You seem to be doing all right." Smitty blew out a long breath and sagged onto a nearby stool.

Tyler paused en route to the other corpse. "I know I brought these guys here." He shook his head. "I just couldn't get past the fact they killed a girl for bringing a car to your shop. Someone needs to speak for her."

"Didn't know it was your job."

"I guess I nominated myself," Tyler said. He left out the part about Alice reminding him of a dead soldier. Smitty wouldn't get it. The second body lay face down. Based on where Tyler shot him, the bullet would have blown through his heart and kept going. The exit wound would be messier than the entrance. Tyler flipped the corpse onto its back, grabbed it under the arms, and dragged it to the SUV. He tossed the second one atop the first. Blood still seeped from the bodies onto the carpet of the cargo hold.

Tyler grabbed a roll of paper towels and set out a bunch near where the liftgate would close. He raided a supply cabinet and tossed a few air fresheners in. Before buttoning up the SUV, he cleaned any areas of the rear he might have touched with a disinfectant wipe. "I realize I've put a lot on your plate," he said to Smitty. "I don't know these guys, but we dealt with drug pushers in Afghanistan. I doubt this will be the last crew they send here. If you want me to stay away for a while, I understand, and I'll do it."

Smitty remained silent for several seconds. "You might as well keep showing up." He rubbed the bridge of his nose. "I can probably get Jake to come in an extra day, too. Someone who can deal with these assholes needs to be here, though, and it ain't me."

Tyler nodded. Smitty was a good mechanic and a capable boss, but he'd never be confused for a fighter. "I'll be back as soon as I can." Tyler took a pack of disinfectant wipes off a nearby shelf and climbed into the Explorer. The bay door lifted, and he drove out, making a right onto Belair Road. Taylor Avenue was the first light, and he made the left barely before the signal went red.

In about a half-mile, Tyler turned right into Parkwood Cemetery. The narrow road wound throughout the grounds, and a small parking lot was set off to the side not far ahead. Tyler scanned the area. The place was mostly empty. Still too early in the day for most funerals. He drove the Explorer to the far side of the property, got out to look around again, and tossed the two dead men's phones into the trees.

He guided the old Ford back near the entrance and left it in the parking lot. The darkened rear window would keep people from noticing the bodies, but either the smell or the fact the vehicle sat in place for a long time would draw attention at some point. Tyler wiped down the interior, paying special attention to areas like the steering wheel, gear selector, and seats. He stayed behind the SUV as a car drove past into the grounds. Once the coast was clear again, Tyler walked into the trees. He snaked his way back to a side street before stepping onto Taylor Avenue.

HÉCTOR ESPINOZA CHECKED his phone again. Nothing from Patricio and Pedro. By now, they'd had plenty of time to drive to the shop and take care of the problematic guy there. He might have taken out one of Todd's amateurs, but Héctor sent a pair of capable men. He tried both their numbers again. No answer on either. Did he underestimate the man at the repair shop?

Rodolfo walked into the living room. Héctor looked up, glowered at him, and went back to staring at his mobile. "Nothing?" the younger cousin asked.

"No," Héctor said without looking up. They waited in silence a few more minutes. "You had to kill your girlfriend."

"You're putting this on me?"

Héctor closed his eyes and counted to ten. "Did someone else beat Alice to death?"

"I can't help it if the guy at the shop is in love with her."

"He wouldn't care if she were still alive," Héctor said. "Even if we took the car back. He's only nosing around because she's dead."

"Maybe Patricio and Pedro are busy," Rodolfo suggested. "Maybe they had to kill this guy and his boss, and now they're covering it up."

"*Quizás.*" Héctor figured the odds were low, but there was a chance Rodolfo was right. His men always answered his calls, but something like dealing with a couple of corpses would be a good excuse not to respond. "I guess we'll wait a little longer." He avoided looking at his screen. *No por mucho madrugar amanece más temprano*, as his grandmother used to say. "No matter how early you get up, dawn won't come any sooner." The gringos he knew would go with, "A watched pot never boils." He liked his grandmother's version better. English was such an inferior language.

Ten minutes passed. Fifteen. Twenty. Héctor looked at his phone. Nothing. He tried calling both Patricio and Pedro with the same results. "I think your optimism is dead, cousin," Héctor said, "much like my men."

Rodolfo put his hands up. "Sorry, Héctor. What do we do now?"

"*We* don't do anything. You go back to being the landscaper. Find some bushes to trim. Try not to get anyone else in trouble."

"Héctor, I—"

"Go." Héctor pointed toward the front door. "I'll handle this. I'll get a couple more men from Mexico. If this guy at the car shop took out two of my men, we're going to change tactics."

11

S mitty busied himself cleaning the service bay floor. Someone came to the door shortly after he started. Smitty's heart raced. Did the cops find out already? Smitty's anxiety eased when he realized it was a customer wanting to drop off a car. He claimed he needed to clean up an oil spill before he could reopen. The man said he'd return later in the afternoon. Smitty heaved a sigh of relief and got back to work.

A few months ago, a large enforcer named Bobby threatened Smitty over Jake's whereabouts. Tyler shot and killed him. It was the first time Smitty saw a fresh corpse up close—not a prepared body at a funeral. Bobby's face still wore a surprised expression below the bullet hole in the center of his forehead. Smitty shuddered at the memory. He learned about cleaning up blood out of necessity and figured he'd never need to use it again.

Then, the events of today happened. Some part of Smitty understood what happened. One of the guys brandished a shotgun, and the other carried a pistol in his back waistband. They came to do one thing, and Tyler did what he needed to do. Still, no one had so much as slipped and fallen in the shop the entire time Smitty owned it. In the last four months, he'd been forced to deal with the fallout of three dead bodies. At least the first one had been his problem. These two came because Tyler couldn't let something go.

Smitty scrubbed the floor clean and then used a bleach spray to finish. He put all the rags and towels into a paper bag, set it in an empty drum outside, and burned it all. While the fire crackled, Smitty returned inside and accessed the security system. The guys coming into the store appeared on two different cameras. The lone one in the bay picked up some of the action, including the second man getting shot and collapsing.

Smitty erased the footage. The system moved recordings to the cloud automatically overnight, but if he deleted something, it wouldn't get archived. He hoped. Smitty dumped the entire day's video so far and started anew. As he sat in the chair, a police car drove by. Smitty watched it keep going up Belair Road. He didn't release his breath until it disappeared from view.

LEXI STIFLED A YAWN. Professor Lord would never be confused for someone interesting or exciting. The same criticism could be levied at economics. Lexi understood money and basic personal finance—her father insisted on it even before she lived under his roof. The rest was a bunch of theory and math she really didn't care about. Putting freshman year and all these gen-ed courses behind her couldn't happen soon enough.

The front door opened downstairs. Lexi glanced at the clock on her PC. It was just past 1400 hours. Early for her dad to be home. She turned off her video—the TA might dock her for it, but half the students showed up as black squares on the screen all the time—and walked to the top of the stairs. "Dad?"

"Down here," he said.

She joined him on the first floor. "You're home early."

"Kind of a rough day." Tyler opened the fridge and grabbed a beer. He held it up. "Want one?"

"I might need one to make it through econ today," Lexi said. Her dad handed her the longneck and took another one out for himself. "Everything all right at the shop?"

A long pull of the amber liquid prefaced his answer. "Not really."

"You've seemed a little distracted for a day or so now." Lexi frowned. "Is Smitty going to fire you from your first real job?"

Her father offered a faint grin. "I doubt it . . . though I couldn't blame him if he did."

Lexi sat at the small kitchen table and invited him to join her. "What's going on, Dad? Does this have something to do with the girl who dropped the car off?"

"Yeah." Her father downed the rest of his beer. Two gulps was a record for him. Something definitely gnawed at his gut. Despite the empty bottle, he joined her at the table. "She's dead. Found in the woods beaten to death."

Lexi felt her eyes go wide, and she drew in a sharp breath. "Oh, my god. You had me look into her boyfriend. Did he kill her?"

"Probably. I'm more convinced than ever now the cousin is in the drug trade." He told her all about his visit to Talbot Lakes and then moved on to the events of this morning at the shop. Lexi gripped the edge of the table as he told her about the man with the twelve-gauge, killing both gunmen, and leaving the bodies in a cemetery parking lot. "When I got back, Smitty was done cleaning up the shop. He suggested I go home, so I did."

"How long do you think it'll take before someone realizes those two are dead?"

"By now, I'm sure their boss knows they're missing," her dad said. "I figure it'll take until the evening before someone realizes the Explorer hasn't moved."

"If you're right," Lexi said, "this Héctor could have cartel connections."

"I know."

"I'm not trying to take Smitty's side, Dad, but he probably thinks you dumped a load of shit in his lap."

"I pretty much did," he said. His head wagged from side to side. "Alice didn't need to die over a car. The cops didn't seem to be motivated."

"So you acted instead," Lexi said.

Her father spread his hands. "Someone needed to." He paused. "You're smart to consider the cartel possibility. Make sure you take your pistol with you if you leave the house. So far, I think these assholes only know where I work, but it's probably a matter of time before they learn the rest."

"You know I'll help you with whatever research you need."

"I know." Her father smiled. "Thanks, kiddo. This isn't your fight just like it's not Smitty's, so I appreciate it." He stood and fetched another beer from the fridge. "How are you? Anything on your mind besides a boring class?"

Lexi considered telling him about her mother reaching out again. It sounded like his plate couldn't hold much more at the moment, however. She could handle her mother. Make a visit to get it over with, and then they could go back to the occasional emails. "I'm good," Lexi said after a moment of consideration.

"You know you can talk to me about anything." He smirked. "Even boys."

"I don't exactly have a lot of prospects at the moment," she said, "but thanks." Her dad stared like he wasn't quite sure he believed her before he got up and went back into the kitchen. Lexi drained the rest of her lager and walked back upstairs to finish her class.

HÉCTOR'S SECURITY cameras picked up the approaching car as it
ascended the driveway. On his monitor, he watched two men get
out. These must have been the promised reinforcements from the
cartel. He'd hoped for at least double their number. The fact they
arrived so quickly meant they probably came from the Texas
operation. Héctor frowned at the thought of adding second-rate
men to his crew. In the end, though, the numbers spoke for themselves. This pair could take the places of Patricio and Pedro.

They knocked on the door a moment later. Orlan Osorio,
Héctor's largest man, opened it. Both did a double take at the
giant standing before them. Orlan moved aside, and they
squeezed past his enormous frame into the house. Héctor sized
them up from the living room. Patricio and Pedro were wiry street
fighters. These two carried more weight. They looked stronger. As
long as they could intimidate people and shoot, they'd be
welcome. "Good evening," Héctor said. A clock struck eleven
behind him.

"We're from *el cartel*," the one on the left said. Both wore
leather jackets over jeans and black tennis shoes. Héctor
wondered if they coordinated their outfits. "I'm Leonel. He's
Juan." The latter offered a single bob of his head. "They told us
you have a problem."

"In a manner of speaking." He wondered what else the cartel
might have told these two. Héctor's idea to expand this far north
got greeted with skepticism when he suggested it. He got a
chance to make it work, but he knew his leash was shorter than
on someone closer to the border. Closer to direct control.
"Someone has . . . taken an interest in righting a wrong."

"We've heard," Juan said in a deep voice. "Is your cousin going
to keep being a wild card?"

Héctor shook his head. "He knows he screwed up. I've taken
him out of action for a while. He won't be a distraction again."

"Good. Bring us up to speed on what's happened today."
Héctor did. Both Leonel and Juan listened quietly, grimacing in

spots but letting him talk uninterrupted. When he finished, Juan said, "One guy at a car repair shop?"

"As far as I know, yes," Héctor said.

"You don't know anything else about him?" Leonel asked.

Héctor wondered if anyone in the cartel fed them these questions. Were they going to report back later tonight? He shook those thoughts from his mind. Their challenges were more local and immediate. "Not yet, no."

"I think we need to figure out who he is," Leonel said.

"And then kill him," Juan added.

12

T yler worked on his second cup of coffee since arriving at the shop. It made for his third overall. A restless night led to trouble waking up. Even Lexi told him how bleary-eyed he looked, and she sometimes stayed in bed until after he left for work. The caffeine finally seemed to be kicking in, and he checked what services the Mustang needed. Its red paint glistened in the overhead lights, and the body looked to be in good repair. The owner clearly took time to care for it.

The list consisted of routine maintenance. Tyler raised the car so he could start with an oil change. Smitty walked through the door from the front part of the building. "Good. I'll tell Ray he can pick his baby up today." Smitty moved to the rear of the vehicle. "Tailpipes look good, too. Probably got a few years left."

"Might be longer than you have left, old man," a harsh Spanish-accented voice broke in. Tyler stepped out from under the car. Two men he'd never seen before grabbed Smitty by each arm. The third man was the giant who accompanied Rodolfo when picking up the Boxster. Tyler reached for the Sig on his hip, but the large guy moved faster than he expected and swatted the gun away before he could bring it to bear. It slid all the way across the shop floor. Smitty disappeared through the door, leaving Tyler alone with a massive foe.

He'd faced someone similar before. His last job for Patriot Security saw him take on a similarly-sized man while trying to recover his missing client. Tyler got the better of his opponent then, though it hadn't been easy. The colossus before him today stood a little taller and a little broader. He could probably play defensive line for most teams in the NFL. Tyler spared a thought for Smitty and what he might be going through before returning all his focus to his adversary. "I'm going to enjoy this," the behemoth said. "You killed two of my friends."

"Don't know what happened to them," Tyler said. "They left in their Explorer."

Instead of saying anything, the giant answered with a punch. Tyler sidestepped the meaty fist. He landed a short cross to the massive man's midsection to no apparent effect. The giant threw a right jab, which Tyler backed away from. Too late, he realized it was a setup, and the left cross which followed it thundered into his face. Tyler fell backwards, keeping his head up to avoid whacking it on the concrete. He felt like David staring down Goliath. If only he had a slingshot. Or a pistol. Or any solid hand tool.

Tyler scrambled back to his feet. His foe looked to be in no hurry. He could have put Tyler in a bad spot by following up there. Maybe he was overconfident. Lulling him into a false sense of security, however, would require taking a couple more punches, and Tyler didn't like his chances to come out of them still conscious. His whole face hurt from the first one. There would be no time for contemplation as another fist rushed at him.

Tyler ducked, took a small step forward, and rose with an uppercut to the behemoth's chin. It rocked him back and made him shake his head, but he didn't fall. If anything, his glare intensified, and the furrow of his dark brows increased. "You were a soldier?" he said as the two men circled each other.

"Yeah. You?"

He shrugged his enormous shoulders. "For a little while. I like this job better." His closed left hand came forward. Tyler shuffled back. The colossus spun on his left foot, however, using his right to slam a powerful kick into Tyler's midsection. He folded in half and collapsed to the floor sucking wind.

This time, his adversary advanced.

ONE OF THE guys shoved Smitty into a chair. The other held a pistol on him. "I'm Leonel," the pushy one said. "My friend who might shoot you is Juan. Why don't you tell us your name?"

"Everyone calls me Smitty."

"How very American." Leonel spoke with only a mild accent. "Do you know why we're here, Smitty?"

"Is it about the damn Boxster we had here?" he said. "The guy who owns it already drove it home. We're not gonna work on it."

"I don't know anything about a Boxster. Two men visited you yesterday, yes? What happened to them?"

Smitty shrugged. "How the hell would I know?"

"Because you killed them," Juan said. His voice was much deeper than Leonel's. "Or maybe your friend did."

"No," Smitty said. He remembered discussing this with Tyler. They'd come up with what to say in case this very situation happened. "They drove here in their Explorer, and they left in it." Which they did, even though they were dead in the cargo hold.

"I'm not sure you're telling me the truth, Smitty," Leonel said. He bobbed his head toward the service bays. "It's not going so well for your friend back there. Orlan's going to beat him to death." Smitty couldn't see through the window. He knew Tyler to be very capable, but how much of a chance did even a trained operative have against the giant these two brought with them? Juan took a step away from Smitty to watch through the glass.

It left no one on Smitty's immediate right. If he could inch that direction, he'd be able to reach the fire alarm mounted on the paneled wall. They tossed him onto a chair with wheels. Smitty straightened his leg an iota, shifting an inch toward where he needed to go. Neither man seemed to notice. "Which way did the men go?" Leonel asked.

"What?"

"When they left here." He banged on the wall, and Smitty sat still. "Which way did they go?"

"I don't know," Smitty said. He heard a tremble in his own voice. Maybe it would work in his favor. They'd think him too scared to do anything—which wasn't far from the truth. "I was just glad they were leaving." He paused. "No offense, but I'll be happy to see you go, too."

Leonel offered a thin, insincere smile. "I'm sure you will. How will you feel about burying your friend, though?"

Smitty scooted another inch or two. He'd be able to make a grab for the lever soon. He couldn't look at the alarm without giving away his plan, so he hoped he remembered its location blind. "No need for anyone to die."

"Two men already have!" Leonel slapped the paneling again. Juan alternated between looking at Smitty and keeping an eye on the action in the bays. Smitty hoped Tyler was holding his own, and he'd be OK to do it for another minute or so.

"I told you they left in their Explorer," Smitty said. He wheeled himself another inch closer. Almost there.

"I think we'll just wait, then," Leonel said. "Once Orlan kills your friend, maybe you'll remember yesterday differently."

A final push got Smitty where he needed to be. His hand reached out. Leonel and Juan realized too late what was happening. Smitty allowed himself to look at his target now, and his fingers closed around the horizontal lever.

He pulled.

~

AN ENORMOUS FIST pummeled Tyler's jaw, bouncing his head off the concrete. Stars swam before his eyes. The giant standing over him smiled like he could do this all day. And he probably could. Tyler, on the other hand, could not. One more blow like the one he suffered a second ago would probably knock him out, and this guy could easily kill him from there. Tyler drew his legs up to his chest and shoved the colossus away.

If he weren't so woozy, he could have capitalized, but when Tyler struggled to sit up, he only got back to his feet with the support of a nearby workbench. His massive adversary bumped into one of the poles supporting the Mustang. The man's jacket hung open, and from his angle, Tyler spotted a grenade strapped inside. What kind of a masochist was he facing?

"Still have some fight in you?" the giant wondered and flashed a grim smile. "They usually do, but it never matters. Tell you what . . . one soldier to another, I'll kill you quick. I won't prolong the beatdown."

"Get on with it, then," Tyler said. He needed to be strategic. Trading punches with this behemoth would be a recipe for failure. Despite his bulk, Tyler's adversary moved pretty well. Strength and speed were out. Tyler would need to prevail with experience and treachery. When his foe advanced, Tyler ducked under a jab and kicked him in the leg. Before he could back away, Tyler did it again.

The principle was simple: a man needed to stand to fight. Take out his legs, and the rest is a lot easier. If he could get the giant down, Tyler could choke him out, beat him to death with a tool, or fetch his M11 and pump a few rounds into him. The big man was no dummy, though. He stayed out of Tyler's kicking range as he brought his fists back up.

Then, a shrill alarm pierced the quiet of the shop.

His brief moment of distraction at the noise cost Tyler another wallop in the face. He tumbled to the floor. His massive opponent stood over him, took out a cell phone, and snapped a picture with the annoying fake camera sound. "Let's go, Orlan" one of the others said as they rushed toward the exit. The colossus followed them.

"I'll see you again," he called to Tyler, patting the grenade as he moved toward their SUV.

Tyler believed him.

13

A t his house, Tyler dumped a couple handfuls of ice into a Ziploc bag. He held it to his aching face and sank onto the sofa. Since he first enlisted in the army thirty-two years ago, Tyler suffered several concussions. This didn't feel like one. His vision wasn't blurry. Turning his head didn't nauseate him. No, he'd undeniably taken a beating, and it had been a while since he found himself in this position.

Orlan. One of the other guys gave the giant a name. Tyler would need to get more information on him. Lots of men his size didn't know how to fight. They didn't need to. No sane person would pick on them. Orlan said he'd been a soldier for a time. The training showed. He knew how to throw a punch or a kick. His massive legs provided all the power he would need. Tyler felt a rematch would be coming regardless of whether he kept pursuing Héctor and his crew.

"Dad, what the hell?" Lexi said from somewhere behind him. She rushed to him and sat.

"Didn't hear you come down," Tyler said, talking around the improvised cold compress.

"Are you all right?"

"Sure. Only hurts when I talk. Or breathe. Or think."

"Not funny." Lexi's brows furrowed as she stared at him. "What happened?"

"Three guys rolled up to the shop," Tyler said. "Two of them took Smitty into the office. The last looked like Andre the Giant." Tyler paused. "He was a wrestler and—"

"I've heard of him," she said, spreading her hands.

"This giant got the better of the encounter. Smitty pulled the fire alarm, and it chased them off." Tyler blew out a painful breath. "It's been a while since I've fought someone his size."

"How long?"

"Almost fifty and a half years," Tyler said.

Lexi punched him in the shoulder. "You shouldn't joke about this."

Tyler laughed, and his ribs protested. He would need to ice them, too. "You're probably right."

"I know you feel bad about what happened to the girl with the Porsche, but it's time you dropped this. These guys are serious."

"I don't think I can." Tyler put up a hand to cut off Lexi's objection. "This isn't me being unable to let something go. Well .. . not entirely. Before they left, the guy who kicked my ass took my picture."

"So?" Lexi said. "They knew where you worked already."

"Sure, but they might not have known my name. I was the guy at Smitty's who didn't want to give the Boxster back to Rodolfo. Pretty soon, I think they'll know all about me."

"And me," Lexi added.

"We should presume they're smart and resourceful," Tyler said. "The military underestimated the Taliban years ago. I've tried to avoid making the same mistake since."

Lexi tucked her knees under her. "What are we going to do?"

"We're going to figure it out. It starts with more intel, though. I'll need your help."

"Of course," she said.

"Get the laptop. We might as well not waste any time."

"ALL RIGHT, DAD." Lexi sat with the computer on her lap. "How are we doing this?"

Tyler took the bag of ice from his face and flexed his jaw. It felt a little better. He'd want soup for dinner at this rate, but there wouldn't be any lasting damage. "It was two guys I'd never seen before plus the massive fellow who came in with Rodolfo." Tyler played the end of the encounter in his mind. The alarm went off. He got battered to the floor. The massive man took his picture. One of the guys called him by a name . . . Orlan. "See if you can find anything about the name Orlan in relation to Rodolfo or Héctor."

She tapped the keys and worked the trackpad. Tyler smiled as he watched her. He'd first asked for her help on something a few months ago. Lexi never used any program on the laptop before then, and she took to it almost right away. She'd gotten a lot better in the intervening time. "I have a hit on an Orlan Osorio." She frowned at the screen and pivoted the device toward Tyler. "Tell me you weren't fighting this guy."

The face of Tyler's adversary stared back at him, and a picture showing the man's fearsome size displayed alongside it. "Age and treachery will always overcome youth and skill," Tyler said.

"Not when youth and skill is twice as big!"

"I'm alive, aren't I?"

"Because Smitty pulled the fire alarm," Lexi said. A deep frown marred her face. "I can't lose you, Dad. Even if Mom weren't in jail, I couldn't, but I definitely can't right now."

"This asshole isn't going to kill me, Lexi." Tyler flexed his jaw again and rubbed the right side of his face. "He might give me some bruises, but I've been through worse. What does the computer say about him?"

Her eyes scanned the screen. "He's committed just about every crime there is. He went into the Mexican Army when he was twenty-one. It doesn't say, but based on what he did in the years before, it probably wasn't his choice."

"Not surprising if it's true," Tyler said. "He mentioned he wasn't in for long."

She shook her head. "Two years. All it says here is he was discharged early. It shows he went back to doing the same stuff as before. Robbery, assault, attempted murder. In and out of jail. During all this, he got hired by Héctor Espinoza as a bodyguard. From then on, he never spent a day in jail again even though the charges didn't stop."

"He enjoyed the protection of the cartel," Tyler said, "and the threat of its lawyers and guns."

"Both Orlan and Héctor were in Mexico until about eighteen months ago," Lexi continued. "Héctor invested in some fancy development in Harford County."

"Talbot Lakes."

"There's no job listed for Orlan once he comes to the States."

"He's still Héctor's goon," Tyler said.

"So now what?" Lexi asked.

"These guys still killed a young woman for no reason," Tyler said. "We're still going to make them pay. Only we're going to be smarter about it."

HÉCTOR GLARED at the face of the mystery man on his computer monitor. He grimaced as if in pain, which made sense after even a brief confrontation with Orlan. Héctor had to give the guy credit for still being conscious. "What do we know about him?"

"He's the one who didn't want to give me the car," Rodolfo said. "*Cabrón*."

Leave it to Rodolfo to point out the obvious. Héctor rolled his eyes. "This is what started his interest in us," he said as diplomatically as he could. "I'm looking for more."

"He's a mechanic," Rodolfo said. "Looks kind of old, too. At least fifty."

"He said he was a soldier," Orlan added in a quiet voice. He didn't speak often—and even more rarely at significant volume—but he usually provided good insight. He was a giant thug when Héctor first met him. Now, he could contribute more than mere muscle to the cartel's operation.

"This is what I'm talking about." Héctor pointed at the image on the large monitor. "You can see it in the hair. A lot of American soldiers keep their hair short." He looked at the eyes and almost flinched. In his years in the cartel, Héctor came across a lot of killers. This man had the same look in his eyes even when losing a fight to Orlan as he did in the first photo Héctor saw of him. "Who is he?"

"I'm running a reverse image search," Fernando Mora said. Héctor recruited him after relocating to Maryland. He wasn't much in a gunfight, but the young man earned his keep behind the keyboard. A smaller image replaced the larger one on the screen, and some text stood beside it. "His name is John Tyler, retired warrant officer. Twenty-four years in, and a bunch of them were in US Special Forces. He's been retired about eight and a half years now." Fernando's fingers flew over the keys. "He's been at the car shop for four months. Before then, he worked for a private security company."

"Now, we know about him," Rodolfo said. "Let's get him."

Héctor closed his eyes and rubbed the bridge of his nose. "One of these years, you'll learn to control your impulses, cousin. Maybe it will even be this year. Have you been listening? This man is dangerous. We can't take him lightly."

"Give me another shot at him," Orlan said.

"In time, maybe," Héctor said. "Fernando, what else can you tell me?"

"His mother is deceased. Father lives in some kind of . . . retirement community, I guess. He has a daughter in her first year at Maryland." The image of a pretty young woman replaced Tyler's. She had brown hair pulled into a ponytail, deep brown eyes, and a classically beautiful face.

"She doesn't get her looks from her father," Héctor said.

Rodolfo now stood next to his cousin. "Let's kidnap her." He slapped an invisible butt in front of himself and moved his hips back and forth. "Have some fun with her before the old man comes looking for her."

"Get out." Héctor thrust his finger toward the door. "You can wait for us in the kitchen. Do the dishes while you're in there."

"But—"

"Out!"

Rodolfo looked to everyone else in the room. He must have seen no support coming, because he frowned and exited the office, slamming the door as he left. "We're all adults now," Héctor said. "Fernando, continue."

"Not much else to tell," he said, "at least not with information I can easily find. You want me to break into the army's network?"

Héctor shook his head. "It's attention we don't want or need."

"Let me beat him to death," Orlan said. "He won't have a fire alarm to save him."

"In time, you may get your wish." Héctor held up a hand to placate his large friend. "This is not just any enemy, however. We can't go after him with just any plan."

14

T yler waited well past nightfall. He left Lexi in the house with a bunch of weapons and got to work. In one of his more paranoid episodes a few years ago, Tyler bought a bunch of security cameras. He'd never used them—the painting therapy took the edge off the worst of his PTSD—but he'd also never gotten rid of them. Now, he planned to use them to keep an eye on the cartel if they sent anyone to his house.

At the first streetlight near his home, Tyler set up a short ladder. He climbed, drilled into the metal a couple feet below the bulb, and mounted the camera. It would capture any vehicles approaching. This was the easy part of the operation. The next part would be more delicate and challenging. The cameras normally ran on USB power. Tyler spliced a USB cable onto a more traditional power wire for each device he planned to install.

He stepped down from the ladder and unscrewed a panel at the bottom of the pole. Simple wiring. The city wouldn't use anything complicated. They'd want the installation and maintenance to be as easy and budget-friendly as possible. Tyler appropriated a couple of the wires and tied his own into them. He finished the connection with a couple of wire nuts and replaced the panel. In theory, this should work. The street light looked a little dimmer.

Tyler got back up on the ladder. A tiny red light glowed on his camera. He called Lexi, who did the wireless setup back in the house before he came out. "We on the air?"

"Ask whoever's on camera to get down," Lexi said. "Maybe someone better looking is nearby."

"You're stuck with this guy, I'm afraid. Glad it works. Thanks, kiddo."

"Sure, Dad," she said. Tyler hung up and carried his equipment about two hundred feet farther down the street. This would be just before the lone bend, and a device here would capture anyone who recently turned onto the road. Tyler mounted this camera just like the first one. When he'd taken the panel at the bottom off, he heard someone approaching behind him. Tyler's hand went around the grip of his Sig.

"Didn't know you worked for city maintenance now," a kind voice said. Tyler turned to see Mister Thompson watching his handiwork. He was a retired black man in his seventies and a bit of a nosy neighbor but very nice. His hair had been white since Tyler moved in and probably years before.

"Kind of late to be out, isn't it?" Tyler said with a grin.

"I ain't the one climbing a light pole."

"I set up a camera." Tyler pointed to the device, and the older man's eyes followed. "One farther up, too, closer to my house. There could be some bad men rolling through here in the coming days."

"Who'd you piss off this time?" Thompson asked.

"A bunch of drug runners. It's a long story, but I'm pretty sure they know who I am now. Only a matter of time before they know the rest."

"What are you going to do if they show up?"

"Kill them," Tyler said.

The elderly man frowned. "Won't they send more?"

"I have a lot more bullets than they have men," Tyler said.

"I don't doubt you. Anything I can do?"

"Nice of you to ask, but I don't think so." Tyler paused. "Maybe one thing."

"Yes?"

"If I'm the one doing the shooting," he said, "don't call the cops. It'd be nice if you could spread the word while you're gossiping with the neighbors."

"Who, me?" Thompson smiled and walked back toward his house.

WITH LEXI'S HELP, Tyler set up alerts in the app the security cameras used. Any person or large object moving past the first camera would send an email to both of them. The same happening at the second camera would send two texts ten seconds apart. Tyler's house was one of three near the end of the street. Someone driving past the second checkpoint wouldn't necessarily be coming to his place, but he found the odds of a false positive acceptable.

Between lingering soreness and wondering if the cartel would send a battalion to his home in the night, Tyler slept fitfully. He finally got out of bed just after 0500. The smell of coffee lured Lexi downstairs, too. She yawned as she poured herself a hot mug. "You're up early," she said as she stirred her java.

"I'm not the only one."

"What are you going to do today?"

"Not much point in sitting around here," Tyler said. "They're either coming or not. I don't want to leave you here alone, though."

Lexi pointed at Tyler and dropped her thumb as if shooting him. "I'm at least as good a shot as you."

"Maybe." Tyler dropped two slices of bread in the toaster. "We don't know how many guys they might send. You might be a heck of a shot, but you don't have experience in these situations. I'd rather you not earn it this way."

Lexi frowned like Tyler knew she would. His daughter was smart and practical. She inherited the former from both her parents and the latter from her father. She would see he made sense. "All right," she said after a few seconds. "The college has some satellite offices set up. I'll go to one of them for the day."

"Good. I'll let you know when I'm coming home." They both ate breakfast and left soon after. Lexi drove the Tesla, and Tyler took her Accord coupe. He left the 442 parked conspicuously in the driveway. If the cartel came by, let them fire bullets into an empty house. Tyler arrived at Smitty's before his usual time.

"You're early," his boss said, peering into the parking lot, "and I didn't hear you coming from a block away this time."

"Changing things up today," Tyler said as he poured himself a cup of coffee. Smitty didn't make it as well as Tyler did, but caffeine was caffeine. He debated how much to tell the older man. Recent events introduced some strain into their normally pleasant working relationship. "The big oaf who kicked me around yesterday took my picture before they all ran out. I'm pretty sure they know who I am now."

"What are you saying?"

"I don't think they'll come back here," Tyler said. "They can go after me at home. I've . . . taken some precautions there."

"Let's hope you're right." Smitty stood and headed toward the service bays. "We have some work to catch up on."

Tyler finished his coffee and joined his boss. He quickly realized it would not be a good day. When Smitty dropped a wrench, Tyler nearly jumped out of his skin. A high-revving motorcycle speeding by produced a similar reaction. Tyler positioned himself with the bay doors to one side and the shop to the other. He could see all the exits. No one could come or go without him noticing. A short while later, another tool clanged off the floor, and Tyler bumped his head on the tire of the Mustang he'd never finished working on.

He needed to paint. Tyler looked at the clock on the wall and counted down the hours until he could leave.

TYLER SET a large pizza on the kitchen counter. He'd clocked out a little early from the shop, and after the second time Smitty called him a jumpy bastard, he figured it was time to pack it in. The security app threw alerts to his inbox several times, and once to text, but it turned out to be the mailman. At least the USPS vehicle came through clearly on the camera.

Lexi padded downstairs and smiled when she saw the white cardboard box. "Good call, Dad." She got two plates out of a cupboard and used one to hold two slices of pepperoni. "You're home a little early."

"Yeah." Tyler pulled a beer from the fridge. He held it up so Lexi could see it; she shook her head. "If you go in early, you get to leave early. Besides, not sleeping well took a toll on me." Tyler joined his daughter at their square kitchen table. "I'm not sure I was doing much good there today."

"If I were home, I would've taken a nap before lunch," Lexi said. "Philosophy was boring. I probably dozed in my chair a couple times."

"You saw the alerts come in?"

She nodded. "If those assholes roll down this street, we'll know about it."

Tyler didn't respond. He busied himself devouring his first slice of pizza. It didn't escape Lexi's notice. "What's going on?" she asked, setting her slice down and crossing her arms.

"We're having dinner. I'm also having a beer." To accentuate this point, Tyler took a long draught from the bottle.

"Don't bullshit me, Dad. You're up to something."

"Fine." Tyler wiped his mouth and leaned back as much as the wooden chair would allow. "I want you to stay with your grandfather for a few days . . . until this mess blows over."

She glared at him. "Seriously? Did you run this by him?"

"No," Tyler said. "I'm sure he'd love seeing someone under seventy on campus, though."

"You're really going to send me away?"

"Think about it. The cartel knows about me, so they also know about anyone connected to me. You're easy enough to find because you live here. Your grandfather's a little harder to get to. The place has a security gate. Guards. Cameras. Sure, they could shoot their way in, but it's not a good tactical play."

"And if they do," Lexi said, "Grandpa has enough guns to hold off a whole regiment."

"Exactly." Tyler nodded. "If they come for me here, it's only me. You'll stay safe, and you can be mad at me all you want, but keeping you out of harm's way is my first job."

Lexi uncrossed her arms and took a deep breath. "You're probably not my favorite person right now, but I get it."

"Good. I want you to take the Patriot laptop, too. We'll probably need to figure out a few more things along the way."

They each ate half the pizza. Tyler pushed his plate away when he finished. He couldn't have forced another crumb. Lexi broke the silence by asking, "Why don't you and Grandpa get along well?"

Tyler let out a dry chuckle. "How much time do you have?"

"I'm serious."

"So am I," he said. When Lexi's stare told him she wanted an answer, Tyler put up his hands. "There's a lot to unpack. The biggest answer is I think he felt I was a disappointment."

"Really?" Lexi frowned. "How?"

"He's tried to tell me all service is good, but I know he wanted me to go into the navy. I would have been the third generation to do it."

"Why didn't you?" Lexi said.

"It's kind of a lame reason." Tyler paused and shook his head. "I get seasick. Always have."

"Really?"

"Yeah," he said. "I'm not a big fan of flying, but I can manage it. Put me on a boat, though, and it's all over."

"Wow. I had no idea." Lexi grinned. "Now I know why you never wanted to go fishing."

Their phones vibrated. A no-frills email showed a car passing the first camera. Tyler's hand went to the Mii on his hip. Lexi fetched a shotgun from the living room. Both their texts went off a few seconds later. The same car approached the end of the street. Tyler moved beside the window and peeked out. The vehicle stopped at their neighbors' house. New homeowners. Tyler didn't remember their names.

A lone man got out, dropped something off on the porch, and drove away. Tyler relaxed. It served as a reminder they couldn't let their guard down until the cartel was no longer a threat.

15

While Lexi packed, Tyler sat in his spare bedroom-turned-studio. A fresh paper waited for him. When he first started therapeutic painting, he tried to force a certain image or design. Eventually, he learned to trust the process. His subconscious would tell him what to draw. It sounded like psychobabble the first time Tyler heard it—and it still did if he thought about it—but he couldn't deny it worked.

He picked up a wide brush, closed his eyes, and took a few calming breaths. When he opened them again, he mixed some colors and painted an ominous blue sky at the top. Using black, he drew the outline of a squat building on the right and a ribbon of road on the left. Tyler rinsed his brushes and waited for another bolt of inspiration.

A thin brush helped him trace the outline of a car, then a figure. He spent several minutes and a few different shades filling everything in. When Tyler finished, he felt mentally drained but also like he unloaded a burden he'd been carrying around. He left the room while everything dried. Lexi assembled a roller bag, a bookbag, and a laptop case near the front door. She rinsed her reusable water bottle in the sink. "I'm still not happy with you," she said as she dried the metal cylinder.

"You'll survive to be unhappy with me another day," Tyler said. "It's what I care about."

"I know." She filled the bottle using the cold water dispenser in the fridge. "I'm sure Grandpa will be glad for the company. I don't expect I'll have a good time, but it's just temporary." She smirked. "When we both survive this, I'll tell you how much of a jerk you were to send me away."

Tyler walked into the kitchen, and they embraced. "Take care of yourself, kiddo. If the worst does happen, listen to your grandfather. He probably has defense plans for just about any scenario. Hell, I'm sure the security director there blocks his calls."

Lexi giggled. "That sounds like Grandpa." She picked up the smaller bags, and Tyler carried the larger one. They loaded everything into the Accord. Tyler figured she took it because charging the Tesla wasn't a guarantee, but he was glad she logged some miles on the car they restored together. "Love you, Dad."

"Love you, too." He waved as Lexi backed out of the driveway and took off down the road. Tyler walked back inside and returned to his upstairs mini studio. He never focused on what he painted as it was happening, but the results always fascinated him after the fact. A stormy sky dominated the top of the paper. A short building looking a lot like Smitty's filled the right side. Behind a sports car, a giant lay dead, his blood running into the nearby street.

Orlan said they would meet again. Tyler knew he'd be ready.

LEXI PUT her stuff in her grandfather's extra bedroom. It was even more spartan than the rest of the unit. A double bed, a small dresser, and a nightstand—all the same boring medium brown—

were the only items in the space. Even the closet was empty. Most people used a spare room to store boxes and piles of extra crap. Not Zeke Tyler. He didn't own extra crap to begin with.

"Will it work?" her grandfather asked.

Lexi smiled. "It's fine."

"Your dad could've phoned me, you know. I would've said yes."

"You know him," she said.

"His whole life." He paused. "What happened? You talked about some cartel when you called."

"Yeah." They walked to the living room, which served as the main area of the condo. It joined a small dining space and average-sized kitchen, and Lexi figured the place touted the "open concept" layout she saw on every home renovation show. Down the hall were the two bedrooms and second bath. The flooring looked like authentic hardwood, and whoever painted the unit did so recently and well. Her grandfather hadn't put up many decorations. A few family photos and some navy memorabilia were it. "A woman dropped off some car at the shop where Dad works."

"Figures this is all over a woman," her grandpa said with a chuckle.

"I don't think it's like that."

"Your father was a bit of a skirt chaser before he met your mother."

"Gross, Grandpa." Lexi fought a losing battle with a shudder at the thought of her dad being a player. It was a long way from the man he was today. Once she pushed past that, Lexi remembered her mom's last email. She needed to reply at some point. Despite leaning against going earlier, she now thought she might as well. Maybe it was lingering anger at her father for shipping her off here. Whatever the reason, she hadn't seen her mother in a long time. "The girl was really into cars," she said. "The problem is her boyfriend got pissed she took it there. She ended up dead, he and dad got into it, two guys got shot in the shop, and now the cartel knows who Dad is."

The old man nodded. "Your father's always had problems letting things go."

"They murdered a woman for no reason."

"I know," he said. "It wasn't your dad's problem until he made it his problem, though. People get killed over dumb shit all the time."

Lexi frowned. "I'm beginning to think I should go back home."

Her grandpa waved a hand. "No, it's probably better you're here. I didn't mean to upset you. You have dinner yet?" She nodded. "All right. I didn't have anything planned for tonight. Just going to watch TV."

"I think I'll do some homework." She offered a small smile. "Thanks, Grandpa."

A grin split the old man's face. "Sure thing. If I don't see you before I turn in . . . good night." He stood, and Lexi heard his knees creak. "Oh, in case anything happens, there's a shotgun under your bed."

"Of course there is," Lexi said. She returned to the second bedroom. Without a desk to work at, her laptop earned its name while she sat on the bed. Lexi opened her mother's most recent email and typed a reply.

Mom,

> I'd love to see you. The next few days probably won't work, so maybe we could do sometime next week? Let me know, and I'll schedule something.
> Love,
> Lexi

. . .

HER FATHER SAID she could do what she wanted with her mom's invitation, but she knew he'd prefer she not go. It felt a little petty, but Lexi liked the thought of making him angry over something.

HÉCTOR GATHERED his men in the living room. He took a color printout of John Tyler's face and taped it to the wall. "This man cost us two of our own. He's our target."

"Let's get him!" Rodolfo said.

Héctor put up a hand to calm his younger cousin. "Before we do, I want everyone to know what's going on. We cannot take this man lightly. Besides killing Pedro and Patricio, he was an American soldier for a long time. He's dangerous."

"Look how many of us there are." Rodolfo stood and started counting.

Héctor cut him off. "I can add, cousin. Sit down. If you talk again, you can go back home." Rodolfo scowled, but he sank onto the couch. Héctor affixed a second paper to the wall beside the first. "This is his street. He lives in Baltimore. There's one way in and one way out. We can surround his house with a six-man crew and take him out." Héctor paused. "He has a daughter." A few of the men smiled and perked up. "She's not part of this. If she ends up a casualty, so be it, but no one is to go after her unless you have to." The enthusiasm dampened as quickly as it rose. Héctor grinned. "If you capture her, I don't care what you do with her. Or how often." It was amazing how quickly morale returned to the ranks.

Héctor pointed at the Google Maps photo of John Tyler's street. "Two vehicles. Three men in each. Danilo and Videl, you head it up." Both men nodded. They were experienced operatives. Some of the younger guys might fly off the handle and get too eager about kidnapping a pretty girl. Danilo and Videl would keep their eyes on the target.

"Get ready," Héctor said. "I want you to roll out in fifteen minutes."

16

L ater in the evening, Tyler sat in his bedroom and sent Lexi a text to ask how everything went at her grandfather's. They'd be a good pair. Zeke moved to an active adult community a few months ago, and he'd basically enjoyed the run of the place ever since. Maybe he sought an audience. Tyler didn't inherit his father's extroverted nature, but he'd seen plenty of people drawn to it over the years. Lexi, by contrast, would be happy to stay in her room, do schoolwork, and listen to music.

If the worst happened, Zeke picked a condo he knew would be easy to defend, and they were both good shots.

Tyler's phone vibrated. Lexi replied. *We're fine. Enjoying a couple beers after shooting a dozen cartel lackeys. How are you?* He smiled and shook his head. She'd gotten the morbid sense of humor from him.

Tyler typed a response. *I hope you took care of at least half. Your grandfather is 75. Don't make him work too hard.* His phone vibrated again. Too fast for another text even considering Lexi's thumb speed. The security app sent an alert. Tyler looked at the feed. Two Jeep Wranglers, their tops open on a pleasant fall evening, drove slowly down the street. Each showed two men in front plus another standing in the back.

With guns.

Tyler slipped a bullet-resistant vest over his head and strapped it on. He turned off the lights in the room and then crouched at an open window facing the street. Another buzz from his phone. The lead Jeep's headlights passed the pole with the second camera. Tyler picked up the M4 carbine he'd left in here earlier. A suppressor protruded from the muzzle, and the weapon was in semiautomatic mode. He activated the night vision scope and surveyed his adversaries.

All looked to be men in their twenties or thirties. The drivers didn't have any guns drawn. Each front-seat passenger held a pistol, and the two in the back both carried handguns, as well. They were likely going to fan out and surround the house. Not a bad tactic, and six men could cut off all reasonable avenues of escape.

Tyler didn't plan to give them the chance.

The Jeeps slowed to a crawl. They remained about a hundred yards away. No one inside seemed to be in a rush to get out. Tyler sighted the lead driver, then his passenger. He avoided the rear vehicle's headlights on the way to the second wheelman, then the second front-seat passenger. Their lips moved. They were probably confirming the plan.

In the army, rules of engagement tied soldiers' hands in some cases. Don't fire unless fired upon. Don't engage without authorization. Here, Tyler felt no such constraints. These men came to kill him, and he would get them first. Simple. The way it should be. Tyler emptied his lungs, put the first driver back in the crosshairs and fired. The man's head snapped rearward. Tyler moved the gun slightly to his left. A muffled report sounded, and the second guy slumped over dead, too.

By this point, the rear driver's face showed he knew what was going on. Tyler sent a bullet screaming into it an instant later.

The passenger turned to his now-dead compatriot in horror, and then Tyler put a shot into the side of his neck. Four bullets, four dead men. Total time: about two seconds. Not bad for someone who'd never been a sniper.

Panicked voices in Spanish came from the street. Tyler stayed low, carried the M4 downstairs, and exited the house via his side door.

WITH THEIR DRIVERS DEAD, the Jeeps remained in place. Tyler switched off the night vision scope and advanced to the crabapple tree in his front yard. He peeked out from it. Nearby driveways sat empty. If the neighbors were out, this would be easier. The two surviving men had a conversation Tyler couldn't understand, but their voices conveyed panic and uncertainty. Someone probably told them they'd surround a house and shoot one man inside. An easy job. Not much chance of something going wrong.

Tyler learned a long time ago how no plan survives contact with the enemy. He was ready for them thanks to the cameras, and now two-thirds of their contingent bled from bullet wounds to their heads and necks. "Night not going how you planned?" Tyler called down the street.

Both voices quieted. "Screw you, old man!" one of them hollered back. "We'll kill you."

"There were six of you a minute ago. If you're going to scare me, you should've done it before I killed four of your friends." They didn't say anything. "If you two don't want to join them, turn those Jeeps around and get out of here."

"Come out, you coward," the other one said. He got off a couple shots which died in the dirt before the tree. Tyler frowned. His suppressed M4 wouldn't alert anyone. The handgun fire could draw attention he didn't want.

The two survivors were close to three hundred feet away. Their pistols could hit a target at this range, but they'd need to be good shots. Based on what Tyler just saw, he didn't think they had it in them. Still, he wore a vest. His weapon was good out to five hundred yards. He exhaled, stepped from cover to the right, and put down a volley of suppression fire through the front Jeep's windshield.

"*Madre de Dios!*" the one inside the vehicle under siege yelled. He covered up and crouched behind the driver, whose body absorbed another couple rounds in the burst. Blood ran from a fresh wound in his abdomen.

"OK, I'm out," Tyler said. "My offer's the same. You want to live, you get those Jeeps rolling back to your boss."

"What do we do with the guys you shot?"

"They're your friends, not mine. I don't really care."

The two men went back and forth in Spanish for a moment. The one closer to Tyler did most of the talking. When the other guy didn't seem receptive, he yelled and made wild gestures to the carnage. After a moment, he said, "Fine, we'll leave. This isn't over, though. You're going to have the whole cartel after you."

"You're down four more men," Tyler said. "I'll take my chances."

He watched as each man pulled the dead drivers into the respective backseats, took their places, and turned the Jeeps around. Both guys stopped and stared at Tyler. He fired a couple rounds into the back of the trailing Jeep. The engines roared, and the two SUVs took off the way they'd come in. Tyler only lowered the M4 when their taillights disappeared, and he kept his vigil for another five minutes to make sure they didn't come back.

17

After putting his vest and carbine away, Tyler waited in the kitchen. He brewed a quarter-pot of coffee. If one of his neighbors farther up the street heard the commotion and called the cops, he'd need to go out and talk to them. The Jeeps ended up close to Mister Thompson's house, and Tyler figured he'd keep quiet. He may have even spread the word. The older man was both nosy and chatty, and while Tyler didn't always appreciate the combination, he thought it could be useful now.

His phone rang while he sipped some hot caffeine. Sara called. "Keeping late hours," he said. "The Pentagon got you burning the midnight oil?"

"It's barely ten," she said in a light tone. "It's not like either of us go to sleep early." She paused. "Especially not when we're together."

Tyler smiled at the lascivious comment. "If you want to come over, I'm just drinking coffee." *And I just shot four cartel men on my street*, he added in his head.

"I don't think I can tonight," Sara said. "I was wondering what you were up to this weekend."

"I don't know. Let me have my girlfriend get back to you."

"Tell her not to take too long. I'm popular."

"I'm . . . sort of in the middle of a situation."

"Do I want to know what it is?" Sara asked.

"Remember the guy you said I shouldn't take on?" Tyler said.

"Yes," Sara said after a moment.

"Well, I'm kind of taking him on. I don't want to get into the specifics right now, but let's just say recent events have made me very unpopular in his house."

Sara took a deep breath, and the exhalation whistled in Tyler's ear. "You know I worry about you. Don't get into more than you can handle."

"So far, I haven't."

"Yes," Sara said, "but I know you and your sense of obligation. You helped me out when three men were in my house despite me being nothing more than a voice on the other end of a phone. It sounds like the dead girl made quite an impression on you. I know you'll see it all the way through."

"I'm glad you understand." Tyler swirled the black coffee around in his mug. "And I'm sorry it's thrown a wrench into making any plans."

"These are the things a woman finds out when she gets involved with a knight-errant." They both chuckled. "Maybe you should call Rollins. I'm sure he could lend a capable hand."

"Officer thinking, Lieutenant."

Sara snorted. "Please. I'm a senior executive. I passed lieutenant equivalency ages ago."

"A simple retired warrant officer like me doesn't understand these things," Tyler said.

"You should talk to your girlfriend more," Sara said. "I hear she's pretty smart."

"She is," Tyler said. "And patient, too, thank goodness."

〜

AFTER HANGING UP WITH SARA, Tyler called Lexi next. Her voice rose in concern, and she even admitted sending her to stay with Zeke for a few days was a good idea. "Nice shooting, Dad."

"They kept me around all those years for a reason," he said.

"You need to call Rollins," Lexi told him.

He didn't divulge Sara said the same thing a few minutes ago. Lexi might be salty at not being his first call. "I had the same idea." They hung up a moment later, and Tyler dialed his old acquaintance from the service. Rollins was retired despite being about a decade younger than Tyler. The man was reliable, selfless, and stealthy enough to break into a lion's den with a pocket full of catnip.

"Little late for someone your age to be awake," Rollins said when he picked up.

"Good thing I already drank my prune juice," Tyler said.

"What's going on? I know you're not making a social call."

Tyler filled him in on everything starting with Alice sashaying into the shop and concluding with four dead men riding out in a pair of bullet-riddled Jeeps. "What'd you do with Lexi?" Rollins asked.

"She's with my dad for a few days. Between the location of his unit and the arsenal he keeps there, I think they could hold off a few men."

"Agreed. What's the next move?"

"I figure Héctor's going to be pissed," Tyler said. "He knows who I am, sent six men to take me out, and two-thirds of them went back dead."

"You don't want to go after him now?" Rollins said. "He's depleted."

"I don't know enough about his operation yet. He could have two dozen men standing by. I think we're in reaction mode for now while we gather some more intel. Then, we make a plan and take the fight to them."

"All right. I'm in."

"Thanks." Tyler paused. "I can't really pay your rates, but we're liable to take out a few men with fat wallets."

"I'll manage." For the first time ever, Tyler heard Rollins stifle a yawn. He wasn't sure the man ever slept. "You said they're in some fancy Bel Air neighborhood?"

"Yeah."

"If the boss gets pissed, it'll be a little while before they roll out on you again. You want me to keep an eye on your place?"

"I set up a couple cameras," Tyler said. "Another gun couldn't hurt, though."

"All right," Rollins said. "See you soon." He broke the connection. Tyler went back to his coffee. He appreciated the weight of the Sig on his hip.

HÉCTOR SEETHED as Danilo and Videl pulled the twin black Jeeps into his driveway. They'd called ahead and talked to Rodolfo, who relayed the bad news. Once the gate swung shut, Héctor and Orlan walked outside to meet them. Two corpses flopped at odd angles in each of the vehicles. Between the bodies and the bullet holes, Héctor was surprised they made it all the way from Baltimore without someone noticing.

"Sorry, boss," Danilo said as he climbed out of the vehicle. "It felt like he knew we were coming. We couldn't—"

Héctor cut him off with an upraised hand. "We'll debrief inside. You and Videl head downstairs."

Danilo gulped. Héctor enjoyed the fear in his eyes. "Downstairs?"

"You have a problem?"

"No, no." Danilo jerked his head, and Videl accompanied him inside.

Héctor and Orlan briefly surveyed the Jeeps and the four

cadavers. "I didn't think we'd underestimated him," Héctor said in a quiet tone. "Six men, Orlan. Six!"

"Let's hear what they have to tell us," Orlan said. They entered the house via the side door and took the carpeted stairs to the basement. The first room held a giant TV, a plush couch, and two next-gen gaming consoles. Danilo and Videl waited there. Héctor beckoned them with a wave. They walked through a door into the next room. It featured bare stone walls and an unadorned concrete floor.

Orlan closed the door once everyone was inside. Danilo and Videl cowered at the far end of the room. They stank of fear and failure. Orlan stood beside his boss and crossed his massive arms. "All right," Héctor said. "We knew who this guy was. I respected him enough to send a half dozen men to kill him. Four came back dead. What happened?"

"I swear he was ready for us," Videl said. "We stopped about a hundred yards from his house to go over the plan. All six of us would surround it. He couldn't get away, and the numbers would get him if he came out." He snorted and shook his head. "The next thing I know, two guys slump over in the front Jeep. I didn't even see where the shots came from. They were quiet, too." He ran a hand through his damp black hair. "Before I could do anything, the two men with me were both dead, too."

"There were still the two of you," Héctor said.

Videl laughed, but there was no humor to be found in it. "He'd just killed four men before I realized what happened. What good were the two of us?"

"What good indeed?" Héctor asked. "Orlan."

The giant strode toward Videl. His eyes went wide, and he held his hands up. "Boss, wait a minute. I—" Orlan's massive fist walloping him in the face cut him off. Videl went down hard. He flexed his jaw and rose to all fours. Orlan glanced back to Héctor, who gave him a single nod. Another punch drove Videl to the floor again.

Danilo recoiled in horror as Orlan rolled the unconscious man onto his back, crouched over him, and rained hammer blows onto his unprotected face. Héctor enjoyed the reaction. Men needed to know the consequences of failure, and if he couldn't inflict the suffering himself, watching his trusted enforcer dish it out came in a close second. Between the beating and the unforgiving stone, Héctor wondered how much longer Videl could survive. His answer came quickly. After several loud cracks, Orlan's blows sounded wet as he pulped Videl's face and burst his skull. The enforcer stood.

"Go wash your hands," Héctor said. The giant nodded and left the room. "Danilo." The man stared at his comrade, now beaten to death only a couple feet away. Héctor followed his gaze. The left side of Videl's head was caved in, and the floor was a red mess. Danilo's hands shook as he struggled to look at Héctor. He'd learned what it meant to come up short where the cartel was concerned. "Will you fail me again?"

"N . . . no, Héctor," he stammered.

"Good." Héctor pointed toward the corpse. "Clean this up. Then do the same with the other four."

"Where . . . where do I put them?"

"Figure it out," Héctor said, "or join them."

18

T yler woke up at the usual time. The security cameras didn't record anything in the night. After he rolled out of bed, he texted Smitty, mentioned an incident late last night, and said he'd be in late as a result. Rollins' idea of striking while Héctor was down four men held some appeal, but Tyler wanted to know more about the operation. How many men? What defenses did they have? Did they keep drugs in the house? He'd been meticulous in planning operations in Afghanistan, too, and it showed in his crews' survival rates.

He would use the morning for surveillance. Rollins would be a good partner here. He could probably get onto the property undetected. Yet with so many unknowns, their consequences could make getting out again difficult. Tyler brewed a half-pot of coffee and pondered the best move. Rollins could keep an eye on Lexi and Zeke. Héctor was still something of a wild card. He could lash out at people close to Tyler after four of his men returned dead last night.

He texted Rollins. *Can you sit on Lexi and my dad for a while? I'm going to try and gather intel at the source.* He also provided Zeke's address. Rollins replied in the affirmative. Tyler wolfed down a bowl of cereal, filled a thermos with coffee, gathered some supplies, and approached the entryway. He slid the M11 out of its holster and held it ready against his thigh. He pushed the door open from the side. No bullets greeted him. Tyler looked around, saw no one, and locked up the house.

Lexi took the Accord to Zeke's, so Tyler hopped in the Tesla SUV. It whirred silently to life, and he enjoyed a comfortable cruise to Talbot Lakes. The huge screen where most cars had knobs and switches still vexed him. Each time he drove the car, he figured he'd get used to it next trip. He'd been wrong every time.

Tyler again parked across from Rodolfo's house. In this environment, the luxury SUV fit right in with its German and Japanese counterparts Tyler noticed all over the neighborhood. The 442 drew the wrong kind of attention. It marked him as an outsider in a ritzy place like this. Residents' eyes would pass over the Tesla, and its tinted windows would prevent them from seeing much inside.

There wasn't much to see, anyway. Tyler kept an eye on both houses, but his vigil was fruitless for a while. Drinking a thermos lid of coffee counted as the most significant event for the first hour. Then, someone walked down the driveway dragging a large trashcan on wheels behind him. Tyler fetched his camera from the passenger's seat. Whenever he used it, Lexi told him cell phones took perfectly good pictures. They did, but Tyler couldn't snap a good zoom lens onto his Samsung mobile.

With help from the lens, Tyler realized the guy trudging toward the sidewalk was one of the men who drove away last night. Sweat and dirt covered his features. He set the can near the curb, leaned against it, and rested for a moment. Tyler wondered what gruesome tasks Héctor forced the fellow to spend the night doing. When the man walked back toward the house a couple minutes later, Tyler followed him with the camera. It allowed him to see a gate about halfway up the driveway for the first time. Trees and bushes hid it pretty well without a zoomed-in view.

All was quiet for another half-hour. Then, a late-model BMW sedan cruised down the street and stopped in front of Héctor's house. The guy who stepped out was a paunchy white American. He ambled up the walkway toward the front door, turned left, and disappeared from Tyler's sight behind a lattice and some shrubs. Probably a side entrance. What did he come here for, though? Windholm wouldn't hire someone so out of shape for security work.

A couple minutes later, the man emerged from the jungle and returned to his car. Tyler noticed he walked faster this time. He got back into his 3 series and pulled away. Tyler turned on the Tesla—it was so electric and quiet, he couldn't think of it as firing it up—and followed at a reasonable distance. It wasn't a long trip as Talbot Lakes didn't cover more than a few blocks. The Bimmer turned left down a short cul-de-sac off the main drag. Tyler swung the SUV in and crept along the short street.

The sedan stopped in a driveway. Tyler curbed the Tesla and retrieved his camera again. He focused on the passenger compartment. After turning the car off, the driver fished a small baggie full of white powder out of his pocket. He produced a mirror from somewhere in the interior and emptied the snowy substance onto it. Next, he used a credit card to make the pile into neater lines before snorting them through a straw. Tyler snapped photos throughout the process. He didn't know who this guy was, but pictures of him snorting coke in his driveway could be useful at a future date.

Previously, Tyler wondered if Héctor kept any product in the house. This confirmed the answer was yes. It didn't need to be a lot, but it created an additional risk if the cops ever raided the compound. Considering the lukewarm response Tyler received when asking about Alice's murder, he didn't think law enforcement intervention was likely. Men like Héctor always kept a few cops on the payroll.

If Tyler were going to take down the cartel, he'd have to do it without any help from the local sheriff's office.

THE EASE at making an appointment to see her mother in prison surprised Lexi. She set it up before she fell asleep, and she got up at the normal hour in the morning. Her grandfather was already awake. He'd brewed a pot of coffee and sat at his dining room table reading the *Baltimore Sun*. Just like her dad. Lexi grabbed a cup, exchanged morning pleasantries with Zeke, and took the java to her bedroom to get dressed.

She emerged with her backpack a few minutes later and inhaled a quick breakfast. "You seem like you're going some-where," her grandfather said.

"Yeah. I have to do something for school in person."

"You sure it's a good idea?"

"I'll be fine, Grandpa," she said.

"You'd better be." She would. Even if the cartel were on to her dad, they wouldn't know to look for her here. A perk of living in a place like this was the security presence. A couple of Héctor's goons couldn't simply drive past the gate and go where they wanted. Still, Lexi would be careful. She knew how to spot a tail while she drove, and she'd packed her Glock in her bookbag.

It took about a half-hour to drive to the jail, a gloomy gray fortress outside Columbia. Barbed-wire fences surrounded the place. A few women exercised in a yard under the close supervi-sion of a man with a rifle. Towers broke the fenceline at regular intervals, and each featured an armed guard surveilling the grounds. Lexi parked her Accord coupe in a space marked for visitors and walked inside.

She passed through a mantrap, showed her ID, and got a

wanding and brief pat-down from a squat, unpleasant-looking female corrections officer. The matron walked Lexi along a short corridor and let her into a waiting room. A few women in prison jumpsuits sat talking to loved ones across ugly plastic tables. Lexi slid onto an unused one. She tried to move the bench, but the whole thing was bolted to the floor.

A minute later, another man walked in. Lexi frowned in recognition. "Uncle George?" He was in his mid-forties, about six feet tall with a full head of blond hair. Lexi remembered him being in trouble often, both with the law and the husbands of women he pursued. The former made him just like her mother. What was he doing here?

"I kinda hoped you'd be happier to see me," he said. He put an arm around her for a side hug, and she gave him a quick pat on the back.

"I'm surprised is all."

"Guess we both scheduled something for the same day." He slid onto the bench across from her.

"And time?" she asked.

He spread his hands and plastered an insincere grin on his face. "A happy coincidence, huh?"

"Sure," she said to placate him. Lexi's dad taught her about coincidences, especially as they concerned her mother. It explained a lot of the things she saw and dealt with as a girl. Uncle George walking into the room today was no happy accident. He and her mother planned it—probably this morning because Lexi made the visitation appointment late last night. She thought she'd feel a little vindication at coming here so soon after her dad ordered her out of the house, but now this whole thing reeked of a setup.

Before she could leave, a guard led her mother into the room. Despite the unease she felt, Lexi grew up with Rachel and hadn't seen her in well over a year. She stood and gave her mom a hug. A nearby officer cleared his throat, and Lexi took her seat again.

Her mother looked a little older, and her blonde hair lost some of its luster under prison living. She was still pretty, though, and she'd maintained a healthy weight during her time inside. "It's so good to see you, Lexi." Her mother sat next to her brother. Being across from both of them felt a little like an interrogation.

"You, too, Mom." She smiled and hoped it looked legit.

"I was surprised you came so quickly."

"Had an opening in the schedule," Lexi said with a shrug. "It's a light class day for me." She was missing English and political science to be here, neither of which constituted any great loss. Her poli sci prof might be grouchy about it, but she maintained a solid A, and he'd just have to get over it.

"Well, it's certainly good to see you. Tell me all about your schooling. How was graduation?"

They chatted about the final year of high school and the first semester of college for a few minutes. Uncle George sat and listened in silence, offering up one of his patented grins whenever the situation called for it. Lexi really didn't like him being here. She'd never been close to him growing up, and as she matured, she realized he brought out the worst in her mother. He always had another plan, another scheme. What could he be after today?

"Did you hear me?" her mom wanted to know.

"What? Sorry, no."

"I asked how your father's doing."

"He's good," Lexi said. "He enjoyed retirement for all of a few weeks before finding his mechanic job, but he's happy with it." She left out the incident with his former commander a few months ago and all the cartel stuff from the present.

"I'm glad he could step up and take you in," Rachel said. Lexi's eyes narrowed at the implicit dig, but she didn't say anything. "Are you going to live with him while you're in college?"

"Might as well. Even when I go on campus, it'll save me the housing expense."

"A smart girl like you didn't get a scholarship?" Uncle George asked.

"Partial," Lexi said. "It covers a nice chunk of the tuition, but I'd be out of pocket for housing."

"I'm sure your father could pay for it," Rachel said. "He's working a job now . . . plus, he has his retirement. If you want to live somewhere with your friends, I think you should do it."

Lexi shrugged. "I really haven't made any friends yet. Maybe when classes aren't over Zoom, it'll be easier."

"Don't let your dad be a cheapskate," Uncle George added.

"He's not."

"I'm just trying to look out for you." Her mother smiled, and it even looked sincere. "It's hard to do from in here."

You might as well get used to it, Lexi thought. Rather than hurl a barb, she said, "I know, Mom."

They talked a few minutes more before Lexi told them she needed to get back to class. "Thanks for coming today," Rachel said. They embraced again, and even with the weirdness of her uncle being here, Lexi missed hugging her mother. "I hope you'll see me again soon."

"I'll try," Lexi said. She left the room, and her uncle walked with her. She figured he would, but she didn't want his company. They signed out together and emerged from the depressing building into the sunlight.

"I'm glad you could make it today," he said. "It's the happiest I've seen your mom in a while."

Lexi wondered what their game was, but putting the question to her uncle directly wouldn't get her anywhere. It was better she kept her suspicions to herself for now. "Good. She looked happy. Probably not many opportunities in here."

"You got that right." He would know, having been behind bars a couple times, himself. Lexi didn't want him to see her get into her car and drive away. She stopped at a nondescript Toyota Corolla. "This is me."

"Good to see you, kid." He gave her another side hug, and she didn't even bother with the back pat this time. Lexi pretended to look for her keys in her purse while her uncle walked farther into the lot. He got into a battered Volkswagen GTI and left without a wave. She watched his taillights move toward the exit before she got into her car.

~

HÉCTOR HATED waiting on the phone. It made him feel he wasn't being taken seriously. Finally, Tomás Quintero came back on the line. "I want some good news."

"So do I," said Héctor. "It's in short supply right now."

Silence served as the response. Héctor wondered if Tomás put the phone down again. After a moment, the lawyer said, "Are you still having problems?"

"We've run into a capable adversary. It's nothing we can't handle, but I'm going to need some more men."

"We sent you more men."

"I know." Héctor sighed. "This man was a soldier. Special forces. I . . . . think the crew underestimated him even though I specifically told them not to. I sent six men to deal with him, and only one came back alive." Tomás lacked a way to verify any of this. Héctor's crew would be loyal to him. Might as well blame Videl's death on the meddlesome American, too.

"You insisted you could handle this expansion north," Tomás said. "We warned you it was a thousand miles from any support. Did we place too much trust in you?"

"No. This is just a snag. If we kill this one guy, we're in great shape. The rest of the operation is humming along."

"Minus a handful of men."

"Unfortunately, yes," Héctor said. "You know we've been holding up our end. The product is moving. We're taking care of the money. Does the boss have any complaints?"

"Only about his women," Tomás said with a chuckle.

"I wish my troubles were so simple."

"Look, Héctor, we can't keep sending you more soldiers. We need to be ready for a war here in Mexico. You remember how it is . . . at least, I hope you do."

"Of course," Héctor said.

"I wish I could be certain. Perhaps your time in America has made you soft."

"What are you telling me?" Héctor asked. He tried to ignore the barb, clenching and unclenching his fists as he paced the room. There were always problems with rival groups in Mexico. Tomás needed to come through. Moving an operation so far north turned out well for the cartel. The lawyer thought as much, and he had Bernardo's ear.

"We'll send you a few men with your next shipment," Tomás said. "This is it, though. No more."

"I hear you."

"I want to be sure you do, Héctor. You solve this problem, or it's over for you. Bernardo's becoming less keen on this idea of yours. You'd better handle your business soon."

Héctor understood. Failure meant death in the cartel's world. He could accept it. He wouldn't fail. "We'll take care of it," he said. "Consider the American dead."

19

At her grandfather's condo, Lexi found it difficult to focus on her work. She watched a recording of a lecture she'd missed due to her morning trek to the prison. It was just as dull when viewed later—if not worse. She scrolled through social media while her professor yammered on. Nothing interested her. She merely needed the distraction. When the video ended, Lexi removed her headphones and walked into the kitchen.

She hailed from a long line of coffee drinkers, so it was never the wrong time to brew more. Zeke joined her when the half-pot finished. She poured both of them a cup. The old man took his black. Lexi added milk to hers. "How was your morning errand?" her grandfather asked.

"Fine." Lexi replaced the milk in the fridge.

"You gonna tell me where you really went?"

"What do you mean?"

Zeke took a seat at the nearby table and invited Lexi to do the same. She did. "Look, I like having you here. It'd be nice if your father talked to me about it first . . . but whatever. I might be an old coot, but don't presume I'm an idiot."

"I wouldn't," Lexi said.

"Good. Now . . . where'd you really go?"

"How do you know I didn't drive to school?"

"No reason for you to," Zeke said. "Bunch of people here have grandchildren in colleges all over the place. If the classes are virtual, everything else is, too. There's nothing you need from your school you couldn't do online."

Lexi frowned. She'd never think of her grandfather as an idiot, but she figured she could get this one past him. "Fine." She sighed. "I visited my mother in prison."

Zeke paused with the mug of coffee halfway to his mouth. He set it back down before saying anything. "Your father know you went?"

"No, but he told me I should do what I wanted. He knows Mom reached out to me."

"Your mother's no good," he said. Lexi started to object, but her grandfather put his hand up. "I know you love her. You grew up mostly with her and not your dad. Take my word for it, though . . . she's no goddamn good. I tried to tell your father years ago, and he wouldn't hear it."

Lexi sipped her coffee rather than say something rude. "You never liked her?" she asked after stewing on it for a few seconds.

"She was always nice enough to me. I could tell, though, how something was off about her." He shook his head. "Hard to quantify, but I'm sure you've met people where you just knew something was wrong."

Her uncle, for one, even if Lexi enjoyed the benefit of hindsight there. "I think everyone has."

"Your dad didn't want to see it. He was smitten." The old man snorted. "He ever tell you how they met?"

"No. They never talked much about each other even when I asked."

"She was a secretary on base when your dad was at Fort Bragg. They dated for a while. She got fired at some point . . . said it was about the contractor downsizing, but I think something happened. Didn't take her long to get a job as a bookkeeper. She got canned again . . . this time while your dad was overseas."

"Was she stealing?" Lexi said.

"Of course," Zeke said. "Your mom's always been smart, so she was able to paper over it. It was a long time ago, so I don't remember what tipped anyone off. I heard she was lucky not to get arrested, though."

"My dad's never told me any of this." Lexi sipped her coffee and leaned forward in the chair.

"He doesn't like to badmouth her. He's too nice when it comes to Rachel." Her grandfather shrugged. "I'm an old man. I don't have time to be nice."

Lexi grinned. "She stayed out of jail for a long time, though."

Zeke nodded. "Sure. She never stayed at a job long enough to get caught. By the time your father came back, she'd been through two other places. Then, she got pregnant."

"You wanted him to leave?"

"No. He wasn't sure about marrying her. I think he knew what she was but didn't want to admit it. His mother was big on not having a grandchild out of wedlock, so he and Rachel got married a few months later."

"I don't really remember Grandma." Lexi frowned and stared at the bare tabletop.

"You were little when she died." Zeke fingered the wedding ring he still wore. "She's the one who spurred your dad to marry your mom, though. It was a mess when they got divorced. The UCMJ isn't very friendly to soldiers, but your dad knew a JAG who found a loophole. Rachel got arrested. Eventually, they didn't charge her, but putting her in cuffs was enough. Your father could divorce her and not lose a chunk of his pension, so he did."

"Wow. I didn't know most of that." Lexi sipped her coffee, which grew tepid during the conversation.

"Like I said, your father doesn't like to badmouth her. I'm not really trying to, even if it might seem like it."

"It kind of does," Lexi said.

"She and I ain't exactly close," her grandfather said. "She knew I was onto her. Your dad was blind to it all for a while. He loved your mother, but in the end, he couldn't be with a criminal, and it's the path she was walking."

"I'm surprised he didn't get custody of me."

"Courts used to favor the women in this stuff. Always have. He got pretty generous visitation, though."

"Yeah." Lexi nodded. "He was around a lot." She glanced at her watch. "I need to get back to my work. Thanks, Grandpa. Interesting stuff."

"Sure." Zeke smiled. She freshened her java and walked back to her bedroom. For a few years before her mother's arrest, Lexi suspected Rachel was a criminal. She also thought—or maybe hoped—it was something new. Not a vocation. Now, more things made sense. The frequent job changes. Her mother's state of near-constant worry. Moving from city to city. Always with Uncle George not far behind. Then, the next apartment and the next plan. Lexi wondered anew what her uncle was doing at the jail this morning and what the two of them were up to.

AFTER HIS TRIP to Talbot Lakes, Tyler went back home. Plenty of work awaited him, and he didn't want to test Smitty's patience by coming in late every day. He'd get there a few hours after his normal time now. Tyler felt bad about leaving his boss there alone, but he also had bigger problems to solve. On his drive into the shop, he called Lexi. "What's up, Dad?"

"I see the two of you haven't killed each other yet," he said. "Progress."

A light chuckle came from the speakers. "We're getting along fine, actually. Grandpa has some interesting stories to tell."

"He certainly does. I'm calling about our friends in Harford County, though. Can you help me with some research?"

"Sure. Let me get your laptop." Her phone thunked onto something solid while Tyler puttered along on Northern Parkway. When she came back onto the line a minute later, he hadn't moved very far. "All right. You're on speaker now, too. I seem to have acquired a research assistant."

"I want to see this fancy machine in action," Zeke said.

Tyler saw an opening in the right lane and surged around a slow-moving white van. He zoomed through an intersection just as the light changed to red. Traffic picked up without the delivery vehicle gumming up the works. "You're watching the right opera- tor, then. I checked out Héctor's neighborhood again this morn- ing. He's moving product from his house, and it's not Amway or Mary Kay."

"Wow," Lexi said.

"Yeah. It's more brazen than I expected. It makes me think he's built some legal protections into what he does. Before, I would kick the door in, but someone else gathered the intel and assembled a report. Now, I need to do my own. Which means you get to do it."

"I follow you."

"All right," Tyler said. He thought back to his first visit to Talbot Lakes. "Héctor might be in business with the property manager up there. Todd Windholm." He spelled the surname for her. "Can you check it out?"

"Sure." Lexi's fingers tapped the keys.

"Wish we had this kind of stuff in my day," Zeke said.

"I take it you have results?" Tyler asked.

"Working on it." After more keystrokes and mouse clicks, Lexi came back on the line. "You're right, Dad—they do have some- thing together. Talbot Lakes Development. It's an LLC incorporated in Bel Air. It's also listed as a wholly owned subsidiary of Windholm Enterprises. A few others fall under the umbrella, too."

"Shell companies?"

"Pretty much," Lexi said. "The address for the parent business is a vacant lot. Another one turns out to be a convenience store that closed last year. There's a lot of crap here."

"Sure, but it gives us another potential avenue of attack. Anything else?"

"Yeah," Zeke said. "Be careful messing with the cartel. They have ways of killing people you and I would never think of."

"I'm pretty creative, Dad."

"He's right," Lexi added. "You know you're on their radar now. You're going to push because it's what you do. I only want you to be smart about it."

"It's the only way I know," Tyler said. "Thanks, kiddo. Bye, Dad." He hung up. Héctor cloaked his operation in the veneer of legitimacy. It could explain the local LEOs not wanting to go after him. Cursory research would reveal a retired imports executive who now developed real estate. Either they lacked incentive to look deeper, or Héctor funded the disincentive.

Tyler checked his mirrors again. All clear. He remained vigilant looking for a tail all the way to Smitty's.

20

W hen Tyler pulled into the lot at Smitty's, he drove around the perimeter and scanned for anyone casing the place. No one stood out to him. He parked in a vacant spot and texted Rollins. *At work. All clear so far. Can you linger in the area in case?* A moment later, Rollins replied in the affirmative. Tyler holstered his Sig at his hip, buttoned his work shirt over it, and walked into the shop. "Nice of you to join us," Smitty said, standing near his desk. Through the window, Tyler saw Jake working on a car in the first service bay. It was about time he showed up.

"I know the cartel stuff is keeping me occupied," Tyler said. "They've been ramping things up recently. I got a visit from six armed men last night."

Smitty sighed, sank onto his chair, and rubbed his forehead. "Let me guess . . . they're all dead."

"Four are. The other two drove the Jeeps away. Saved me the cleanup and questions."

"And here you are today." Smitty jerked his thumb toward the service area. "Jake's here, for Christ's sake. What if they come to the shop?"

"They're down four men," Tyler said. "They're regrouping right now . . . maybe getting some reinforcements. I think we're all right. Besides, I have a friend who's going to be keeping an eye on things."

"This friend as good as you?" Smitty asked.

Tyler smiled. "Almost."

"I sure hope so." The boss checked a paper on his cluttered desktop. "Why don't you hoist the old Chevy pickup in the lot onto number two rack for a peek at its tranny?"

"Sure." Tyler walked through the door into the work bays. He and Jake shook hands. It was good to see him here, though he seemed to be coming less and less every week. While fixing old cars was in Smitty's blood, the trait didn't pass down to his son. Current events made Jake a good coworker. He'd spent years in the army and only recently left the reserves. He could handle himself and protect his father if the cartel's goons came calling.

Tyler found the mid-'eighties S10 and pulled it in. Even on such a short jaunt, the hesitation at takeoff and jerky ride told Tyler the transmission needed work. Most people didn't check or change the fluid, so Tyler started there. It was old and gunky, and he replaced it with a new synthetic blend. Tyler backed the truck out and did a circuit of the lot. It drove better but still didn't feel right.

As he steered it back toward the bay, he noticed an older pale green Cadillac with blacked-out windows pull to a stop on the side street running alongside the shop. The engine revved and then cut off. The driver's side glass went down, and a Hispanic man stared at Tyler. He put the tinted window up a few seconds later, but the short time was enough to send a message.

Tyler guided the truck back in. Jake helped him do some maintenance work while he kept an eye on the car. It didn't move, and no one got out. When he and Jake took a break, Tyler walked inside and told Smitty. "I saw them on the camera," the owner said. "Looks like your friends are back."

"I'll deal with them if they start anything."

Jake and Tyler finished the pickup about an hour later. Smitty ordered a pizza delivery for lunch, and each man sat at his desk and ate quietly. If Jake noticed the Caddy, he didn't say anything. Tyler wondered if his dad told him about the Boxster and the cartel problems it started. Despite wanting the mess resolved, he might have kept it close to protect Jake. Maybe the son's appearance at the shop today had been a happy coincidence of scheduling.

Toward the end of the work day, the sun set behind the houses across Belair Road. The Cadillac rolled to the end of the side street. "I'm going after them," Tyler said.

"You sure it's not a trap?" Jake asked.

"No. If anything, it probably is. Guess I'll find out."

"Be careful," Smitty called as Tyler jogged from the shop to the 442. He fired it up and pulled onto Belair Road three cars behind the Caddy.

AT THE TAYLOR AVENUE LIGHT, Tyler grabbed his phone and tweaked the settings. Then, he called Rollins. "A car showed up at the shop today," he said after Rollins, as usual, picked up on the first ring. "One of the cartel guys stared me down. He just left, and I'm following."

"You know it smells like a trap, right?"

"Check your phone. I shared my location data with you." Tyler learned how to do this out of necessity when Lexi came to live with him. He wanted to know where she was in case she ever found herself in a bad spot. Being her father's daughter, she insisted he share his data with her, so he did. Now, Rollins could track him, too.

"I see you," Rollins said after a few seconds. "I'm probably about five minutes behind you. Try not to get yourself killed before I show up."

"I'll do my best," Tyler said, and he hung up as the light flipped to green. Tyler followed the Cadillac deeper into the county. They passed the McDonald's where he'd shared lunch with Alice. It seemed like months ago rather than a few days. The Caddy sped by the Baltimore Beltway exits and dueling shopping centers on each side of the street. They went up a long hill. A derelict car dealership sat at the top. Tyler remembered his dad buying a Dodge there some thirty years ago.

After driving most of the way back down the other side of the hill, the Cadillac turned into another abandoned business. This one featured a much smaller building in pretty serious disrepair. They drove to the rear, and Tyler followed. Here, traffic on Belair Road wouldn't see them, and fencing around the lot would keep any nearby prying eyes off them, as well. It was certainly a good place to spring a trap.

The sedan pulled near the chain link at the far end of the lot. Tyler stopped the 442 about two hundred feet away. If the guy in the other car—and any friends he may have brought—carried pistols, they'd be less effective at this range. Tyler felt confident in his ability to make it across the blacktop and take out a couple guys with handguns. If they brought the heavy artillery, he left his car close enough to the exit to get away.

No one moved for a moment. Tyler held his M11 in his lap. He kept an eye on the rearview in case another cartel vehicle rolled up behind him. Rollins should be here soon. Even if these assholes brought reinforcements, Tyler liked the odds of him and Rollins taking out a bunch of them. The driver's door on the Cadillac opened, and a wiry Mexican man stepped out. Another guy, a little heavier, emerged from the backseat.

Then, Orlan got out of the passenger's side.

Tyler stepped out of the 442. The giant promised they would

meet again, and here they were. Everyone stayed near their respective vehicles. "Told you we'd get another chance," Orlan called
down the lot. "How about it, old man? You and me. *Mano a mano*.
My two friends here will make sure you don't go for your gun."

"How do I know they won't just shoot me?"

The large man raised his hand. "My word."

"You really expect me to take your word for it?" Tyler said.

Orlan said something to the other two in Spanish. They
scowled at Tyler and their massive comrade, but both got back in
the car. "Better?" He doffed his enormous jacket. "I'm unarmed.
Toss your gun back in your car, and we can settle this like men."

Tyler was a good shot, but sixty-odd yards with a pistol on a
breezy, dusky evening was asking a lot. Orlan presented a large
target—a point in favor of shooting him. The other two could
pull out automatic weapons, though, and Tyler would quickly be
outgunned. A point against. Orlan got the better of him last time.
Tyler fought larger foes before. The thought of pummeling the
giant to death held a certain primal appeal. He set the Sig on the
driver's seat and took a few steps forward. "You can come to me,"
Tyler said. "I don't trust your friends."

Orlan spread his hands, nodded, and walked forward like he
had all the time in the world. His long legs quickened their pace
as he drew closer. A hundred feet. Tyler planned out his opening
salvo. Orlan held many physical advantages, and his time in the
army meant he knew how to exploit them. Tyler's edges lay in
intelligence, experience, and specialized training.

Seventy-five feet.

He couldn't get into a slugfest with a colossus like Orlan. He
needed to be cerebral about it. The large man knew how to derive
power from his legs. If Tyler could take them out, Orlan's advantages would shrink.

Fifty feet.

Targeting the lower body alone wasn't enough. Tyler needed
to get Orlan off his feet. On the ground, he could use his experi-

ence and knowledge of holds. Tyler's hands clenched at the thought of choking out his huge foe.

Twenty feet.

A few long strides closed the distance. Tyler dropped low as Orlan threw a punch right away. As he felt the breeze, Tyler stuck his leg in front of the giant's feet, used the other to kick him in the back of the knee, and pulled on his waistband to help topple him forward. Tyler untangled himself and hammered the big man in the hamstrings. Orlan grunted in pain and rolled to his side. Tyler got in one more kick before a quick backhand made him step away.

Orlan got back to vertical sooner than Tyler thought he could, but his huge opponent's grimace said the blows to his legs were at least somewhat effective. Tyler plotted how to get the giant off his feet again. Orlan's advantage in reach meant he could keep Tyler at bay while his hamstrings recovered. A few punches told Tyler this was the plan. Orlan never overcommitted, however, and Tyler couldn't slip inside his defenses.

Tyler spread his feet as he parried a jab. Orlan fired off a hook. Tyler blocked it while dropping to a crouch. Before he could pummel his adversary in the leg, however, Orlan kneed him in the face. Tyler saw stars as his head snapped back, and he crashed to the asphalt. He rolled out of the way when Orlan tried to stomp on his head. Out of the corner of his eye, Tyler saw the two cartel guys standing near their car. They seemed content to watch, probably confident in Orlan killing the meddlesome American.

Orlan went for another knee, but Tyler blocked it while in a crouch. He grabbed at the big man's other leg, which made him step back. Tyler regained his feet just in time to get clobbered in the face. This time, he felt his nose snap, and blackness crept into his vision as he fought to stay on his feet. Orlan showed a sinister smile. Tyler turned away a couple jabs, but a strong right cross to the gut folded him in half and drove the breath from his lungs.

Orlan hammered him across the back and sent him onto the
asphalt again, this time face-first. Tyler's limbs felt leaden, and he
struggled to get air.

An engine roared from his left. Rollins' full-sized pickup
surged onto the lot. Orlan scampered out of the way, spared a
glare for Tyler, and took off toward the Cadillac, seemingly
unhampered by the blows to his legs earlier. The two other guys
tried to get in the car. The driver made it. Rollins' grill slammed
into the passenger, who rolled onto the windshield and roof
before crashing back to the blacktop like a broken doll, his arms
and legs splayed at odd angles.

Orlan dodged the pickup again as Rollins circled back for
him. The giant made it into the Cadillac, which took off with
screeching tires. Right toward Tyler. He rolled to the side and felt
the breeze again as the car zoomed by. Its tires squealed as it
made a left out of the lot, then a right onto Belair Road.

Rollins drove closer to Tyler. He got out and approached at a
quick jog. "You all right?"

"Sure." Tyler's voice sounded odd in his own ears. His nose
was broken. "I always try to lie down in a parking lot at least once
a day."

Rollins crouched beside him. "You look like hell."

"It matches how I feel," Tyler said.

21

"I had things well in hand," Tyler said as he struggled to a seated position.

"If I'd gotten here thirty seconds later," Rollins said, "your funeral director would've had things well in hand."

"Yeah, yeah." Rollins extended an open palm. Tyler gripped it and accepted the boost back to his feet.

"We should go somewhere else." Rollins glanced around. "There's a corpse here, and those guys might be smart enough to call the cops and try to jam you up."

"Good call," Tyler said. He wobbled en route to the 442.

"You all right to drive?" Rollins asked as he followed.

"Sure. Let's try to stay close, though."

Tyler got in his car and waited for Rollins to pull up in his truck. The windshield sported a nice crack in the center. Closer inspection could reveal blood or other evidence someone recently spent a few seconds on the hood. The pickup left the lot, and Tyler followed. They drove north up Belair Road, which was smart to get away from here and away from Smitty and Son. About three-quarters of a mile up the street, Rollins made a left into a church lot. They parked behind the building.

"Let me see your nose," Rollins said when they were both out of their vehicles.

Tyler tilted his face up so the slightly taller man could get a better look. "Why a church?"

"Figured we could get you last rites while we're here."

"Very funny," Tyler grumbled.

"Churches tend to help people, not the police," Rollins said.

"I knew I called you for a reason." He winced as his rescuer touched his face. "Pretty sure it's broken."

"You didn't need much help getting uglier." Rollins put his left hand across Tyler's upper jaw. "I'm going to put it back in place. It's gonna hurt."

Tyler took a deep breath and said, "Go ahead." Rollins used his right hand to pull Tyler's nose up and push it back into place. Even though it took less than a second, it hurt like hell. "Shit!" Tyler bit off a string of even worse curses which left Rollins shaking his head.

"I bet your father's never said some of those things."

"You'd be surprised." Tyler sat on the hood of his Olds.

"I'm a little surprised you're still alive," Rollins said. He retrieved a water bottle from his truck and tossed it to Tyler, who caught it. "Andre the Giant there could have picked you up and snapped you over his knee. He probably enjoys hurting people. Likes to drag it out and maximize the pain."

"He's a real charmer." Tyler opened the water and swigged half of it. "This is the second time I've tangled with him."

"I take it you're oh-for-two?"

"Yeah. Third time's the charm."

"Lot of dead people thought the same," Rollins said.

"You must be fun at parties," Tyler told him.

"I'm happy to do this with you. Getting rid of a cartel helps everyone. You and me might not be enough, though."

"You think we need more men?"

"Can't hurt. I'm pretty sure we're badly outnumbered, and the big bastard you fought with should count for three or four guys."

He was right. Rollins had been a great help against Braxton, but Tyler knew his former commander and the men he would recruit. The cartel was an unknown, but their brutal history spoke volumes. "I'll see if I can pull someone else in. Maybe somebody with experience taking on groups like this."

Rollins nodded. "Good. It can only help." He frowned at Tyler's face. "You good to drive?"

"Yeah."

"How about I follow you home anyway?"

"I won't tell you no," Tyler said. He clapped Rollins on the shoulder and climbed into the 442. From the church, he picked up Route 43. Once there, he could take I-95 into the city. It was far from the most efficient way to his house, but it was less likely to attract attention from Orlan or the cops. Tyler pondered who else he could recruit to the cause as he drove down the highway. Not many names came to mind.

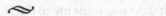

HÉCTOR CHECKED the shipment at the alternate location. He kept as little product in the house as possible. Some neighborhood people bought from him, and he maintained enough stock to keep them happy. A hidden alcove held it all, and even a police dog wouldn't find it. Here, they could store as much as they wanted, and no one would come looking for it.

Mexico held up its end of the bargain. Four cartel soldiers accompanied the drugs. They all looked to be in their thirties save one guy who was clearly on the downside of his career. He worked equally as quickly as his younger and stronger brethren, though, so Héctor couldn't complain. Once the men unloaded everything and put it away, Héctor gathered them around. "The SUV is stolen?"

"Yes," Danilo said. "I boosted it earlier today."

"Good. Drive it far away from here and torch it. We'll meet back at the house when it's done." The guys moved toward several vehicles. "Danilo, wait."

He stopped, and Héctor smiled when the man shuddered. Watching Videl get beaten to death made Danilo a better soldier. The dead man's subtraction made the entire organization better, and now Danilo understood the same thing could happen to him. "Yes, Héctor?"

"Before we came here, Orlan told me what happened with the American. He's not working alone. Orlan was close to finishing him off, but someone saved him."

"You want me to find out who the other guy is?" Danilo asked.

Héctor rolled his eyes. If he wanted research done, he paid Fernando for his computer skills. "I want to reduce his options. We know where he lives, and we know where he works. He seems to go between the two whenever he wants. Alice took the Boxster to the repair shop. She made a mistake, but something so simple started this whole mess."

"What do you want me to do, Héctor?"

"Wait until after midnight," Héctor said. "Take someone else with you. Burn the shop to the ground."

22

S mitty drank a mug of warm milk before bed. His father taught him how good it was for sleep many years ago. Now, whenever he felt stressed as the evening wore on, he heated a cup. It was probably hokum, but in case it actually helped, Smitty kept it up. He'd been raiding the fridge for the white stuff to heat more often ever since the Canadian girl dropped her damn Boxster off at his shop.

The more he thought about it, he realized the added stress began when Jake went on the run. Men soon came calling for him. Smitty didn't have a way out of the situation until John Tyler wandered into his shop looking for a job. He never knew he was hiring Rambo, but Jake came back safe and sound. Since then, Tyler proved himself to be a good and knowledgeable worker.

Smitty took a sip and tried to relax with deep breaths. For his many attributes, Tyler couldn't let things go. When the girl turned up dead, he'd taken offense. He couldn't have been sweet on her—she was barely older than his daughter. For whatever reason, Tyler couldn't abide her death, and he made it his job to get revenge for her against the cartel. Which was all well and

good. Smitty didn't like criminals. He also didn't like getting
caught in the crossfire, a place he increasingly imagined himself
as the cartel sent men to case the shop.

With thoughts roiling, the breathing didn't do much. Smitty
rinsed his cup out and settled in to bed. As he drifted off, he
thought the warm milk probably helped. His phone trilling on
the nightstand shocked him out of a slumber some time later. He
looked at the device as he picked it up—1:33 AM. What the hell
could be going on at this hour?

When he put his glasses on and read the alert, his heart sank.

A fire alarm went off in the shop. The system was new. It
shouldn't produce a false positive. Smitty opened the app
allowing him to view the security feeds. Flames blazed in the
office area of the building. "Shit," Smitty said. The camera cut out
before he set his phone down. The alarm would also alert the fire
department. They might be able to save the shop. He'd owned it
for years, and nausea gripped his stomach at the thought of
losing it now.

Smitty got dressed faster than ever before in his life and
hustled out the door.

THE PROPRIETOR SAW the flashing lights from a block away as he
sped toward his shop. Two fire engines sat in the lot behind the
service bays, which were still on fire. Orange flames spilled out of
what used to be windows. "The chemicals," Smitty said to his
empty car. All sorts of flammable liquids were clustered on
shelves waiting to be poured. A few other FD vehicles dotted the
lot, along with the police cars whose swirling red-and-blues he
saw on the approach.

After turning onto a side street and curbing his car, Smitty
watched. He couldn't tear his eyes away from it. Everything he'd

worked for now lay in ruin. He'd toiled for years as a mechanic under other men. Some imparted useful lessons, and others taught him things he should avoid. Twenty-four years ago, he took everything he'd learned and opened the shop. A business owner before he turned forty. Smitty's parents would've been proud. He certainly was. So many of his friends worked jobs they hated. Smitty loved what he did, and he liked to tell people he had the best boss in the world.

Now, he felt numb as he watched his hard work burn. The building itself remained intact. It was solid stone. The interior would be a total loss, though. Some of the equipment in the service area might survive. The combined smoke and water damage, however, would make it unusable. Smitty wiped at his eyes as he climbed out of the car and trudged toward the shop. He explained to a cop in the lot he was the owner. A plainclothes detective invited him inside the yellow tape perimeter a minute later.

The man looked Hispanic, and Smitty immediately thought of the cartel. They did this. There was always a tiny chance some electrical fault would turn the place into a conflagration, but no. The cartel torched his shop, and they did it because of the girl with the Boxster and Tyler. "Did you hear me, sir?" the detective asked, jolting Smitty from his thoughts.

"Sorry, no."

"I said I'm Sergeant González, Baltimore County Homicide." He showed a badge. Smitty frowned.

"Homicide? Was someone inside?"

"No. I was close, and a lot of the guys in our arson unit are investigating something across the county. They'll be here when they can." González wore a sharp suit and looked alert despite the hour. His spiky black hair showed a few spots of gray. Smitty guessed him for forty. His voice only held the hint of an accent. "Were you here at your shop today?"

Smitty nodded. "Everything was fine. We closed up around the usual time."

"When is that?"

"Anywhere from five to six," Smitty said. "Depends on how much work we have. Today was probably closer to five."

"You said 'we?'" González asked.

"Me and another guy work here. He left a few minutes before I did."

"What's his name?"

Smitty told González as calmly as he could. "John Tyler."

"You and Mister Tyler get along?"

"Sure. If you want to know if I think Tyler would do this . . . absolutely not."

González nodded and flipped a page in his small notebook. "All right. Can you think of anyone who would?"

Flames licked the exterior of the building. The stone would survive, but the paint wouldn't. Something else to be fixed or replaced. Smitty hoped his old insurance policy would cover everything. "Mister Smith?" González prompted.

"I'm here. Not every day you watch something you built for twenty-four years go up."

"I'm sorry," González said. "Can you think of anyone who might've wanted to set your business on fire?"

He couldn't tell González about the cartel. It would be a jurisdictional issue for one thing, and he didn't think the cops would be able to do much about them. Besides, if they did all this before the police got involved, what would their playbook look like after? "No." Smitty shook his head. "I can't think of anyone. Are you looking at this as arson?"

"Too early to say. Our fire inspectors should be here soon. They'll be able to tell you more. I just like to cover all the bases. How's the wiring?"

"Solid," Smitty said. "Got it upgraded a few years ago when I put in new lifts. Everything runs like it should. No shorts, no faults."

"All right." González jotted a few notes. He handed Smitty a business card. "I might not end up as the investigator, but in case I do, there's my number. You call me if you think of anything."

Did González believe him? Maybe this was something he told everyone at a crime scene. Smitty's hand shook a little as he accepted the card and stuffed it in his pocket. "Thank you, Sergeant."

"The arson guys should be here soon. I'm sorry about your business."

Smitty nodded and watched as the fire department gained control of the blaze at the rear. Flames receded into the building. About fifteen minutes later, they were out completely. The area smelled of carbon and chemicals, and Smitty's nose burned when he took a deep breath. Two more county types showed up a short while later. They were both middle-aged white guys. Smitty told them much of what he'd said to González. They also asked about the electrical work. Once they finished their questions, they promised Smitty a full investigation into the blaze. He nodded his gratitude, stuffed his hands in his pockets, and walked back to his car.

Once inside, he took out his phone and dialed John Tyler. A sleepy voice picked up on the third ring. "Smitty?"

It took him a few seconds to find the words. "They got to me, Tyler."

"Who?" His tone sounded louder and more alert.

"Who do you think? I'm sitting outside my shop. The fire department and police are still here. It's a total loss."

"Smitty, I—"

"Twenty-four years and no problems. Jake got caught up in that crap with his old CO a few months back, and I'm grateful you got him out of it. Always will be, but this is payback for the

Porsche, the men you shot here, and whatever else you've done since."

"Let me—"

"No. You've done *more* than enough. I have to hope I can rebuild after this." Smitty covered his voice cracking with a deep breath. "I'll be going it alone. You're fired." Before Tyler could respond, Smitty hung up. He started his car and drove back home.

23

R ollins knocked on the front door the agreed-upon amount of times. Tyler let him in. "See anyone outside?"

"Only a nosy neighbor," Rollins said.

"He's harmless. Coffee?"

"Sure."

They both walked into the kitchen. Tyler brewed the pot about ten minutes ago. He poured himself a second cup and Rollins his first. "There's milk in the fridge if you want it," Tyler said. Rollins added a little to his and joined Tyler at the table.

"You said something happened overnight?"

"Yeah. The cartel burned Smitty's shop down."

Rollins paused with his cup most of the way to his mouth. "You know it was them?"

"I guess it could have been some faulty wiring," Tyler said, "or a lightning strike. But the electrical work in the building is good, and there were no storms last night."

"You thinking of backing off?" Rollins asked after a sip.

"Not at all. I want to keep going after these bastards."

"What about Smitty? You don't think they'll go after him again?"

Tyler shook his head. "They didn't go after him this time. It's about me. Héctor's trying to get to me. Smitty and Son was collateral damage." He paused. "I hope he has good insurance. He's owned the place for a while. I'd like to see him get a chance to rebuild."

"What if his policy doesn't cover it all?"

"Good thing we're going after people who run a cash business," Tyler said.

"They don't exactly leave it out in the open," Rollins said. "Some, sure. Enough to work with. But they put most of it in accounts, and someone needs to clean it for them. You find out who they're using, you can probably get all the money you want."

Tyler swigged some coffee. "Something else to put on the list."

"You haven't thought much about it, have you?"

"Not really," Tyler said. "I tend to focus on kicking in doors and shooting assholes. It's what I'm good at."

"Might want to remember what you're good at the next time you see the giant."

"Yeah." Tyler smirked, and his hand brushed the outside of his nose. It still hurt, though he could breathe better through it today. "I'll deal with him."

"I have to say," Rollins pointed out, "you don't have a good track record there."

"I didn't have much of a plan the first time," Tyler said. "The second time, I did, but I stuck to it too much. I didn't change tactics when I should've."

"Let's focus on the money. You got any idea who takes care of it for the cartel."

"No."

"Got a plan for figuring it out?" Rollins asked.

"Sure," Tyler said. "Kill enough cartel bastards, and someone will eventually tell me." Rollins arched an eyebrow. "It worked against the Taliban."

"Let's hope it does here, too," Rollins said.

DIPLOMACY WAS a key part of any modern military operation. Tyler didn't have much use for it—and didn't consider himself very good at it—but he figured he would give it a try. Not with the cartel directly. They were too riled up, and he didn't think they'd be content to burn Smitty's shop down and walk away from all hostilities. Instead, he drove to Talbot Lakes and parked the Tesla outside the model home.

Inside, Todd Windholm wore the same suit and sat at the same desk. He wiped across his top lip when Tyler walked in, and his brows pulled down a second later. "Miss me?" Tyler asked as he sat in the guest chair.

"Not really."

"Don't worry, Todd, I didn't miss you, either. Still, you might be useful today. Maybe we can even help each other."

Windholm picked up his phone and scrolled through something. "I don't see how."

Tyler leaned across the desk, snatched the phone from his hand and stuffed it into the back left pocket of his jeans. "Can't have you calling for reinforcements. Let's just be two guys sitting down to have a conversation."

"Fine." Windholm scowled. "What do you want?"

"I know you and Héctor are pretty tight," Tyler said. He held up his hand when Windholm gestured and opened his mouth. "No point in objecting. You basically told me yourself the last time I was here. I'm coming with a proposal I'd like you to take to him."

"Why should I?" Windholm nodded at Tyler's face. "Looks like they've gotten to you already. If I wait it out, you'll go away."

"Maybe. There's the matter of the guys I've killed, however. I think we're up to six now. I admit it's kind of ghoulish to count, but you seem like the kind of guy who appreciates accuracy." Tyler paused as Windholm's frown deepened. "They were trained cartel operatives. What kind of a chance do you think you have?"

"I'll listen to your idea," Windholm said after a few seconds of useless deliberation. He didn't have a choice here, and he knew it.

"It's simple," Tyler said. "I'll leave Héctor, his men, and his operation alone. In return, he ceases what he's doing in Maryland and lets me deal with Rodolfo."

Windholm snorted. "You expect him to agree?"

"Honestly? No. I know he can't. Nevertheless, I'm making the offer. It'll save him the trouble of burying a bunch more guys."

"I don't like to speak for Mister Espinoza," Windholm said, "but I'm confident he will decline your offer." He scratched at the bottom of his nose. "If he had any reason to be concerned, of course."

"Save it for the rubes," Tyler said. "We both know what goes on here. I'm sure you've seen people go to his house and score drugs." Windholm stared at his keyboard. He couldn't sit still, however, and his nose wrinkled over and over as his hands clenched and unclenched. Tyler smirked at getting the confirmation. "Maybe you've even sampled the product yourself."

"Me?" Windholm said right away. "Never."

"Whatever you say." Tyler made a show of looking around the interior. "Mind if I check the place out? If I'm going to be a constant presence in Héctor's life, maybe I'll buy a house in the neighborhood."

"I think we're out of your price range."

"And I think I could come across this desk and cram your phone down your throat." Tyler stood. "It's a model home. I'm going to look around." A door immediately inside the entry was open enough to reveal a powder room. Too high a chance of discovery there. The public would use it on their way in and out.

Tyler bounded up the carpeted stairs. The plushness continued on the second level. He entered the master bedroom. It was staged well, with a king bed and enough medium brown furniture to pretend a boring suburban family slept here.

Tyler nudged the door open for the attached master bathroom. An *en suite* as he learned from the house shows Lexi sometimes inflicted on him. In the army, Tyler encountered soldiers who succumbed to addiction. With opium being so plentiful in Afghanistan, someone getting hooked on it was a formality. Windholm probably liked cocaine a little too much, and he would need to stash it in a place people were unlikely to spend much time.

Browsers would look around at the bathroom but probably not use it. There wasn't even any toilet paper or a roll on the dispenser. It sent a clear message: go downstairs. Tyler slipped a pair of thin black gloves on and lifted the lid of the toilet tank. Duct taped to the inside was a bag of white powder. He removed it, dumped its contents into the bowl, and flushed. Tyler replaced the bag and dropped Windholm's cell phone into the refilling tank. Then, he replaced the lid and left the room.

He removed his gloves as he walked downstairs. They'd need a good washing later in case any residue stuck to them. Windholm sat in his chair gripping the edge of the desk hard enough to turn his knuckles white. "You'll want to thank me," Tyler said. "Some asshole left drugs in the bathroom upstairs. I flushed them for you. You wouldn't want the cops to find it and presume the worst."

Windholm took a slow breath and pushed it out through pursed lips. "Will there be anything else, Mister Tyler?"

"No. You might want to check the water resistance of your phone, because it's in the same place someone left the drugs." He paused. "I hope you know where it is."

Tyler let himself out while Windholm seethed in the chair. He climbed into the Tesla and sped out of the swanky community. As he took a circuitous route back to the highway, he thought he needed someone besides Rollins to help with this—a person with practical knowledge of the cartel and how to hurt them. Luckily, he knew someone who might be able to help.

HÉCTOR LEANED back in his leather executive chair and reviewed a series of spreadsheets. He paid accountants and bookkeepers to handle the work—and compensated them well for their silence—but he also liked to look things over himself. His first accountant skimmed a little off the top. The guy probably figured his boss was an uneducated foreigner and wouldn't notice. He died from blood loss after twelve hours of torture. Héctor showed choice clips of the man's agony to the next people he hired. He'd experienced no troubles since.

His vibrating phone interrupted him. Héctor scowled at it. Windholm. The man had his uses, but there were days he was almost more trouble than he was worth. "Yes?"

"Mister Espinoza . . . I thought you'd want to know the American was here recently."

"What?" Héctor shot forward in his chair. "When did he leave? Why did you let him go?"

"He took my phone and dropped it in the toilet tank," Windholm said. "I'm a little surprised it still works."

"Why did he come see you?"

"He presented an offer. I declined."

The American probably made a one-sided proposal in his own favor. Still, Héctor didn't like Windholm answering for him. "What did he say?"

"He'd leave you alone if you stopped all your operations here and let him have Rodolfo."

"Ridiculous," Héctor said. Rodolfo got them into this mess, and Héctor wasn't above sacrificing him to get out of it. Abandoning his business—the cartel's business—would never happen. Just as he figured, the American made an absurd suggestion which didn't even deserve to be called an offer. "You were right to decline. I want a straight answer—how long ago did he leave?"

"Maybe ten minutes," Windholm said. "I waited for him to drive away. Then, I needed to find my phone, dry it off, turn it on—"

"I don't need the whole list," Héctor said. He sighed. Ten minutes could put the troublesome American anywhere. "Thanks for letting me know."

"One more thing," Windholm said in a small voice. "He ... uh ... found my stash and flushed it. I'll need more."

Héctor rubbed his forehead. "You should have been more careful with it. I have a lot to deal with right now, including the best way to find and kill this man. You'll get more when I have some to spare." Before Windholm could object—or worse, grovel —Héctor hung up. Burning down the place where he worked didn't deter the American. He represented a growing threat to Héctor and the cartel. He needed to die. Héctor imagined him suffering at least a full day of torture before begging for death, and the thought made him smile.

24

Tyler drove past Baltimore and headed into Columbia. It was the largest city in Howard County, one of the most prosperous electoral districts in the country. Tyler remembered it as a "planned community" and wondered how much the original design changed in the intervening years. In addition to expensive houses located on streets with pretentious names, the area boasted of a good restaurant selection. He parked in a garage near Clyde's to meet Sara Morrison for lunch.

She waited in the lobby when Tyler walked in. She smiled at him, and they shared a tight embrace. "How are you?" she asked, frowning at his nose. It looked black and blue in the mirror this morning, and he figured it hadn't improved since.

"I tried out a new cosmetic surgery technique," Tyler said. "I don't recommend it."

Sara grinned as a hostess led them to a secluded table. They sat against the large windows and enjoyed a nice view of the manmade lake behind the restaurant. People strolled about it, and an occasional bird swooped from the sky to pluck an unsuspecting fish from the water. "What happened?" Sara said as she opened her menu.

Tyler looked around the restaurant. He took the seat allowing an easy view of the main entrance. A corridor at his four o'clock led to the restrooms, and the kitchen was at his two. At least one would have a door to the outside. Tyler angled himself on the chair so he could keep both the lobby and kitchen in sight. "The cartel has an enforcer," he said in a hushed tone. "He and I disagreed about a few things."

"Looks like he won the argument."

"We both lived to see another day."

A young waitress approached their table. Sara ordered a fancy-sounding salad. Tyler, who'd never even opened his menu, chose a burger and fries. "What if they didn't have what you wanted?" Sara said.

Tyler shrugged. "Then, I'd watch you eat, and I'd get food from a more sensible place."

A spark of happiness danced on Sara's face, but it left as quickly as it came. "I got the feeling this wasn't entirely a social call."

"You're right," Tyler said. He kept his voice low even though no one else sat close enough to overhear them. "I need someone else's help with the cartel. It's gotta be somebody who has some actionable intelligence on them. Preferably a person who can shoot straight if it comes down to it. None of my old army buddies have the knowledge I'd need. I was hoping you could make a recommendation."

Sara frowned and took a long, slow breath. "I can think of a few people right away. I'm simply not sure the information you want is . . . public domain."

"I wouldn't ask anyone to divulge something secret. I took an oath to protect classified information, too, and I know it's a lifetime obligation."

"Have you considered dropping this?" Sara sipped her water. "I understood Braxton because of your connection to him. This isn't your fight."

"Someone needs to speak for Alice," Tyler said. "The cops don't seem to want to do it. People like Héctor need to know they can't get away with everything. I didn't tell you yet, but the bastards burned down Smitty's shop."

Sara nearly dropped her water glass. "That's terrible! What's he going to do?"

"I'm not really sure." Tyler crossed his arms. "He fired me. I don't blame him. This wasn't his mess, but he got caught up in it." He shook his head. "Héctor and his cronies have hurt way too many good people. I'm drawing a line in the sand."

"You really are a knight errant," Sara said.

Tyler shrugged. "I kick down doors and shoot people. Labels aren't for me to worry about. Can you help?"

Sara lapsed into silence. Worry creased her forehead and pulled her brows down. Tyler wasn't surprised she wanted him to drop this. He'd gotten her away from Braxton, and it served as an unconventional beginning to a relationship. Tyler never considered himself marriage material, though. He cared about Sara, but he couldn't let the matter of the cartel go. Even if Sara couldn't understand why. "I think so," she said after a moment. "I know someone who might be precisely who you need. I'll see if he's interested."

"Thanks." Tyler smiled. He put some effort into it and turned the brightness up. Sara didn't share his good spirits.

NATANIEL WAITED IMPATIENTLY as Raul peered through the binoculars. They sat in a Jeep outside the Evergreen Acres retirement community. The American's father lived here. The place sat about ten minutes from Héctor's house. Nataniel didn't understand why Raul kept looking at everything. This was a complex full of elderly people. They could drive in and be done with their target in a few minutes. "What's taking so long?"

Raul took the binoculars away from his face. His long black hair grayed at the temples. Of all the men who came north with the last shipment, Raul was the oldest and most experienced. Maybe he saw something significant. "This won't be easy," he said.

"What do you mean? Everyone here is a hundred years old."

"There are two guards at the gate."

"So?" Nataniel said. "We could kill them before they knew what was happening."

Raul nodded. "Maybe. We would then need to raise the gate ourselves. There are three cameras at the entrance. We'd be seen. If anyone is watching, they'd call the police."

"So we would need to work quickly."

"You're not getting it," Raul said with irritation in his voice. "There is another guard patrol in a golf cart. I've seen a different sentry go in and out of each building. We would not be unchallenged."

"You and I each have an AK," Nataniel said.

"I'm telling you a frontal assault won't work. It's way too risky."

"Fine." Nataniel waved a hand. "We'll try it from another side."

Raul turned in his seat. "Do you know what building the old man lives in?"

"Six," Nataniel said after a moment of thought.

"Right." Raul nodded. "Now show me which one is six." Nataniel stared at the compound. "You looked through the binoculars before I did."

"I know, Raul!" He sighed. "I guess I didn't notice."

"Good thing I did," the older man said. "It's on the right. There's a guard station at the side of the road just before it, and it's protected by trees to the side."

"You're afraid of walking through the forest?" Nataniel asked.

Raul rubbed the bridge of his nose. "Did you listen when Héctor told us about the man who lives here?"

"He's the American's father, and he needs to die. What else do we need to know?"

"Maybe the fact he spent his career in the American navy," Raul said. "He's the registered owner of enough guns to start his own security force. Considering his son was in the army, do you think they haven't spoken? Do you think we'd be taking him by surprise?" Nataniel didn't say anything. "I think he's expecting us. He doesn't know when, of course, but he's prepared."

"He's one geezer in an apartment," Nataniel said.

Raul made a sweeping gesture with his hand. "By all means, then . . . you try to walk through his front door."

"I'm calling Héctor." Nataniel slipped his phone out of his pocket. When the boss answered, he put the call on speaker. "We're outside the old man's place."

"Why isn't he dead yet? I want to show the American a video of his father bleeding out."

"Raul is chicken."

"I'm cautious," Raul said. "The area is well-guarded. The building we want is protected by trees. It would be hard to come from the side. Our target is well-armed. Even if we made it past everyone, he'd be ready for us."

"We can do it, *jefe*," Nataniel said.

"I don't think we can," Raul said. "Not easily, at least. It's too risky."

Héctor's sigh hissed through the speaker. "Fine. Abort for now. We might try this again later with more men. Come back to the house." Héctor broke the connection. Nataniel sat in the driver's seat staring ahead at the complex.

"You heard him," Raul said. "It's not worth it. Let's go back."

"You're scared of a bunch of old people and a few guards."

"I'm cautious. I've seen a lot of easy situations go bad. One day, you'll know better."

Nataniel fired up the engine and put the Jeep in gear. "Screw you," he said as he steered them away from Evergreen Acres.

TYLER PLAYED the two encounters with Orlan in his mind. He gave up a lot to his adversary in terms of size, strength, reach, and youth. Experience and treachery would need to cover the gaps. Orlan knew how to use his size and throw a powerful punch. He could have ended a lot of fights with one hit, but the last one showed he liked to let things play out and go for maximum pain.

It could be his downfall.

Tyler believed in ending fights as quickly as possible. Knock out, disable, or kill within the first few seconds. He'd need a major infusion of luck to do any of those to Orlan. The giant proved himself to be a skilled adversary. Tyler needed to make a plan and stick with it. He understood no plan survived contact with the enemy. He'd need to adapt based on what Orlan did. Tyler was too rigid last time. Too inflexible. He felt lucky to get out of it with a broken nose and a few bruises.

Trading blows with someone of Orlan's size and strength would be suicide. Tyler would need to wait for the long arms to finish swinging, then move inside and get his hits in. If he stayed close, he would lessen the big man's advantage in power. The new plan called for quick strikes and the ability to shift to defense in an instant. Tyler opened his basement door. He'd work out the finer points on the heavy bag.

Before he got downstairs, his phone rang. An unknown number with a DC area code. He returned to the main level, kept his Sig handy, and picked up. "John Tyler?" a man's voice said in a light Hispanic accent.

"Who are you?"

"Lorenzo Aguilar. Sara Morrison asked me to reach out to you."

Tyler relaxed and holstered the M11. "Thanks for calling. Did she mention what I needed your help with?"

"You use Signal?" Aguilar asked.

"What?"

"The messaging app."

"Oh," Tyler said. "Actually, I do. My daughter suggested I download it."

"Good. I'll call you in it. Give me a minute." He hung up. Tyler checked his phone and confirmed he'd installed Signal. Half the apps on his mobile probably came from Lexi's suggestions. He still didn't understand Spotify despite her constant reminders of its greatness. A few seconds later, a white and blue box popped up and showed an incoming call. Tyler answered.

"We're secure now," Aguilar said. "They encrypt end-to-end with no central server."

"Sure," Tyler said as if he understood what this meant.

"Tell me what's going on." Tyler relayed the story from the beginning, naming the key players and events along the way. "It's only you and one other guy?" Aguilar asked.

"In our defense, we're both pretty damn good."

"You'd better be to take on the Espinoza cartel."

"I've taken out six guys so far," Tyler said. "My friend got one. I haven't told him I'm keeping score yet."

"They have a lot more men back in Mexico."

"How many could they send without weakening themselves? These assholes always face challenges at home. Someone's trying to move in on their territory or whatever. He can't simply snap his fingers and get two dozen guys."

"Fair point," Aguilar said. "He could probably replace the ones you killed, and you're still only three when you count me. Long odds."

"We need to plan and execute well, then," Tyler said. "I've been in this spot before. Outnumbered by the Taliban. IEDs all over the damned roads. I'm still here. Unless I've missed my guess, you've probably been through something similar."

"A time or two," Aguilar said after a pause. "I did a tour in Iraq before I left and moved into intelligence."

"What area did you specialize in?"

"South America. Narcoterrorism."

Tyler grinned. Sara hit a home run. "I'm sure you dealt with a lot of classified information, then. I won't ask you to break your oath."

"Good," Aguilar said. "I wouldn't do it. Even avoiding anything secret or top secret, I think I can help you. Police can't do much against organizations like Espinoza's because they're normally attacking endpoints. Reacting to low-level stuff. I can tell you how to take the fight to them before they make it to Maryland . . . if you're willing to get on a plane, of course."

"To where?"

"Texas."

"Yeehaw," Tyler said.

25

R ollins knocked on the door about an hour later. He held up a brown bag stuffed with takeout as Tyler opened up and let him in. Tyler checked the street out of habit, even though Rollins would've noticed anything amiss. "Where'd you go?" he asked as he joined his friend in the kitchen.

"Kabab Stop."

"Good place. Thanks for picking up dinner."

Rollins grunted. "I told them you'd be paying for it with your charm and good looks. They tried to charge me double."

Tyler grinned. "Sounds like you got off light." Neither he nor Rollins cared about eating on plates. Tyler grabbed a beer from the fridge. He held the bottle up toward Rollins, who shook his head. "Sorry, I don't know how to make a cosmopolitan."

"Just because it's the official drink of the gays," Rollins said, "doesn't mean I like it." He caught the bottle of water Tyler tossed him. "You said someone called you earlier?"

"Yeah. Sara put him in touch with me. I think he's going to help us."

"He got any friends who can shoot?"

"Probably." Tyler opened the white cardboard container

which was already damp with steam. The aromas of beef, rice, and grilled onions made it past his battered nose. "This is the first thing I've smelled in a couple days." The container also held grilled red pepper and a small salad. Condensation rolled off the inside of the lid and onto the tabletop. Tyler focused on the two skewers of seasoned beef, sliding the chunks off the thin wooden spears. "I want to keep the operation lean, though. Héctor can't have a lot of men here, especially with the ones we've already taken out."

"You think he can't get more from Mexico?" Rollins opened his dinner. The scent of lamb hit Tyler's nose, and he wished the break would prevent him from smelling again.

"I think cartels face challenges in their own country." Tyler speared a chunk of beef onto the crappy white plastic fork and ate it. When he finished, he added, "Even if he's replaced everyone we've killed, he can't have more than a dozen or so."

"You and me against twelve men?" Rollins said.

Tyler nodded. "Personally, I'd make us three-to-two favorites."

Rollins bobbed his head. "Sounds about right. You talking to this guy again?"

"I'm going to call him back when we finish eating," Tyler said. "He's given me some info already. I want to make a plan and take these bastards out."

Fifteen minutes later, Tyler opened Signal and called Aguilar. "Your friend with you?" he wanted to know after picking up.

"I'm here." Rollins introduced himself in brief. Tyler felt he underestimated his own military career, but Aguilar didn't notice or mind.

"I've done small-team work before," he said, "and I suspect both of you have, too. I know what's going on south of the border. I can tell you how they get their product into the country, where it probably goes when it's off the plane, and when the next shipment is coming in. What I don't know is the local operation. How much have you seen?"

"Not a ton," Tyler admitted. "Héctor has a fancy house in a swanky community. He's at the end of the main road with a gate around the property. Basically advertising he's someone important. As far as I can gather, he's an investor in the building and development. The property manager is a toady."

"It's a chance to wash his money, too," Aguilar said. "One thing at a time in any event. We need to know more about how he does things locally."

"Why don't we all go in the morning?" Rollins said. "I'll sneak in and see what he's got. Then, we can put something together."

"When's the next shipment come in?" Tyler asked.

"Few days," Aguilar said. "They don't finalize it until the end in case someone's listening. And someone's always listening." He paused. "You thinking about hitting the transport?"

Tyler swigged the last of his lager. "I'd rather deal with it when it's off the plane. The guys are more relaxed by then. They've taken it someplace they know . . . a facility they control." This was true of the Taliban and Afghan opium producers more than a decade ago. Tyler figured it would apply to the cartel, too. People let their guard down in familiar locations.

"I like it," Aguilar said. "I'll keep an ear out."

"Let's scout their local operation first," Tyler said. "Like you told us . . . one thing at a time."

～

A VOICE PULLED Lexi from her sleep. She mumbled something incoherent and rolled over. "Alexis . . . wake up." She recognized her grandfather's voice. Why was he rousing her? Did something go wrong? Lexi shot up in bed, her heart pounding in her ears.

"What? What's going on?"

Zeke put his hands up. "Relax. Everything's fine."

Lexi grabbed her phone off the nightstand and glanced at it.

"Why are you getting me up at seven-thirty, then? I don't have a class until ten."

"When was the last time you went to the range?"

"I don't know." Lexi rubbed sleep from her eyes. Her grandfather clearly wasn't going to let her go back to bed. "Ten days, I guess."

"Good," he said. "We're going today. Get dressed. I made toast and eggs." He closed the door on his way out.

Even her father would've let her remain asleep. He might have gone shooting himself at this hour, but he'd never drag a sleeping student out of bed and make her tag along. "Dammit." She tossed the covers back and stood. Lexi took some clothes to the second bathroom, freshened up, tied her hair back into a ponytail, and joined her grandfather at his table. He'd already poured her a mug of coffee, and the color indicated he added the right amount of milk. She forced a smile and took a sip.

"Gotta keep your shooting up," he said. "I picked a pretty good unit here, but these cartel bastards might come, anyway."

"Your place isn't that big, Grandpa." She spooned some scrambled eggs onto her plate next to the toast Zeke put there. They looked yellow and fluffy, and the smell made her realize how hungry she was. "I'm pretty sure I could hit someone from the end of the hallway."

"Pretty sure ain't the same as sure. Certainty keeps you alive."

"Could it let me sleep another hour next time?"

Her grandfather looked over the top of his glasses at her. "Range isn't crowded in the morning. We might also catch the cartel napping. We'll leave when you finish your breakfast."

Lexi wolfed down two pieces of toast and all the remaining scrambled eggs. She wanted a second mug of coffee, but she figured Zeke would try to put her over his shoulder and carry her downstairs if she made him wait any longer. "I'll just get my pistol." She fetched the Glock 19 from her bag. "Do I need a carrying case?"

"Normally, yes," her grandfather said. "I know these guys, so they won't hassle us." He picked up a large duffel bag, and metal clanged inside as he carried it toward the door. "You drive."

They took the elevator down to the lobby. Zeke insisted on walking out first, and he scanned the area in both directions when he did. Once he gave her a thumbs up, they walked to the Accord and got in. "I'll keep an eye out for anyone following us," Zeke said after he buckled up. Lexi guided the car out of the complex and listened to her grandfather's directions. They took Route One north, drove across the Conowingo Dam, and entered Cecil County. Despite his vigilance, Zeke didn't raise any alarms, so she presumed the coast was clear.

Trees and open spaces dominated the landscape. Lexi couldn't tell the roads apart here. Her grandpa knew where he was going, however, and it turned out that what looked like another farm was actually a gun range. She parked the car, and they walked inside. The burly man behind the counter, who looked like he could fix a misfiring rifle by bending it with his bare hands, smiled when they entered. "Chief Tyler!"

"Barry, how are you?" The two men bumped fists. "Bringing my granddaughter here to get some shooting in."

"She know what she's doing?"

"She does, in fact," Lexi said. She looked at some paper targets tacked to the wall. Very tight groupings. "I can do as well as anyone you're displaying up there."

Barry offered an appreciative nod. "All right, all right. Why don't you two take stalls four and five. You need a box of ammo?"

"Yes."

"You go ahead, Lexi," Zeke said. "I'll pay for the ammo and join you in a couple minutes."

She took a set of ear protectors and the box of bullets to the fourth stall. A small stack of paper targets sat on the slapdash table. The range operators already set them up on the fifteen-yard and twenty-five-yard boards. She slipped the ear protectors on, racked the slide on her Glock, and took aim at the closer marker. Her finger slid inside the guard, and the pistol fired as fast as she pulled the trigger. When the slide locked back, Lexi looked at her target. A very tight grouping.

After prepping another magazine, she sighted the twenty-five-yard target. Her dad first took her shooting when she was twelve, but she didn't tell her mother about it until she was sixteen. If someone kicked in the door to her grandfather's place, she knew what to do. Nineteen more bullets screamed down the range. When she'd emptied the clip, Lexi looked at another cluster of holes around the bullseye.

Her grandfather took his spot in the next stall a moment later. In the past, she'd seen him bring large rifles. Today, his bag held a pistol, an AR-15, and several spare mags for each. They both blasted targets for another hour or so. Lexi's box ran out, so she watched Zeke pepper a bullseye with the AR-15 from two hundred yards. He did better at close range, but every shot at the farther target would have been debilitative to a person. "Let the cartel come," she said when they walked back across the parking lot.

"Don't be bloodthirsty," her grandpa said. "We'll be ready for them." As they put their stuff in the Accord and got in, Lexi noticed one of the range workers climbing onto a motorcycle. Zeke followed her gaze. "I told Barry a little about what was going on. He was an ensign when I first made it to chief." The old man smiled at the memory. "Anyway, the guy on the bike is going to follow us back to my place and make sure we don't have any issues."

"You think we will?" she asked as she put the car in reverse and backed it out.

"If we do," Zeke said, "I think the three of us will handle it."

Lexi glanced over at her passenger and grinned. "Don't be bloodthirsty, Grandpa."

26

R ollins arrived early, a few minutes before seven. The coffee pot beeped its completion a moment before he knocked on the door. Each man sat with a mug in front of him when another knock came on the front door. Tyler moved to the entryway and peered through the peephole. A Hispanic man waited on the porch. "Name, rank, and serial number," Tyler called after moving to the side.

"Lorenzo Aguilar," the man answered. "Civilian. No serial number, SKU, or barcode."

Tyler opened the door, and Aguilar entered. He was tall and lanky, probably six-three but only about a hundred seventy pounds. His short dark hair matched the fresh stubble on his face, and a few wrinkles and worry lines marked him as being in the neighborhood of forty. Tyler made the introductions, and Aguilar helped himself to a cup of java. "Today's recon day?" he asked as he joined Tyler and Rollins at the small table. Three wasn't a crowd, but four would have been.

"I'm going to sneak closer and get a better look," Rollins said.

Aguilar nodded. "I brought something I think can help, too."

Tyler poured the remaining coffee into a thermos, grabbed a

few travel cups, and the three men walked outside. "We'll take the SUV," Tyler said. "It's quiet."

"A Tesla?" Aguilar said. "Someone's fancy."

"I didn't buy it." Tyler unlocked the doors. "I . . . acquired it from the original owner."

Aguilar pulled up the gull-wing door and climbed into the back. "Did he die tragically?"

"I strangled him with my belt," Tyler said. "No tragedy involved."

"I hope there's some backstory there."

"You have no idea," Rollins said from the passenger's seat.

Tyler backed the Model X out of the driveway and guided it down the road. He remained vigilant for cartel hitmen. No one stood out to him. After a little traffic on the Baltimore Beltway, they picked up I-95 North and made good time to Bel Air. A few minutes later, Tyler turned off Route 543 into the swanky Talbot Lakes community. "Héctor's house is at the end of this main road," he said. "There are a few smaller streets farther down. A toady works in the model house on the last side street."

"You think we can be unobserved?" Aguilar said.

"Look around," Tyler said. "Just about every car carries a luxury badge of some sort. The Tesla will blend in." In short order, they passed a Cadillac Escalade, an Audi Q7, and a Jaguar sedan parked in various driveways. "I brought my car here the first time. It stuck out."

"Good thing you murdered a rich guy and took his car," Aguilar said.

"If we get any fancier," Rollins said, "I got dibs on finding someone with a Bentley."

Aguilar shook his head. "Rolls Royce all the way. One of you two can chauffeur me about."

"Very good, sir," Tyler said in a bad British accent.

The end of the road appeared as they rounded a bend. Tyler swung the Tesla around and curbed it a few houses from Héctor's

—facing out of the neighborhood in case they had to make a quick getaway. From this vantage point, they had eyes on Rodolfo's and Héctor's houses, and Rollins reported he could see the model home from the passenger's side. They remained in the car, and each man watched a different part of the operation. After a half-hour, they'd seen no car or foot traffic. "I think it's time to get a closer look," Rollins said.

Tyler nodded. "Be careful. Keep a line open."

"Roger that." Rollins opened the car door, closed it with barely a sound, and padded off toward Héctor's property. Tyler watched him in the rearview mirror. He walked down the sidewalk, hands in his pockets like he was just another person from the neighborhood. When he came to a large tree at the edge of the house, Rollins scampered behind it. From there, he looked around, kept low, and headed toward the fenceline. Tyler lost him in the other trees and foliage a moment later.

His phone buzzed, and Tyler put the call on speaker. "I'm at the fence," Rollins said in a whisper. Looks like there's a gate on the driveway side. Got a guard about ten yards away. I'll see if he's walking a patrol."

"How many guys you think Héctor has here?" Aguilar asked from the back seat.

Tyler shrugged. "It's a guess. We've taken out seven of them. I figure he's gotten some replacements by now, but in terms of actual cartel soldiers, he can't have more than eight to ten on hand."

"What about the guy in the model home?"

"He's in business with Héctor," Tyler said. "But he's an American toady, not a fighter."

Aguilar grunted an affirmative. A moment later, Rollins spoke up again. "He's moving around the back. I'm gonna hop the fence and see what's going on."

"Roger," Tyler said.

"He a ninja or something?" Aguilar said.

"More or less. I'm not sure I've ever worked with someone who could make like a ghost quite the same as Rollins."

"All well and good, but what if they happen to spot him?"

"He has a vest and a gun." Tyler patted the steering wheel. "And this baby has a ton of instant torque."

"I'm getting some pictures," Rollins whispered. "Pretty standard house . . . just big. I definitely think things are happening in the basement. I've looked through a window and seen people go up and down stairs."

"There a walkout anywhere?" Tyler said.

"Negative." Rollins paused. "Not so far, at least. I haven't made it to the gate side yet. Most houses put them in the back, though. My guess is Héctor made a deliberate choice not to have one."

Aguilar dropped the other rear seat and reached into the cargo hold. "What I brought can help." He opened a large duffel bag and slid a white and gray drone out. It had four blacked-out propellers and a small camera mounted on its underside.

"Rollins, come on back," Tyler said. "We're going to use Aguilar's drone."

"On my way." Tyler kept an eye on the mirror. A couple minutes later, Rollins hopped over the fence, moved in a crouch to the tree, then straightened and walked back toward the Tesla. He climbed into the passenger's seat. "I got some pictures. I'll share them with you later."

Tyler popped the lift gate. Aguilar used the remote to fly his small aircraft out of the SUV. He guided it over the trees and above Héctor's house. "The video is live," he said. "It goes to an app on my phone and gets backed up to the cloud almost in real time." Aguilar glanced at his mobile. "I see the guard. He's looping away from the gate now." His thumb pushed the left joystick to the right. "Normal slider. Looks about five feet high and reinforced. I doubt you could ram it down with a civilian vehicle."

"What about a basement exit?" Rollins said.

Aguilar shook his head. "Nothing. I think you were right. He didn't want one." Both his thumbs slid up. "I'm moving it higher and taking it around to the back." Tyler half-turned in his seat, but it was difficult to make anything out on Aguilar's small screen. "Bringing it down. I want to try and see inside the house." A moment later, large windows came into focus on Aguilar's phone.

"Can it zoom?" Tyler asked.

"About as ably as a phone camera," Aguilar said. "It's not a super advanced setup, but it works pretty well." He paused. "Shit. I think someone spotted the drone." He navigated it up. A shot rang out from somewhere on the property. Another soon followed, and the video feed cut out. Tyler fired up the Tesla and drove it away from the curb. Once they rounded the curve, he stomped on the gas, and the electric motors surged the SUV ahead. At the end of the road, he turned left on Route 543—away from the interstate—and pulled into the next development a half-mile up. He turned around in the cul-de-sac and left the Tesla pointing out. After a few minutes, it became clear no one was following.

"Can they trace anything back to you?" Tyler said.

Aguilar's head wagged from side to side. "It's all anonymous. The purchase, the wireless setup, the accounts . . . all of it."

"Can we still access the footage?"

"Up until right before the drone took a bullet, yeah."

"You want to call it a day?" Rollins asked.

Tyler grinned. "Not yet. They haven't found us. Let's go raise a little more hell."

THE THREE MEN watched the drone footage on Aguilar's phone screen. Tyler wished there were a way to beam it to the Tesla's much larger display. There might've been, but he didn't know it, and he didn't want to lose time searching in the event the cartel's goons showed up. The footage showed a large house, but Tyler thought the grounds looked a little small. The forest the development butted up against limited Héctor's backyard. Still, he owned the largest home in the community, and could boast of a gate and armed men to keep prying eyes at bay.

"I'm surprised there's no walkout," Rollins said as the camera zoomed in on the driveway. It continued past the gate, turned left past the rear wall of the house, and ended at the patio. "If someone's delivering something, they have to take it into the house first. It would be more efficient to drop it off in the basement."

"If cartel people can come in, so can the cops," Tyler said. "I think Héctor's trading efficiency for access control and an early warning. If law enforcement kicks the door in, whoever's upstairs is going to raise hell. Plenty of time to conceal things in the basement."

"Makes sense," Aguilar said. "I know a lot of Americans like to paint foreigners as uneducated, but the cartels know what they're doing."

The rear of the house didn't look like anything special. A large bay window allowed the camera to see inside. Past the dining room, people used a door in the hallway to enter and exit. It must have been the stairs to the lower level. The drone elevated suddenly, and the second story flew by in a blur before the feed cut out. "Sorry about your toy," Tyler said.

Aguilar shrugged. "I'll put it on your tab."

Tyler looked at Rollins. "This is getting to be an expensive operation. No more picking up dinner."

"On a serious note," Aguilar said, "I'd like to take a stroll around the neighborhood. You mentioned Héctor and his crew deal to some people who live nearby." Tyler bobbed his head. "Good. They know who you are, so you can't go. No one's seen me before, and I have the benefit of looking like I might work for the cartel."

"Keep a line open," Tyler said. "Call if you think you're made. We'll come get you."

"Roger." Aguilar climbed out of the Tesla and jogged back to Route 543. A few minutes later, he dialed Tyler's mobile. "I'm on the main drag. Not much activity." A couple more minutes passed in silence. "Okay, I'm closer to Héctor's. I can sort of see it around the bend."

"Don't give away your position," Rollins said.

"I'm crouching in someone's backyard," Aguilar said. "They don't appear to be home." He paused for a moment. "Here comes a customer now. White guy in a track suit walking away. I'm gonna talk to him."

A strange voice came through the speaker a short while later. "Who the hell are you?"

"No need to be alarmed, sir," Aguilar said. Tyler thought he heard a bit more of an accent in his voice now. "I noticed you leaving Mister Espinoza's house."

"What?" the other man said. "No. No, I just . . . I thought it was my friend's place."

"You thought your friend lived in the biggest home on the street? Come on now. Just tell me what you were doing there."

"You can't search me. You're not the cops!" The sound of shoes clapping against concrete filled the car.

"He's running away," Aguilar said.

"So we gathered," Tyler said. "You going after him?"

"Negative. Trying not to stand out too much. I'll go back to where I was before."

Silence resumed. The minutes ticked by. Tyler and Rollins exchanged a few glances. Right when Tyler thought about packing it in, Aguilar came back on the line. "Got another one. They did this deal out of the back. Bigger guy. Looks like he might've played football in college."

"Don't let him tackle you," Rollins said.

Aguilar snorted. "I think the only thing he's tackled the last fifteen years has been the buffet line. Standby."

Again, a surprised voice spoke next. "What? Who are you?"

"Neighborhood watch," Aguilar said. "Can I ask what you were doing at Héctor Espinoza's house?"

"I was dropping something off."

"Didn't look like you were carrying anything on approach. Maybe you are now, though."

"Get away from me!" the man said. "I'll ... I'll ..."

"What? Call the cops? Better do something with the drugs in your pocket first."

"Screw you!" This fellow ran away, too.

"I could catch him," Aguilar said. "It's kind of hurting my pride not to try. I'll see if anyone else comes by in the next half-hour or so."

No one did. Aguilar said he'd return, and he rounded the bend from 543 a few minutes later. Once he was back in the car, Tyler said, "Sounds like they denied everything."

"Yeah." Aguilar nodded. "It seemed a little beyond just fear of being busted. I think those people were scared of Héctor . . . namely, what he might do if he thought they gave him up."

"Ruling by fear," Rollins said. "Machiavelli would approve."

"Machiavelli's dead," Tyler said. "It's about time Héctor Espinoza joined him."

27

L exi and Zeke didn't run into any cartel soldiers on the drive back. The guy on the bike waved goodbye as he left. Upstairs, Lexi settled into her schoolwork, including watching a recording of a lecture she'd missed. She frowned as she realized the due date for a ten-page paper loomed five days away. She'd written precisely zero pages so far. Saving assignments like these until the last night or two worked in high school. Her dad told her she'd need to use her time better in college, and she had until this mess with the Espinoza clan.

While Lexi wanted to at least draw up an outline for the paper, her eyes glazed over the more she looked at it. Political science was boring. She thought it would at least be an interesting way to get three easy credits out of the way. Maybe a different professor could have livened things up, but Doctor Boyd droned on like he wanted to cover the late shift on C-SPAN. Lexi clicked away from her assignments and checked her email.

A message from her mother stood out. She opened it.

DEAR ALEXIS,

It was so great to see you recently. I hope you'll come again soon.

I know you were probably surprised to see your uncle George. He's been a pretty frequent visitor. Still, I didn't expect him to show up when he did. I hope you were happy to see him in the end. He loves you, too.

By now, I'm sure you've mentioned our exchanges to your father. I hope he's supportive. I always wanted you to have a relationship with him when he was deployed. Please give him my best. I know things went south for us years ago, but I wish him well, and I hope the two of you are getting along.

Let me know when you're coming by again. It's always great to spend time with my daughter.

Love,

Mom

LEXI FROWNED AT THE SCREEN. "Hell of a guilt trip," she whispered to the empty room. "For me and for Dad." In fact, she had definitely *not* been happy to see Uncle George, even though she wouldn't tell her mother. Lexi dug her dad's laptop out of her bag and fired it up. She logged in and typed her uncle's name into the app specializing in digging up info on people—cleverly named DIRT by whoever wrote it and put it on the machine.

George Goodson, aged forty-four, did not live up to his last name. He'd been arrested eight times, all for fraud or theft. Only two of them turned into actual charges, and he managed to avoid serious jail time, doing a total of four months. The months and years of some of his arrests matched up with times Lexi remembered moving as a kid. Her mother and Uncle George were always close. Were they running some sort of scheme, and he took the fall?

"What's your game, Mom?" She stared at the screen and tried to make sense of her uncle's misspent life. Whatever they were cooking up, it wouldn't be good for her father. She wouldn't let them get to him.

HÉCTOR HAD no problem keeping Todd Windholm waiting. Lackeys needed to know their place. Ten minutes after he'd been told the man wanted to see him, Héctor finally emerged from his office and entered the living room. "What is it?"

"I think our American friend is at it again." Windholm lounged on a comfortable couch, leaning back into the soft pillows and spreading his fat arms wide. He looked far more comfortable than Héctor wanted him to feel.

"What do you mean?"

"Someone accosted a few of our customers today."

Héctor dropped onto a nearby chair. "Explain."

"Two people came to me and told me someone hassled them about stopping here," Windholm said. "The description doesn't sound like the man you're after, though."

"John Tyler?" Héctor asked.

"They said this guy was Hispanic. Both of them thought he worked for you at first until he started grilling them."

"What was he saying?"

"Basically accusing them of buying drugs," Windholm said.

Héctor sighed. "It wasn't Tyler. He could have some associates, though. He's smart enough to recruit a Latino to try and bring me down."

"What are we going to do about it?"

"We?" Héctor glared at Windholm until the other man looked away. "We are not going to do anything. You are going to report to work in your model home every day and work on the side of the business you can control. The men and I will take care of Tyler. If we kill him, his friends will scatter."

"Of course, Mister Espinoza."

"Good day, Todd." Windholm extricated himself from the couch and hustled out. When the front door shut behind him, Héctor stood and pushed a button on the intercom. "Nataniel, Raul . . . to the living room."

The two came up from the basement and joined Héctor. Both remained standing even though he sat. He appreciated this. They didn't overstep or try to get too familiar. They knew their places in the hierarchy. "What can we do, boss?" Raul asked.

"I think our American friend is sticking his nose where it doesn't belong again," Héctor said. "We have a shipment coming in soon. I don't want any trouble."

"What should we do?"

"Go to his house tonight," Héctor told them. "Do it quietly. Not like last time. Make him suffer. Bring him here alive if you can. I'll make sure he begs for death for hours."

Nataniel smiled. "We'll take care of it. Consider it done."

28

After dinner, Tyler retired upstairs to paint. He used to think of it as winding down, but the creative—and sometimes cathartic—process usually amped him up for a little while before the inevitable crash. It only took a moment of reflection on recent events to get the brush moving. Tyler soon lost himself in the work. In his younger days, he used to scoff at writers who talked about the muse. A few years of therapeutic painting served to soften his opinion.

He narrowed his eyes to focus on finer details. He could see them in his mind, and while his limited skills never let him capture things exactly as they were, Tyler turned out some good representations. He rarely shared his output with anyone. Lexi had seen most of it, though she discovered it on her own. Sara knew Tyler painted, but she'd never glimpsed a sample. Maybe he'd show her one of these days.

A deep breath cleared his mind, and he finished the painting with a few broad strokes. A large house sprang up from green grass. A large foreboding black fence surrounded it. Blood ran from many of the spikes atop fenceposts. It was a version of Héctor's house but heavily influenced by compounds Tyler helped raid during his years in Afghanistan. The Taliban and the most notorious opium traders knew how to set up a facility to discourage visitors and prying eyes.

Tyler showered before bed, and his creative spurt predictably left him tired. He fired off a quick text to Lexi, asking how she was and received a short reply saying all was good. Next, he sent a message to Sara thanking her for the Aguilar introduction and promising to be less errant and more knight when all this mess was over. His eyelids grew heavy, and he was asleep before a response came in.

An alarm jolted him from his sleep.

It took him back to the sirens in Afghanistan. Tyler shot upright in bed. The security app on his phone sounded the alert. Because the rear half of his backyard was concrete, Tyler covered it in turf and had pressure plates installed when he bought the place. A night-vision camera above the back door showed two armed figures creeping closer to the house. Between the time it would take them to reach the door and bypass the excellent lock, Tyler figured he had three minutes.

He slipped a black T-shirt on and strapped a bullet-resistant vest atop it. His black sweats would be fine. Tyler hooked a knife onto his vest and held the familiar M11 in his hand. He screwed a suppressor onto the end. No need to wake the neighbors if he could avoid it. These were cartel guys here to do a job. They'd be thorough. There were plenty of places to hide on the first floor, so at least one of them would have to search it. Better to clear it in a pair. They'd probably ignore the basement.

Tyler could take a position at the top of the stairs and pick them off. It was the only way to reach the second floor. He wondered why the guys were here. Killing him was the easy answer—too easy in Tyler's opinion. He knew he'd pissed Héctor off. No way someone like a mid-level cartel boss would farm out the torture and murder of a troublemaker to a couple of hired guns. No, Héctor would want to do it himself. Which meant these two assholes weren't here to kill Tyler. Héctor would want him alive.

They needed to hold back. Tyler didn't.

Downstairs, the rear door of the house swung open. Tyler's security app beeped. He silenced his phone. The two guys would be searching the lower level. Tyler slid open the door to his walk-in closet and stepped in. He stood amid a collection of suit bags, the serrated knife now in his hand. Then, he waited. He'd always been good at waiting. Younger soldiers lacked patience, and even though Tyler told them it would keep them alive, their attention spans betrayed them. Silence and darkness were a prepared soldier's allies.

Footsteps came up the stairs. Two sets . . . one trailing close behind the other. Lexi's bedroom was the first door they'd come to. One went in, and the other entered the bathroom directly across the hall. They both emerged a moment later. Tyler's door came next. His extra bedroom turned studio was the last along the upper hall. A pair of footsteps went in each direction. The thought of some cartel lackey seeing his paintings boiled Tyler's blood.

The man in the bedroom took his time. He walked a circuit of the bed, spent more time in the connected bathroom than he needed to, and finally came to the closet. He nudged the door open. Tyler saw the outline of a slender man poke his head in. The suppressed barrel of a pistol moved ahead of him. Tyler hid in his collection of suits on the right side of the closet. The guy turned his head away.

Tyler slipped his left hand over the man's mouth. At the same time, his right arm moved atop the other's, pinning it to his body as he drove the knife up through the gunman's ribs. A wet burble escaped his lips, and blood ran over both Tyler's hands. He pulled the knife out and eased the dying man onto the carpeted floor. The gun fell from his grip as he expired.

A single pair of footfalls moved toward the bedroom. Tyler

scampered from the closet and crouched at the end of his dresser. He set the knife down and eased the Sig from its holster. "Raul," the second guy said as he tiptoed into the bedroom. "Raul?" The closet door remained open. No lights were on, but Raul's fate would become apparent soon enough. Tyler pondered what to do with this second gunman. He could kill him. It might make his pending interaction with the police a little more complicated. Two dead bodies would draw a lot more attention and questions.

"Oh, no," the man said. He gave no indication he saw Tyler at his four o'clock as he crossed the room to the open closet. Tyler picked the knife up again and put it in his left hand. If he wounded this one and took him alive, they might be able to learn more about the Espinoza cartel's operation—including the upcoming shipment Aguilar lacked specifics on. "Raul, you idiot. You were supposed to be the cautious one." Tyler slipped up behind this new assailant.

He clobbered him in the back of the head with the hilt of the knife. The man grunted and slumped forward. He remained conscious and swatted ineffectively at Tyler, who whacked him in the head with the butt end a second time. This one turned the lights out. Tyler rolled the guy over and checked for a pulse. A bit of blood dampened his hair, but he was alive.

Tyler grabbed his phone and called Rollins. "Get to my place quick," he said when his friend's sleepy voice came on the line. "The cartel sent two guys here. One might still be useful to us."

"I'm on my way," Rollins said.

29

R ollins' pickup screeched to a halt in front of the house a few minutes later. He backed the large vehicle into the driveway. Tyler opened the front door, and the two men carried the unconscious gunman downstairs and outside. Once they tossed him onto the back seat, Rollins bound the man's wrists and ankles with a zip tie. "You got someplace you can take him?" Tyler asked.

Rollins nodded. "I'll text you the location later. You calling the cops?"

"Yeah. I'll get rid of them as soon as I can." Rollins drove away, and Tyler reported the home invasion via 9-1-1. He sat in his living room and waited. It didn't take long for the first two Baltimore Police cruisers to roll up with their lights flashing. "It's open," Tyler said when he heard the officers at the door. Four men walked in.

Tyler went over the very basics with them. His name. Yes, he was alone. No, he'd never seen these guys before. Yes, he was a registered gun owner. A white van arrived at the end of the preliminary questions. A man and a woman in white Tyvek suits entered, conferred with one of the officers, and walked upstairs.

"Detectives are on their way," Officer Jennings said. He and another cop, Brennan, sat with Tyler in the living room. They might try to pass it off as being personable, but he understood it was to keep him from leaving.

Two more men entered a few minutes later. Tyler recognized one of them: Sergeant Rich Ferguson. He'd faced the man's questions after the bloody end of the Braxton mess. Ferguson wore the same charcoal suit today he'd sported back then. His partner looked like a failed rocker in desperate need of a cut to contain his sandy mop of hair. He wore a blue blazer, gray pants, and shoes Tyler would have been embarrassed to present for inspection during his early enlisted days.

Ferguson sat near Tyler on the couch while his partner went to the second level. "Mister Tyler." He nodded. "I kind of hoped we wouldn't need to talk under these circumstances again."

"No offense," Tyler said, "but me, too."

"Let's start at the beginning." Ferguson held a notebook and pen. "Tell me what happened."

"I was asleep. An alarm in the backyard woke me. A couple minutes later, two guys were in the house. I took up a position in my closet. One of them nosed around and found me, so I stabbed him."

After jotting a note, Ferguson asked, "What about the second one?"

"He got away." Ferguson frowned, and Tyler spread his hands. "They woke me up. I wasn't exactly dressed in full tactical gear. I also wasn't going to shoot at a man while he ran away."

"You ever see these guys before?"

"Nope."

"Know why they might've come here?"

"Home invasion, I guess," Tyler said. "Maybe they wanted to rob the place."

"Anything missing?" Ferguson said.

"I don't think so, but I haven't checked. Once the second guy split, I dialed nine-one-one. I figured I'd leave the investigation to you."

Ferguson showed a wry smile as he recorded a few things in his notebook. "Good choice. Did either man say anything to you?"

Tyler shook his head. "The first guy turned toward me with a gun. He never said a word. The other one bolted once he saw what happened."

"Can you describe the second man?"

"A little," Tyler said. "I didn't get a long look at him. He was Hispanic . . . I guess in his twenties. Younger than the guy upstairs, definitely. Probably a little taller than me . . . thin. He wore jeans and a dark jacket."

"Not bad for a short look," Ferguson said.

"Pretty sure you had a lot of the same training I did. It never leaves you."

"Maybe I'll find out in about twenty years." Ferguson flipped his notebook shut. "Why'd you stab the guy?"

"He found me in the walk-in," Tyler said. "He had a gun. What was I supposed to do? Invite him downstairs for tea?"

"I might have done something similar in your place," Ferguson said. "I know you own several guns. I guess I'm curious why you didn't shoot him."

Tyler couldn't tell him the real reason—he'd hoped to keep the whole thing quiet so the neighbors would be unaware. When he decided to KO the second gunman, the plan changed, but the first guy had already bled out. He wondered where Rollins took the survivor. "I guess I hoped to avoid bloodshed if I could. If he hadn't opened the closet door, I wouldn't have needed to do anything."

Ferguson stared at Tyler a few seconds before pursing his lips. "You know the drill. We might have more questions later. Probably a good idea if you stayed in town."

"Like I told you last time, Sergeant," Tyler said, "I'll go where I want unless a judge tells me otherwise." Ferguson shrugged, stood, and walked up the steps to join his partner. About a half-hour later, the crime scene technicians left, followed by the uniformed officers. Ferguson's partner handed Tyler a card. Paul King was his name.

"In case you think of anything else," he said.

"Sure," Tyler said. His phone buzzed in his pocket.

"You get many texts in the middle of the night?" King asked.

"Probably just an email." He frowned but left with his partner. When they pulled away and their rear lights were out of view, only then did Tyler check his phone.

TYLER READ the address as he fired up the 442. It resolved to a derelict repair shop on Harford Road. He used his phone's GPS to plot a route. Making good time in the middle of the night proved easy. Tyler swung his car into the lot about twenty minutes after he left. He parked it beside Rollins' truck. The building would hide their vehicles from anyone driving by. A couple of old cars sat in the lot. Tyler wondered if their owners even remembered they were still here. The rear door opened a crack. Rollins peeked out and left it open wider when he spotted Tyler.

Inside, the cartel guy was awake and tied to a metal chair. A strip of duct tape served as a gag across his mouth. It didn't stop him from yelling incoherently. "He's chatty," Tyler said. He couldn't look at any one area of the interior too long. There was no organization system. Maybe there had been before the place closed, and people broke in and trashed it. Tyler wasn't compulsive about being clean and neat, but he kept his tools and work areas arranged a certain way.

Rollins grunted. "I thought about knocking him out again. The other side of his head doesn't have a knot yet."

"He might be willing to tell us something useful." This triggered another flurry of muffled yelling from their captive.

"Let's find out." Rollins ripped the duct tape free. The man in the chair had to pause his forthcoming rant to scream in pain.

"*Puta*," he said after a moment, spitting at Tyler's feet. "I'll never tell you anything." His nasal voice carried a moderate accent but was easy to understand.

Tyler moved closer and stared down at the man. Across the shop, metal clattered as Rollins searched for something. "What's your name?"

"Nataniel."

"Nataniel, I'd like to point out two things. First, you just told me something." His face twisted into even more of a scowl. "Second, a lot of people in Afghanistan swore over and over they'd never talk, and they ended up singing like canaries."

"Because you tortured them!"

"Me?" Tyler said. "No. I've never had a problem killing people, but I don't like 'enhanced interrogation,' as they liked to call it." Rollins found what he'd been looking for and approached from Nataniel's six. "Now, if other people did it . . ." He trailed off and shrugged.

A blowtorch hissed to life as Rollins walked around the chair. Nataniel's wide eyes followed the two-inch blue flame. "I'm not as principled," Rollins said. "If you don't want to talk, there's a lot of fuel for this torch." He held it within a few inches of Nataniel's face for emphasis. Tyler kept his expression neutral. He knew Rollins was playing bad cop, but he hoped Nataniel wouldn't call the bluff.

"Héctor will kill me," he said. To his credit, Nataniel hardened his expression, but the tremor in his voice gave him away.

"What do you think we're going to do?"

Nataniel shook his head. "Screw you. I'm not talking."

Rollins shrugged. "Have it your way." He moved the flame closer to the captive's face. "How do like your beard? I wonder if burning it would catch the rest of your face on fire? Let's find out." The blue fire inched closer. Nataniel moved his head back as much as the chair allowed. He tried to squirm back but couldn't. Smoke rose from the bottom of his beard, and Tyler frowned as the horrible scent of burning hair reached his nostrils.

"All right, all right!" Nataniel said. "*Madre de Dios!*"

Rollins killed the blowtorch, and the flame winked out. "Smart decision, kid."

Nataniel's saucer-like eyes flicked to Tyler. "What do you want?"

"We need information," Tyler said. "How many men does Héctor have right now?"

"I don't know." Nataniel shrugged as much as his restraints would allow. "I guess about eight."

"Could he get more?"

"The cartel already gave him me and a couple other guys. I don't think they want to send anyone else."

"What about a shipment?" Rollins said.

"Soon," Nataniel said. "Two days, I think."

"Where?" Tyler asked. Nataniel clammed up. "Where?" The hostage continued staring at the dingy floor. "Rollins, fire up the torch again."

"Sure thing."

No sooner did his hand touch it than Nataniel ended his silence. "All right. The cartel avoids major airports. Stuff comes in to some little one in Texas just outside Houston. Then, they drive it to another place to process it."

Tyler crossed his arms and glared at Nataniel. "What's the place called?"

"I don't know." Tyler looked at Rollins and nodded. "I don't! I swear. I've only been a couple times. It's a nice facility. The security team takes money and doesn't ask questions. It's pretty high-tech."

"How far is it from the airfield?"

"Ten minutes."

"Which direction?" Tyler asked. Nataniel turned his hands up.

"We can figure it out," Rollins said. "Can't be too many places checking all those boxes. I'm sure the other guy can help, too."

"All right," Tyler concurred. "What are we doing with this guy?"

"I say we kill him."

"I told you what you wanted!" Nataniel's voice grew high-pitched.

"You sure gave it up easily," Tyler said.

"This is just a job. I'm not in the Espinoza family. They offered me work in Mexico. I took it. I've mostly fought the other cartels. They would've done worse to me than you did."

"We can't have you going back to Bel Air and talking."

"Please." He folded his hands and begged. "I won't make any trouble. I won't tell anyone what happened. You . . . you knocked me out, and it took me some time to wake up and drive back."

"Héctor would never buy it," Tyler said. Nataniel shook his head, silently pleading. "You have a passport?"

"What?"

"A passport," Tyler said. "*Pasaporte*. Do you have one?"

"*Sí*." Nataniel nodded. "It's the ID I use."

"Good. I'll give you a choice, then. My friend here will drive you to the airport. You get on a plane to Canada, and no one ever hears from you again." Their captive remained quiet. "If you don't like those terms, we'll shoot you in the head and burn your corpse in one of those rusted-out cars in the lot. I don't care which one you pick."

"I will get on the plane."

"Good decision."

Rollins jerked his head to the side, and Tyler followed him to the far wall of the shop. "You sure?"

"What do you mean?"

"For a man who's never had a problem killing people," Rollins said, "I'm surprised this clown is still alive."

Tyler shrugged. "Maybe I'm getting soft in my old age. I think he told us the truth. He's more afraid of us—well, you and your blowtorch—than he is of Héctor and the cartel. We did our job."

Rollins grunted. "Fine. If he gives us trouble, I'll remind you we had this conversation."

"Fair enough." Tyler grabbed Nataniel's phone and looked at the screen. Two missed calls. Neither displayed a number, but they had to be from someone in Héctor's house. He glared at Nataniel. "If you give my friend any problems, he'll get rid of you. He's not as nice as I am."

"No problems," Nataniel said.

"If I hear about any word reaching Héctor—" Tyler jabbed Nataniel with his own mobile for emphasis—"I'll fly to Canada, kill you, and feed your body to a moose."

"I won't say anything . . . I swear."

"All right." Tyler nodded at Rollins. "Thanks. Let's figure out a plan later. I feel a trip to Texas coming on."

"I guess I'd better buy a Stetson," Rollins said. Tyler left the derelict shop and climbed back into his 442. He headed farther into the city. As he drove, he memorized the number for the contact which had now called three times and dialed it. When a voice answered in Spanish, Tyler said, "Sorry, this asshole can't come to the phone right now. Or ever again, really."

"You must be Mister Tyler," replied a voice dripping venom.

"How many more men, Héctor? Can't be too many. It'll be down to you and me soon. Maybe I'll even see you in Texas."

It took a couple seconds for Héctor to say anything. "Orlan will kill you and piss on your corpse."

"Orlan's had two chances. He won't get a third." Tyler broke the call. Traffic was still light this early, so he tossed Nataniel's

phone out the window, turned around, and headed back the way
he came.

HÉCTOR HELD his cell phone in a white-knuckle grip. The temptation to fire it across the room gnawed at him. He held back,
regaining some measure of calm with a few deep breaths. In his
younger days, he had been impulsive like Rodolfo. The cartel
made him into a man. A man found solutions to his problems. He
didn't lash out like a child. Héctor used his laptop to run a few
searches. Several sites posted the details of police calls. If anyone
dialed 9-1-1 in or near Tyler's house, these so-called police blot-
ters would have it. It didn't take Héctor long to find what he was
looking for.

He stood and pushed an intercom button on the wall. "Orlan.
Come downstairs."

A sleepy reply came through the speaker a moment later.
"Boss?"

"I need you downstairs."

"All right." Orlan sounded a little more alert now.

A couple minutes later, the giant walked down the steps. He'd
changed into sweats, and he rubbed at his eyes as he walked into
the living room. "I know it's early, but we have a problem."

Orlan's face darkened as he sat at the opposite end of the
couch from Héctor. "Let me guess. Tyler survived."

"He did. There was a nine-one-one call from his neighborhood. Police responded to his house. One man found dead
inside."

"Which one?"

"I don't know," Héctor said. "But only one is the problem. If
either got away, they'd come back here. I think Tyler captured the
other. When I called Nataniel's phone, it went to voicemail a few

times. Tyler called me back about ten minutes ago. He mentioned something about seeing me in Texas."

Orlan ran his hands through his short hair. "You think he knows everything?"

"I think he knows enough."

"The facility is secure."

"We seem to keep underestimating this man," Héctor said. "I'm not going to do it again. You go to Houston and oversee the shipment. Make sure you're there."

Orlan nodded. "Okay, boss. What if Tyler shows up?"

"Kill him. Beat him to death but take your time. He's caused us a lot of problems. I want him to die in agony."

"I'll make it happen," Orlan said.

30

A couple hours later, Rollins and Aguilar joined Tyler in his kitchen. They all waited for the coffee to finish brewing. It reminded Tyler of many mornings in the Army. The coffee mess was always a popular spot. Conversations never flowed until every man partook of his first cup just like today. Once the machine beeped and everyone held a hot mug, the morning began in earnest.

"Why do you want to hit the shipment?" Aguilar asked.

Tyler enjoyed a long sip of coffee. "A couple reasons. First, I want to show Héctor his organization isn't as strong as he thinks it is. Then, once we have a bunch of his product, we have something to negotiate with."

"To what end?"

"If he wants it back, he leaves Rodolfo to me and clears out of Maryland."

"You think he'll go for it?" Rollins said.

"I think the cartel will murder him if he loses their drugs," Tyler said. "After a long round of torture, of course. Héctor knows what he'd be staring at. He'll want to avoid it."

Rollins grunted. "I guess. I don't much like blackmailing a drug dealer with his own stuff, but it could work."

"We'll probably thin his ranks some, too. He won't be in a position to do much but agree."

"Before we celebrate ridding the area of Héctor," Aguilar said, "we need to figure out where the shipment gets processed. I know these guys avoid major airports. Too much scrutiny. Too many people to pay off. They'll fly in to someplace small." He took a paper out of his pocket and unfolded it, flattening it on the table-top. "This is the greater Houston area. I marked the major airports already—Bush Intercontinental, Hobby, and Ellington. What do we know about where they take the product?"

"Like you figured, the guy we talked to says they pick just enough runway to set down and take off again," Tyler said. "Wherever they go from there is a high-tech place within ten minutes."

"Did he say which direction?"

"He didn't know," Rollins said.

"Water limits the distance in the southeast." Aguilar tapped Galveston Bay and the Gulf of Mexico with his pen. "Still a lot of ground to cover. There are several possibilities."

"It can't be too big," Tyler said. "The cartel will want to have some control of it. They won't want to share it with a lot of other people. Not much traffic in and out."

"All right." Aguilar nodded. "This eliminates ports and any kind of large processing place. If it's high-tech, we can probably presume it's fairly new." He took out his phone and scrolled through a screen of search results. "Astro Airfield is a good possibility." Aguilar made a large blue dot with his pen east of Houston. "Small enough to get only a few flights a day. People who work in places like that aren't rich. Toss some money at them, and they won't see or say anything." He glanced at Tyler. "You have a compass?"

Tyler snorted. "Sure. In the same drawer as my protractor and slide rule."

"I'll figure it out, then." Aguilar held his pen up to the map key and used it to estimate distances from Astro Airfield. "I'd like to go smaller, but I want to cover ten miles in the directions we can. If they pick up Route 90 or another highway, they could cover a decent distance in ten minutes." He made more dots on the map and then connected them with a rough circle.

"Lot of ground to cover," Rollins said. "Even so, I think we can narrow it down. They'll want to avoid downtown Houston. Too much traffic . . . too many other people."

"North, south, and east, then," Tyler said. "Makes it easier."

Aguilar tapped on his phone. "This would be easier on a computer."

"Lexi has the good one."

"I'll make do," Aguilar said. "I got good at Google working in counterintel." His thumb scrolled through a results page, and he added six marks to the map. Two sat to the north, three east, and one to the south near the bay. "Let's see if we can winnow this list."

"I'll get my laptop." Tyler picked it up from his small desk in the living room. When Lexi got her new model, Tyler took her previous one. She said she did things like wiping and reinstalling applications, which all sounded very good. It was a couple years newer than the one he'd been using. He set it on the kitchen table and logged in.

"You could have brought it a few minutes ago," Aguilar pointed out.

"I wanted to hear you complain a little more first," Tyler said. "I'll take the ones to the east." Aguilar texted Tyler his search results.

"I'll look over your shoulder," Rollins said. "Old people and tech don't mix."

Tyler grinned. "You'll be fifty in about eight years."

"And still better with a computer than you."

He looked up each of the places east of Houston. Rollins provided the keyboard shortcut for opening a new browser tab. A few minutes later, the three compared their results. "I like one of the spots we found," Rollins said. "It's about six miles from the airfield, mostly a straight shot. Their website talks about how locked down the building is before anything else. Looks like it would be hard to breach."

"Sounds more promising than what I got," Aguilar said.

"Iron Tower owns the facility and makes the security system. They sell it in Texas. I don't know all the specs, but if the cartel turns it on once they're inside, we'll have a problem following them."

Aguilar looked up. "It's gotta be the one. I heard chatter about *Torre de Hierro* around the cartel. They must be using it."

"I guess that means Iron Tower," Tyler said.

"*Sí. ¿Habla español?*"

"No. I studied Pashto." Tyler looked at the map. "We probably can't hit them en route. Too many major roads. Unless their plane comes in the middle of the night, any assault would be too visible."

Aguilar tapped the dot representing Iron Tower on the map. "We need to crack the security at their facility, then."

"Won't be easy," Tyler said.

Rollins looked at his watch. "I know a guy. He's probably not up yet, but I'll get him to help us."

"You sure he'll want to?"

"I've done him plenty of favors," Rollins said. "He'll play ball."

ROLLINS WAITED inside the Daily Grind coffee shop in Fells Point. It sat right on Thames Street and proved to be a good spot for prime people watching. The tables were small but spaced out, so he enjoyed plenty of room. People hustled by in every direction. The constant smell of coffee and steaming milk went from pleasant to tolerable. Rollins normally got his order to go in places like this, and the overpowering aromas were the reason.

A few minutes past the appointed hour, C.T. Ferguson walked in. He stood about six-two and was built like a runner or lacrosse player. His dark brown hair looked freshly cut, and he wore a Hilfiger jacket over jeans and tennis shoes. "You're late," Rollins said.

"Three minutes. It's early for me. Need a refill?"

Rollins shook his head, and C.T. got in line. A couple minutes later, he sat opposite Rollins. "I've already marked this day on the calendar . . . you asking me for help."

"It's definitely some role reversal," Rollins said with a nod.

"If you're going to play my part," C.T. said, "you'll need to dress better."

"I'll do my best." Rollins sipped his chai. It smelled great, and it carried exactly the right amount of spice. Holding the cup closer to his face drowned out the dominant aroma of coffee. "You ever hear of a place called Iron Tower?"

"You mean the one in Germany?"

"No," Rollins said. "This is a facility outside Houston."

C.T. shook his head. "Can't say I have."

Rollins glanced around. Tables were filling up, and a half-dozen people waited in line for drinks. "Let's walk and talk." He put the plastic lid back on his cup and headed for the door. A block later, the two men climbed into Rollins' pickup. "Better not to have this conversation in there. I have a friend who needs my help. Long story short, he's taking on a drug cartel selling out of Harford County."

"Sounds like a suicide mission." C.T. frowned. "If your friend wants to die, you don't need to go with him."

"We've actually done pretty well," Rollins said. "Eight guys down so far. We have someone else working with us, too. He knows all the intel about these bastards. We figured out they're getting a shipment soon, and they'll be processing and packing it at a place outside Houston."

"I've always wanted to see Texas," C.T. said. "I'm not really a raid-the-cartel-compound kind of guy, though."

Rollins waved a hand. "We'll take care of the raiding part. The place sells itself on being high-tech. I thought you could help us from behind the keyboard." From experience, Rollins knew C.T. to be a very capable hacker. He didn't know if something like this would be in the man's wheelhouse, however. If not, he'd need to scramble for an alternative.

C.T. grinned. "Sure. Let me do some research on it and get back to you. Iron Tower, you said?" Rollins nodded. "All right. I'll let you know what I find. When were you all planning to undertake this fool's errand?"

"A day or two."

"I'd better read fast, then." C.T. opened the passenger's side door and climbed down. "I'll be in touch."

"Thanks," Rollins said. He drove back to Tyler's house and told him and Aguilar he'd be hearing from his contact soon. In the meantime, the trio looked at Google Earth data to get the lay of the land around the facility. About an hour later, C.T. called. Rollins stepped into the living room to answer.

"They're definitely leaning hard into security," he said. "Selling a proprietary system raises an alarm for me. Pun intended."

"Of course it was," Rollins said. "Does this mean you think you can get past it?"

"As far as I can tell, they're running a stripped-down version of Linux. It's a few years old, and they've removed a lot. Someone breaking in will find a lot of familiar commands gone. Fortunately, I found a review of their beta code with some clever Googling."

"Why wouldn't they delete it?"

"Most companies are bad at document control," C.T. said. "The good thing for them is a lot of their competitors don't know how to take advantage of it."

Rollins followed this part of the conversation, at least. "But you do."

"Sure. They've done a good job. I have to give them credit for it. I'm pretty sure I found a way in, however."

"Do I want to know the details?"

"Basically, the system will only accept a shutdown command issued with a few parameters. It puts everything in maintenance mode for two hours. I don't think I can shut it down for longer."

Rollins placed his hand over the phone's mic. "You guys think two hours is enough?" he called into the kitchen.

"We'll go full auto and save time," Tyler said. Aguilar grinned and nodded.

"It'll work. I'll let you know when it's showtime."

"I'll be ready," C.T. said, and the two hung up.

"Who is this mystery helper of yours?" Tyler asked.

"A local private investigator," Rollins said. "He's good with computers."

"All right." Tyler bobbed his head. "We know where, and we know how much time we'll have to get in and get out. Now, we just need to get down there."

"I know a guy who could get us there," Aguilar said. "He usually flies rich assholes around, but I'm sure he'll work with us."

"Good," Tyler said. "Let's pack. I'd like to see this place in the light of day."

31

By mid-afternoon, Tyler, Rollins, and Aguilar were wheels up and winging for Houston. They'd fly into Astro Airfield like their targets did. If the cartel used it a lot, there could be value in scouting it. In advance, they'd given all their weapons to Aguilar's friend Bowman who would fly them down. His bag didn't get searched at the tiny airport they flew out of, so he carried a massive roller packed with guns.

Tyler gripped the armrests hard as the plane continued its ascent and leveled off. He noticed Rollins chuckling at him. "What?"

"Didn't think you'd be afraid of flying," Rollins said.

"I'm not," Tyler insisted. "I just . . . don't like it very much."

"We probably could've taken a boat."

"You know I get seasick. Why do you think I fixed tanks and Hummers? I wanted four wheels or two treads on the ground at all times." Tyler tried to relax. The small plane remained steady during flight with only a few small pockets of turbulence. Lush green dominated the view out the tiny round window. This was another mark against flying in Tyler's opinion: much of the

country looked the same from thirty thousand feet and five
hundred miles per hour.

After about three hours and fifteen minutes in the air, they
touched down at Astro Airfield. Bowman parked the plane on the
tarmac, and the four walked into a small terminal. Rollins
wheeled the weapons bag behind him. An employee met them
inside, hoped they'd enjoyed their flight, and offered cold bottles
of water. The place looked unremarkable to Tyler. It was small
enough to be claustrophobic. There wouldn't be any place for the
cartel to stash any product or cash.

The main area of the building continued the miniature motif.
A single computer and scale handled people and luggage flying
in. A bored middle-aged employee sat behind a desk to the side.
The tin badge pinned to his shirt meant he pretended to be the
security detail. Considering how little he seemed to care about
his job, Héctor could pay him off easily with a stack of bills. This
was an amateur operation—easily exploitable but not criminal.

By six PM local time, the trio arrived at a nearby car rental
business. Aguilar paid cash and scored a GMC Yukon SUV. As
they loaded up the spacious rear, Tyler asked, "You're not worried
about this coming back on you?"

Aguilar shook his head. "It's not my name on the license. If
they wanted me to hand in all my cover IDs when I left, someone
should have kept a list."

"Fair enough." Rollins climbed in the driver's seat. Tyler was
happy to sit in the back. The ample legroom allowed him to sit
low and still keep an eye out. It made him less likely to be spotted
if they ran into any of the cartel's men near the Iron Tower. The
SUV didn't have a GPS, so Rollins used his phone. Eight minutes
later, the Yukon slowed as they approached a foreboding black
fence. The rest of the area remained undeveloped, and a small
hill provided a good sniping spot about three hundred yards
away on the opposite side of the road.

The barricade featured close-set iron posts at least twelve feet tall, spikes at the top, and barbed wire angled out to provide a further deterrent. No one could slip through the narrow gap between the poles and climbing their sheer surfaces would be nearly impossible. Even if someone made it over, Tyler spotted several cameras which would see the whole thing. They rolled on and came to the gate. It looked just like the rest of the barrier save for massive hinges and a keypad setup nearby. "Your friend's going to get us past this?" Tyler asked Rollins. He looked at the building beyond, which seemed less impressive than the barricade surrounding it.

"He says he can." Rollins kept the Yukon moving so the cameras wouldn't see anyone stopping to case the place. "I believe him."

"He ex-military?"

"No," Rollins said.

"A former cop?"

"Nope."

"How the hell did he come to be a PI, then?" Tyler said.

Rollins grinned in the rearview mirror. "You'll have to ask him yourself. I'm not the man's agent." They drove past the far end of the complex. The building itself stood two stories tall and looked to be about the size of a typical large supermarket.

"You said we'd have two hours?" Tyler said. Rollins nodded.

"We might need it," Aguilar said. "Pretty big place."

With the Iron Tower behind them, Tyler sat up more. "Let's confirm the shipment details once we're checked in to a hotel. There's a lot of square footage there, but I think the cartel guys will be easy enough to find once we're inside."

"What if Héctor sent his big bastard down here?" Rollins said.

"I'll deal with him," Tyler said. Rollins glanced into the mirror. Tyler didn't see a lot of confidence in his eyes.

~

"I DON'T THINK you should do it."

Lexi looked up at her grandfather. "They're up to something."

"Your mother was always up to something," he said. "The best thing to do is not engage. Ignore her and her asshole brother, and they'll go away."

"I'm not so sure." She grabbed her dad's old company laptop. "I don't know what they're after yet, but I'm gonna find out."

Zeke sighed and sat beside her on the couch. "Do you want to have a real relationship with your mother when she gets out?"

Lexi stared at the screen as the computer booted up and displayed a login prompt. "I don't know." She let out a dry chuckle. "I loved her so much growing up. She was always there, you know? Dad was deployed a bunch. After they split up, he made sure to see me at least every weekend. I thought it was cool, but now I think he did it because he was concerned about her raising me."

"He was. It was one of the reasons he left the army."

"Really?" Lexi's fingers hovered above the keys. "I thought it was all tied to the Braxton mess."

"I think Braxton gave your dad an easy out," her grandfather said. "He didn't tell me this, of course. I'm speculating. My guess is he wasn't going to re-up when the time came out of concern for you. When the Braxton crap hit the fan, it was the final confirmation he needed to know he'd made the right decision. And none of the brass would question it after what went down."

"I've never heard that side of the story," Lexi said. She logged in to the laptop using her dad's credentials.

"He wants you to have a normal relationship with your mother." Zeke paused. "As normal as possible, I guess."

Lexi's eyes narrowed as several distinct memories of her mom bad-mouthing her dad rushed to the front of her mind. *He's deployed too much. He loves the goddamn army more than he loves us. Why do you need to spend the whole weekend with him?* "We might have passed the point of no return there."

"You're an adult," Zeke said. "You should do what you think is right. Besides, your generation doesn't want to listen to an old man like me. If I were you, I'd just ignore them. Don't answer emails or calls. Don't visit. Let them fade away."

"What if they're running some kind of scheme?" Lexi said.

"Same advice." Zeke stood. "It's ultimately your call, y'know." He left the living room and walked into the kitchen. Lexi cracked her knuckles and got to work. Uncle George was the real unknown. She now understood her mother's shady past. Past a few sketchy details, however, she didn't have much on her uncle. He was always nice enough, but they'd never been especially close. She ran a public records search for him. The Patriot laptop checked many sources with a single click and compiled the results, so it saved a ton of time versus checking multiple repositories.

Uncle George owned a poor credit score, a fair bit of unpaid debt, and a criminal record. Most of his arrests didn't lead to conviction, but Lexi noticed the last three—all in different jurisdictions, of course—were for fraud. She explored each for more details, and the laptop provided the police reports and other legal records each time.

Attempted pension theft.

Attempted pension theft.

Attempted pension theft.

"So that's what you're after," Lexi whispered. "Grandpa, can you tell me again about my dad's pension?"

He walked back into the main room. "Normally, when there's a divorce, a soldier has to give half to his ex-wife. Certain circumstances can prevent it, though, and your dad argued your mother's criminal record meant he could divorce her for cause or something similar. It worked. His pension's all his . . . or yours one day." The old man frowned. "You think they're after it?"

"It fits a pattern with my uncle," Lexi said. "Somehow, he's avoided going to jail for it."

"What about this time?"
She closed the laptop. "I'm going to burn him down."

32

The next morning, Tyler looked at his phone. A text from Lexi came in after he went to sleep. *Mom reached out to me because she's going after your pension. Don't worry, I'm all over it.* "Hell," he muttered, rubbing his face in an effort to wake up. He'd long suspected Rachel of being salty because she couldn't stake a claim to his money. Her own poor choices led to it, of course, but people rarely blamed themselves for their own mistakes.

Tyler sent a reply. *I'm in Texas. Be careful. Your mom may be in jail, but she could call her brother. Your uncle is a grifter who probably knows some people. Love you.*

He showered and dressed. The plan was to meet Rollins and Aguilar for breakfast at a nearby diner at 0730. They would all arrive and leave separately. It all seemed a bit silly to Tyler—they'd be sitting together, after all—but he shrugged and went along with it. Leaving the hotel, Tyler walked a circuitous route. No one followed him, and he pushed the diner door open at 0729.

Rollins sat at a round table in the back. Customers crowded the counter, but not many people gathered around a proper table to eat. Rollins' spot was near the hallway leading to the restrooms. It dead-ended with no emergency exit. Tyler joined him, sliding onto a chair which would afford him full view of the entrance. The kitchen to his left would lead to another way out, and he could keep both in sight.

Aguilar walked in a moment later and sat to Tyler's right. A middle-aged waitress with a huge hair bun poured them coffee without asking. Tyler liked this place already. He ordered sausage, eggs, and toast when she came around again. Aguilar chose some fancy-sounding omelet, and Rollins opted for oatmeal. After the waitress walked away, Aguilar leaned in. "It's coming tonight. I got confirmation a short while ago."

Tyler nodded. "Do we know when?"

"Touchdown is at twenty-one hundred hours. With time for processing and handling, we should expect them about a half-hour later."

"Processing and handling?" Tyler grinned. "Now, I feel like I need to pay fourteen-ninety-five."

"All contributions are welcome," Aguilar said.

"We'll call C.T. once we're back at the hotel," Rollins said.

The waitress dropped off their breakfasts and refreshed their coffees. The three ate in silence, paid their tabs separately, and left a couple minutes apart. Tyler took a random route back to the hotel. Rollins and Aguilar waited in the hallway when he stepped off the elevator, and they all filed into his small room. Floor space was at a premium, but the bed and desk chair offered spots to sit. Rollins bounced a quarter off the mattress, smiled, and sat.

"Did I pass?" Tyler asked.

"Barely." Rollins slid his coin back into his pocket. "You're rusty."

Tyler positioned himself on the opposite corner of the bed. "Let's call your friend."

Rollins took out his phone and called C.T. on speaker. "It's going down tonight," he said following an initial exchange of pleasantries.

"I'll be ready. Let me know when."

"Have you done this before?" Tyler said.

"Gone after this specific facility?" C.T. said. "No. Have I taken out other alarms before? Yes."

"What makes you think you can do it?"

"Probably the same thing which makes you think you can storm a secure building, shoot a bunch of drug dealers, and drive away."

Tyler spread his hands. "All right."

"You got everything you need?" Rollins asked.

"I could get technical on you," C.T. said. "My guess is you don't want to hear about things like code review and Linux command aliases. Let's just say I'm good to go."

"Thanks. We'll be in touch later." Rollins ended the call.

"All right," Tyler said. "We have some time before we roll out tonight. Let's make sure we're all well-rested and fed. We could be in for a long evening."

"Let's take these bastards down," Aguilar added. He and Rollins adjourned to their own rooms. Tyler thought about the plan. They'd seen a Google Earth view of the Iron Tower. He and his fellow soldiers raided similar compounds in Afghanistan. He'd be doing it with a smaller force tonight, but they'd also be facing less opposition. Aguilar would snipe at first and then join the raid once they'd neutralized all outside sentries.

Tyler figured he'd run into Orlan again. Considering the recent losses in his organization, Héctor may have sent his trusted colossus to ensure this shipment went off without a hitch. Tyler baiting the man by mentioning Houston probably helped. If so, mission accomplished. The huge enforcer got the better of him twice now. Tyler thought about how their next meeting might go. He wanted to stay close to Orlan and take away his advantages in strength and reach. He practiced short punches and elbow strikes as he kept reviewing the attack plan in his mind.

An hour after dusk settled, Tyler, Rollins, and Aguilar headed to the Iron Tower. The SUV was unbothered by rough terrain, so Rollins drove it off the road. He left it behind the hill across from the facility. The three men got out, geared up, and conducted a final weapons and comms check.

A few minutes later, four Suburbans rolled up to the gate. They drove inside, and the foreboding iron barrier slid shut behind the last vehicle. They drove a narrow, poorly-lit path to the main doors. Tyler watched them through night-vision binoculars. Three men exited each SUV, including Orlan from the one in the front. "Looks like the cartel sent a few guys to help them process everything," Tyler said.

"They might stick around," Aguilar said. "Not a lot of chatter about violence in Mexico right now."

"We'll make up for it. There'll be plenty of it here."

Two of the men removed M16s from the rearmost Suburban and stood watch over the operation. Orlan directed everyone else. One by one, they each carried bricks of drugs inside. The whole thing took about fifteen minutes. Tyler wondered how many kilos there were and what kind of street value it would translate to. It must have been tens of millions. "We're not going to get all this out of here," he said. With all the product inside, the two sentries walked the perimeter of the building.

Aguilar shrugged. "Siphon gas from their SUVs and burn the rest."

Tyler nodded. "I like the way you think." He glanced at Rollins. "Call your friend."

Rollins did. "We're in position."

"All right," C.T. said, and his voice came through their earpieces. "I've discovered something about maintenance mode on the system, by the way."

"What is it?"

"The cameras still record unless they're disabled locally. It's a good fail-safe. Probably designed as a countermeasure against this very weakness."

"What are we going to do about it?" Tyler asked.

"*We* are going to sample five minutes of footage," C.T. said. "I can feed it back to the central video controller. They might catch on if someone watches it all, but I doubt it would happen until you're out of there."

"Do it," Rollins said. "We can spend a few minutes checking everything out, anyway."

"All right. I'm going to put it in maintenance mode in a few seconds. You'll have two hours less five minutes to storm the castle."

"Understood. Text me when we can go." Rollins hung up.

Tyler used a pair of night-vision binoculars to check out the Iron Tower. The dearth of exterior lighting made things easier. The compound only provided enough illumination for two men to walk the perimeter. Even then, Tyler guessed half their steps were in what remained of the natural light. "Looks like it takes one guy about four minutes to make it around."

Aguilar set up a tripod and his suppressed M4 carbine. "I'll be ready. The way they're staggering the patrol, you'll have two minutes until the second asshole sees the body. I think you should be in position at the gate when I drop the first one."

"We will," Tyler said.

Rollins' phone buzzed. "We're on," he said after reading the message. "He also sent me the admin codes for the gate and the front door."

"One-stop shopping," Aguilar said as he took his position. "You guys go."

Tyler slid his Sig out of its holster. "All right. Radio silence unless we need to talk. Good luck, guys. And . . . thanks."

Rollins clapped him on the shoulder, and the two moved in a crouch. They dashed across the road and approached the gate.

From Tyler's right, a sentry walked around the far corner and moved toward the front of the building. Before he could worry about the man spotting them in another fifty yards, a muffled report sounded from behind them, and the guard fell over dead. Rollins entered the code he got from his friend, and the gate slid back. It made more noise than Tyler would have liked. No one inside would hear it, though, and the other guy on patrol would be in the back of the building. They ran through as soon as it was open wide enough.

Rollins went first up the narrow road. Behind them, the black barrier slid shut. A large column stood on either side of the front door. Rollins hid behind one, and Tyler took up position behind the other. A minute later, the second man walked past them, oblivious to their presence. Tyler leaned out to watch him. He stopped a few feet later—probably when he spotted his partner's body. Before he could raise an alarm, however, another quiet report came from across the way, and a single shot to the head dropped the fellow where he stood.

The gate slid open and closed again as Aguilar joined them. Rollins entered a code into the keypad. The lock disengaged with a click. He pulled the door open, and the three men slipped inside the Iron Tower.

33

I t wasn't much brighter inside the building, but it definitely felt cooler. A small lobby greeted visitors. Past it, a single door led deeper into the Iron Tower. Tyler knew from photos they would encounter office spaces first. Those emptied into a pair of large packing and processing areas. The place would have been a nice setup for a warehouse or shipping company. Instead, Héctor and the cartel were the sole lessees.

They moved on. "Let's clear the offices," Tyler whispered. "They're likely to be empty, but we want to be sure."

"I'll take the second level," Rollins said as he headed for the stairs. Tyler pointed to himself and then the left. Aguilar nodded and went to the right. Tyler opened each door, his Mii leading the way. Most of the rooms didn't even contain a desk. The owners didn't even bother pretending anyone used the office space. Cartel money must have spent really well.

When he'd finished clearing the rooms, Tyler moved on to the door leading to the rest of the building. Aguilar joined him in a moment, and Rollins came down the stairs a minute later. "All clear," he said. "Most of them were totally empty." A keypad restricted access. Rollins entered the same code as before. The red light flashed green. He pushed the door open just enough to pass inside. Aguilar, the last one through, held the door while it closed quietly.

Rollins stayed low and went to the left. Aguilar followed him. Tyler hugged the right-hand wall. Factory machines dominated the floor. Most were off, but a few conveyor belts ran. It added to the noise, which only helped. Tyler didn't see Orlan, but a bunch of guys clustered around the center of the room with kilos of cocaine. They all wore jackets against the constant cool of the air conditioning. A small alcove immediately ahead held a water fountain. Tyler ducked into it as a man broke from the pack and walked into the nearby restroom. No one followed him. Tyler slipped inside, holstered the Sig, and drew a serrated knife from a scabbard on his left hip.

The man stood at a urinal focused on the task at hand. Tyler padded close behind him, put one hand over his mouth, and cut his throat from ear to ear. He let the body fall, and blood spurted and pooled on the bright linoleum floor. Tyler wiped his knife on the dead man's shirt. He'd barely slid it back into its sheath when another man walked in. He gaped at the scene and stared at Tyler with wide eyes.

Tyler sprang forward, punching the newcomer in the stomach and doubling him over. He drove an elbow into the man's temple, then grabbed him by the hair and slammed his head into the sink. A bloody smear traced down the porcelain. The guy stirred. Tyler dragged him into a stall, propped him on the toilet, and also slit his throat. He cleaned his blade a second time before replacing it with his pistol.

No one else came in. Someone would notice these two were missing before long. Tyler couldn't see a way to lock the bathroom door from the outside without a key. Hopefully, they'd thin the herd before anyone else decided to take a piss. Tyler stayed close to the wall as he moved farther down. Some of the workers opened the bricks of coke and mixed it with another white powder. Once the ratios were good, another group repackaged it. Tyler observed one brick turn into four once the contents were blended.

He approached the end of the processing area. The smooth concrete passage continued to the left, and stairs led to a lower level. Tyler crouched and took a step to the left when someone grabbed him and pulled him toward the steps. He leaned forward and into a roll, coming up in a crouch. Orlan smiled at him. "I told you I'd see you again," the giant said. "This time, I'll kill you."

TYLER ASSUMED a fighting stance and inched away from the stairs. They were bare metal, and he didn't want to go down them the hard way. "You've had two chances. The third time won't be the charm."

Orlan puffed his chest out and stood at his full height, about ten inches above the top of Tyler's head. "I'm bigger, younger, faster, and stronger." He grinned. "I almost like your American cowboy attitude. How do you think you'll win?"

"Experience and treachery," Tyler said.

"I'll carve it on your tombstone . . . right after I finish pissing on your grave." Orlan scoffed. He wore a bullet-resistant vest like Tyler. They were meant to blunt high-velocity projectiles, but they also afforded some protection against punches and kicks. In addition, he sported a pistol strapped to his hip. Tyler also spotted the grenade he'd seen in their first encounter. It peeked out from under his vest inside his windbreaker. At the time, Tyler thought the huge man to be a psychopath. He still believed this, but now he saw it as a potential vulnerability.

Orlan threw a powerful right hook. Tyler stayed out of his range and stepped back from the blow. He needed to get inside the colossus' reach to have much of a chance. Another hook and an uppercut kept him at bay. Orlan followed them with a left cross Tyler sidestepped and a side kick he blocked. The big man wasn't even breathing hard despite his opening salvo. A lot of the massive opponents Tyler faced over the years wore themselves out in the first minute. Orlan had the stamina they lacked, and an extended fight favored him—a fact Tyler was certain his foe understood.

Another long hook afforded Tyler the chance to duck and scamper closer. He launched a couple punches at Orlan's sides below his armor. He shrugged off the blows and brought his hands closer. Tyler pressed the offense. He reached high to wallop the giant in the face. The punch turned his head but didn't stagger him or knock him down. Tyler blocked a jab and clobbered the bigger man again. This time, a line of blood spiraled from his lip. He grunted and shoved Tyler away. "First blood." Orlan wiped his mouth. "I didn't think you had it in you."

"I ran into some drug dealers in DC a few months ago," Tyler said. "The boss there kept a big asshole like you on the payroll."

Orlan raised his fists again. "What happened?"

"I beat him to death with a rolling pin in his *jefe's* kitchen."

"You're down to your fists here." Orlan circled and fired a left cross. Tyler leaned away, but Orlan grabbed him around the neck with his right hand. He lifted Tyler off the ground and used his left to hoist him all the way up. Tyler knew what was coming—the giant planned to toss him down the stairs. He stuck his middle knuckle out and socked Orlan square in the eye. He staggered, and Tyler fell behind him. The impact rattled him. Thankfully, Orlan was slow to turn around, and he rubbed at his eye when he did.

Tyler capitalized. He rose to one knee and punched Orlan in the groin. As he bent in half, Tyler stood. He elbowed Orlan in the head twice, then knocked him flat with a solid right. When he moved forward, Orlan recovered quickly with a kick to Tyler's midsection. The vest soaked up some of the impact, but it still forced him to take a couple steps back. Orlan regained his feet and glowered. "Now, you die." He spat at Tyler.

"Get on with it, then," Tyler said. Orlan stalked closer, breathing hard for the first time. Tyler blunted his first jab, which lacked a lot of power. The cross thundering behind it came in at full speed, and Tyler's arm stung when he blocked it. Orlan went for a kick, and Tyler stepped to the side, then rushed in before the big man could get both feet under him again. He hammered some short punches into Orlan's exposed midsection. The giant grunted as each found the mark. Tyler turned to the side, elbowed him directly in the navel, and reached under his adversary's jacket. When Orlan leaned down, Tyler shot up, hitting the giant in the mouth with the crown of his head. With Orlan staggered, Tyler kicked him hard in the chest, sending him stumbling backwards and down the metal steps.

He landed with a crash at the bottom. Despite the drubbing the stairs gave him, he rose to one knee right away. "I'll enjoy beating you to death."

Tyler held up the grenade pin and shook it back and forth. Orlan's eyes widened and he reached for his side in a panic. "Experience and treachery," Tyler said.

He turned his back. A wet explosion boomed behind him, and the force knocked Tyler down. He drew his M11 and stood. They'd lost the element of surprise now, but Orlan was dead, and Tyler still had two capable operatives on his team.

He liked the odds.

34

Rollins stayed low and kept close to the wall. The lines of conveyor belts and other machinery would make him difficult to spot if he kept in a crouch. Aguilar went ahead. Rollins looked across the large room. A guy walked into the men's room. Tyler followed him. Another went in maybe a minute later. Only Tyler walked back out.

A smooth but narrow walkway encircled the production area, ending in stairs at the far end. The work space looked slightly larger than a hockey rink. Even four large SUVs worth of cocaine couldn't put a dent in its capacity. With the cartel as its only client, Rollins wondered who built the Iron Tower and what they hoped to do with it. Maybe he would ask C.T. to look into it when this was all over.

Near a large machine he couldn't identify, Rollins ducked low and watched the workers. He could have taken out the three closest to him, but it would cost everyone the element of surprise. Better to wait and see what happened. Tyler preached patience on a mission, and Rollins was a believer. The first people to run off and do their own thing usually turned out to be the first casualties.

The men turned a brick of pure cocaine into four which could be sold on the streets. He wondered how they planned to get it all out of here. Bringing the drugs in took a quartet of Suburbans. Were a dozen more on standby? Would they roll the product out in shifts? A man approached his position. Rollins wouldn't get those answers anytime soon. He crept back a few steps. The guy sidled around the machine, grabbed a crumpled pack of cigarettes from his pocket, then locked eyes with Rollins.

The knife slipped between his ribs without a sound. Blood burbled on the dying man's lips, but he made no noise as Rollins lowered him to the concrete. With the pair Tyler dispatched in the bathroom, they'd taken out three. The odds were getting better. Rollins' phone vibrated. He looked at the text from C.T. on his watch. *You have an hour and fifteen minutes.*

Rollins still hadn't seen Orlan, and he wondered if the big man found Tyler. Considering how their previous two encounters went, he hoped Tyler possessed the good sense to shoot the giant on sight. Ahead, Aguilar caught Rollins' eye. He held up five fingers and pointed into the work area. Rollins held up two. Aguilar checked the area again. This time, he held up his thumb and first two fingers. The middle dropped, then the index. When the thumb folded into his fist, Aguilar stood, and Rollins did, too. They both scampered toward the workers. Cries of surprise went up, and Rollins shot the two men closest to him before they could reach their weapons. With gunshots coming from farther down, also, the rest of the men scattered and took cover where they could.

Rollins crouched near a conveyor belt. Four cartel workers bolted for the stairs on the left. Aguilar followed. "Dammit," Rollins muttered, but he sprang to his feet and gave chase. He'd almost made it down the stairs when a nearby explosion rocked him from his feet.

AFTER THE GRENADE explosion killed Orlan—a fact Tyler confirmed by looking at the grisly scene below—many of the men above scattered. From his vantage point near the stairs, Tyler saw Aguilar and Rollins pursue a bunch down the other set of steps. Judging by the raised voices, a few remained on the main level. Considering how pear-shaped things turned out for them, they must have been considering cutting their losses.

Which would mean leaving with the drugs.

Tyler advanced. One man shouted in Spanish at three others. Tyler didn't know what he said, but he pointed at the processed and unprocessed bricks of cocaine. Each man held an AK-47 in one hand. If they were going to carry anything, they'd need to set the guns down. Tyler hunkered down and waited. Sure enough, two of them dropped their rifles and gathered the coke into the boxes they used to bring it inside.

Tyler stood and stepped out into the open. One of the men spotted him, and he managed to get a couple syllables out before a 9MM slug entered his head and killed him. The second was slow to react, and Tyler pumped two bullets into his center mass. He fell beside his mouthy friend. The other two scampered for cover. Tyler was outgunned, so he dashed for the end of the conveyor belt. The large control panel would give him at least as much cover as they enjoyed.

Automatic weapons fire cut through the silence a few seconds later. The idiots were firing blind. Even if they happened to see where Tyler hid, he wasn't exposed to them, and their bullets wouldn't make it through a large steel electronics panel. Rounds thunked into metal and pinged off other surfaces. Tyler holstered his Sig and took the Kel-Tec KSG shotgun off his back. These two morons would eventually come to him. They'd either think their barrage proved successful, or their curiosity would overwhelm them. As usual, Tyler took the patient approach.

He heard one of them step out of cover. The guy was probably trying to be quiet, but the soles of his shoes squeaked on the bare floor. He approached from Tyler's right. Slowly. One short step after another. Tyler repositioned himself so he could go on the offensive right away. Following another squeaky pace, Tyler leaned out, landed on his side, and aligned iron sights on his target. One twelve-gauge slug took him down. Tyler fired two more in case the other fellow got brave before he moved back into cover.

Silence prevailed. If the other guy ran for the door, Tyler would hear it. He would have to give pursuit. It allowed for a better chance to escape, making it the superior play. The other three were dead. If their plan had been to steal the drugs and sell them, the survivor would keep all the money. No four-way split. It would take either a fool or someone very loyal to the cartel—or both—to stick around for a shootout.

A single footfall told Tyler this man was a loyal fool. Unlike his fallen comrade, the remaining flunky went to the left. He'd be less exposed. If he reached the other end of the conveyor belt, Tyler would have a problem. The AK would be good from those hundred feet. The shotgun might be marginal. Tyler was a good enough marksman with the Sig to hit a target from such a range, but one miss would expose him to a hail of gunfire.

Those weren't the odds he liked.

When the other guy's footsteps grew quieter past the machinery, Tyler slid around to the front of the panel. He peeked over the top. His adversary took a cautious approach, clearing each potential hiding spot before moving on to the next. Probably former military or law enforcement. When he passed the other end of the conveyor, Tyler moved around to the front. He kept low and advanced to the opposite end, the KSG held out in front of him.

He moved around the far end. The belt whirred to his right, going through the motions and carrying nothing. The guy with the AK checked everywhere Tyler could be hiding. Everywhere except behind him. Tyler sighted him up. He'd be shooting him in the side based on the way he currently stood. The gunman turned his head, and his eyes narrowed at Tyler an instant before a slug blasted him to the floor. Tyler approached, firing a second round into the man's chest to be sure he was dead. He slung the shotgun over his back again and drew the Sig. Bodies lay around him, and he heard no movement.

"Looks clear up here," he said into the small microphone in his collar. "I'm heading your way."

"Roger," came Rollins' quiet reply.

Tyler walked toward the stairs. He made it about halfway before another explosion knocked him off balance. It came from the lower level. Tyler sprinted toward the steps and took a position behind the wall nearby. "Rollins, Aguilar . . . do you copy?" Nothing. He waited a few seconds. "Repeat. Rollins, Aguilar . . . do you copy?" No reply. "Shit." No one else tried to come up the stairs.

Tyler took a deep breath. It felt like a bigger explosion than Orlan's grenade. Rollins and Aguilar were pros. They wouldn't set off a trap. They could get cornered in a room and have a bomb tossed in after them, however. Tyler's heart sank. Rollins had always been so helpful over the years, and he never let the raw deal he got in the army affect him. Aguilar seemed like a good man, and Sara would be furious if Tyler led him to his death. He tried the comms one more time. "Rollins, Aguilar . . . do you copy?"

Silence was his only response.

35

L exi sat in her Accord coupe in a bar parking lot. Uncle George had been inside for almost two hours now. Every fifteen minutes, Lexi turned the engine on to get a little heat in the cabin, but she turned it off quickly. Running cars often drew attention. Finally, about five minutes later, her uncle walked out. His gait looked a little unsteady. A responsible person would call a cab or summon an Uber.

George Goodson, however, would never be mistaken for a responsible person.

He climbed into his GTI, fired it up, and headed toward the exit. Lexi started the Accord and waited for him to make the right turn out of the lot before she went after him. She tried to hang back, a task made easy due to her uncle's reckless speeding. Thanks to some cooperation from the traffic lights, he made it back to his small house in Rosedale in about ten minutes. It looked the same as Lexi remembered it, though her current knowledge of the man made her think of it as little and shabby. She was surprised he owned a house. Grifters rarely put down roots.

She drove by, turned around in a nearby driveway, and parked across the street. Uncle George got out of his car—which was crooked in the driveway—and walked across the lawn to his front door. He dropped his keys, picked them up again, fumbled for the right one, and finally made it inside. When Lexi saw a light come on through the windows, she called him. "Hello?" he said in a slow, skeptical tone.

"Uncle George, it's Lexi." She tried to inject warmth and happiness into her voice.

"Hey, kiddo. It'ssh a little late, ain't it?" He slurred his esses when he talked.

"I guess," she said. "Don't tell me you're keeping regular hours now."

He chuckled and hiccuped. "Of coursshe not. What'sh up?"

"I was just wondering when you were going to visit Mom again. I was kind of surprised to see you both at once, but it was really good, too."

"Oh," he said. "I dunno. In a day or two, I think."

"All right," Lexi said. "I'd like to meet you there if you don't mind."

"It'll be great." He sounded happy now. Lexi almost felt bad for him. "Your mom will really love it, too."

Not for long, she won't, Lexi thought. "I'm looking forward to it. Good night, Uncle George."

"Good night."

She hung up and drove away.

TYLER LED with the Sig as he descended the metal stairs. Despite his best efforts to be quiet, he could hear his own footfalls, so he presumed someone else could, too. When he got to the bottom, Tyler waved dust out of his face. A cloud of it compromised his visibility of the lower level. He hugged the wall and advanced.

Drywall, wood, and floor tile formed a trail of debris consistent with the explosion he heard from above.

No one lurked in the main corridor. Tyler followed the trail of dust and smoke to the right. "Rollins, Aguilar," he whispered into his collar mic. "You all right?" They still didn't answer. Three doors yawned open on the left. Tyler cleared each of the rooms. A fractured door on the right opened into a conference room. Smoke billowed out of it, and Tyler waved it away from his eyes as he walked in.

Rollins and Aguilar lay on the floor, a large conference table shattered and broken nearby. Tyler rushed to them. Aguilar stirred. Tyler felt the unconscious Rollins' neck, and he found a pulse. "Take it easy," Tyler said as Aguilar raised himself onto his elbows. "You all right?"

"I think so." He looked at Rollins and frowned.

"He's alive. What happened?"

"We were clearing this area," Aguilar said. "I went to the left . . . . he took the right. My side was quicker, so I met him in this room. Two guys ran down, tossed a satchel charge in, and shut the door."

"Holy shit." Tyler took in the remains of the conference room. The rear corner was in ruins, with chunks of the wall missing. A TV lay in pieces all over the area. Cabinets which once held supplies got blasted from the walls in the explosion. "What did you do?"

"We figured we only had a few seconds." Aguilar eased into a seated position. "So we stuck as much on top of the explosives as we could. The TV and its cart, mainly. Then we shoved a big table over and took cover. I guess it worked." He chuckled, which turned into a cough. He held his hand out, and Tyler helped him to his feet.

"You got lucky."

"There's a little bit of luck in any successful operation," Aguilar said. He took a couple of unsteady steps before finding his balance. Across the room, Aguilar rooted through the remains of a cabinet before emerging with a first aid kit. He found the smelling salts and held them under Rollins' nose. His eyes shot open a couple seconds later.

"At ease," Tyler said, putting a hand on Rollins' shoulder. "You got knocked out when a bomb went off."

Rollins blew out a deep breath. "Wow. Our blast shield worked."

"Yeah. You think you're all right?"

He nodded slowly. "It rang my bell, but I'll be fine."

Tyler took a few steps back and flipped his friend the bird. "How many fingers am I holding up?"

"The most important one," Rollins said with a grin. He sat up and found his pistol on the floor beside him.

"You two scared me when you didn't answer. I . . . thought the worst might've happened."

"Almost did," Aguilar said. "Putting as much in the way of the fireworks as we could was his idea." He gestured at the seated Rollins. "I figured we were cooked. The explosion probably knocked out our comms."

"I want to clear this level," Tyler said. "Whoever tried to kill you might still be down here."

"You two go," Rollins said. "I'll be all right." He patted his gun with his left hand. "Anybody comes in, I'll shoot them."

Tyler bobbed his head. "Anybody but us, you mean."

Rollins smirked. "Better hope I recognize you, then." He jerked his thumb toward the door. "Go. Don't let these assholes get away."

"Roger," Tyler said. He and Aguilar returned to the hallway. "I'm going to look upstairs and see if they've made it up there."

"Comms are out," Aguilar pointed out.

Tyler shrugged. "If you hear gunshots, come running."

"Copy that."

Tyler climbed the steps back to the main level. He didn't see or hear anyone, and he spent a couple minutes confirming no one occupied the main area. It looked just like he'd left it. He rejoined Aguilar downstairs. "We're good. Let's go." With the dust and smoke dissipating, Tyler spotted a corpse about ten feet down. "You guys shoot one?"

"Don't think so," Aguilar said. "The blast must've gotten him."

As he approached, Tyler saw the large wooden shard sticking out of the dead man's left side. An impressive pool of blood already formed. He checked the corpse for weapons and found only a pistol and a grenade. Tyler took the latter, and he and Aguilar continued. The hallway ended at a T intersection about fifty feet ahead. As they neared the end, Tyler heard voices coming from the left. They spoke in Spanish. "Can you hear what they're saying?" he whispered to Aguilar.

Aguilar cupped his hand to his ear and stood as close to the corner as he could. "They don't have any more ordnance." He paused while the voices kept chattering. "No cell coverage down here. Phones are out." Another pause. "They're planning another assault."

"Let's beat them to it," Tyler said, and he moved out to the left. One door waited on either side of the hallway.

"On the right," Aguilar whispered even though Tyler already figured it out.

"Got it." He put the Sig away and held the dead man's grenade. "Cover me." Aguilar nodded. The door was open. Tyler held the spoon firmly and pulled the pin. As he counted to three, Aguilar moved past him and pointed his gun into the room. Tyler took a step to his left, tossed the grenade in, and shut the door on the surprised voices yelling at them. He and Aguilar dashed down the hallway. An explosion went off behind them.

"You think they're dead?" Aguilar asked.

"Let's check." Tyler drew the M11 again, and they approached the room. It was mostly empty. A few bits of furniture, damaged in the blast, lay strewn about the room. Two men near the explosion were already dead. Tyler stepped over an arm blown off one of them to a lone man on the far side of the room. He coughed weakly. As Tyler approached, he scowled.

"*Puta*," he said, and followed it with a string of Spanish Tyler didn't understand.

"Reap what you sow, asshole," Tyler said, and he shot the guy in the head.

"He posed some serious questions about your mother's promiscuity," Aguilar said.

"Look where it got him." Tyler looked around, opened a few cabinets and drawers, and discovered a stash of cash. He held up the stacks.

"Nice. We can use it to fly back. I'm sure there's a pilot around here who will swallow his questions for twenty grand."

Tyler estimated they were the proud owners of about eighty thousand in hundred-dollar bills. They left the room, cleared the rest of the lower area, and returned to where they'd left Rollins. He'd pulled himself back to his feet, and he didn't shoot when they entered. A double win.

"We have a half-hour," Rollins said. "Reception sucks down here, but I want to call C.T. once we're back upstairs."

They returned to the main level. No one else arrived in the interim. "Let's get as much as we can," Tyler said. "We'll burn the rest."

Rollins made a call and put it on speaker after a few seconds. "We've taken out the guys here."

"I never had a doubt," C.T. said.

"We want the money man now," Rollins said.

"Good call. The cartel is a cash business. They need to clean it somehow. I'll do some digging."

"We're probably headed back tomorrow," Tyler said. "You think you'll know by then?"

"Only if you double my rate," C.T. said.

"You're doing us a favor," Rollins said.

"I tried. Yeah, I'll probably know something by then."

"Great. Thanks." Rollins hung up, and the trio loaded as much as they could into one of the Suburbans. They'd transfer the contents to their Yukon. With about ten minutes remaining until the alarm system came back on, Aguilar and Rollins pushed the remaining bricks together while Tyler siphoned some gas from one of the vehicles they wouldn't use. He let it drain into a water bottle, then carried it inside and spread it around the rest of the coke.

Aguilar took a lighter from his pocket. "Never know when you're going to be asked to light a pretty girl's cigarette," he said.

"Or light a drug lord's cache on fire," Tyler said.

"All things being equal, I'd prefer a couple pretty girls to you two."

"I understand." Tyler handed Aguilar a hundred and then took out his phone to record a video. Aguilar lit the bill and tossed it onto the pile. The small flame grew to a large blaze right away. Tyler filmed it for about twenty seconds before the smell of the burning drugs grew pungent. They torched two of the cartel's SUVs, left the Iron Tower in two hot-wired Suburbans, and drove back to their Yukon across the road.

AFTER LEAVING THE IRON TOWER, the three men checked into two different motels across the street from one another. The night passed uneventfully. In the morning, Aguilar picked up McDonald's for breakfast and a bottle of Tylenol for Rollins' headache and everyone's lingering aches and pains. After breakfast, they drove to Astro Airfield. Rollins still had an old MP badge, and Aguilar carried at least one ID from his past work. Between those and the promise of twenty thousand in cash, they found a pilot who promised discretion.

Tyler and Aguilar loaded the boxes containing bricks of coke onto the plane while Rollins drove off in the Suburban. When he returned about fifteen minutes later, Tyler noticed a plume of black smoke in the distance. Aguilar arranged a couple of large SUVs to meet them. They'd be flying into a different airport, one the pilot said wouldn't ask questions if there was more cash to go around.

About three hours later, they gave a stack of bills to the swarthy guy at Southern Maryland Airpark. Aguilar and one of his men each drove an SUV to Tyler's house. There, they unloaded everything into a room in the basement. Tyler expanded his underground storage when he bought the house. It held his mementos from the army, along with enough guns and ammo to hold off an invasion for a month. He never expected to house a cache of drugs in it, but regardless, it was difficult to find and impossible to access without knowing how.

Once the stash was secure, Aguilar paid his comrades with some of the remaining drug money. Tyler texted Lexi and brewed a pot of coffee while Rollins called C.T. Ferguson on speaker. "I have an answer for you," the private eye said. "A couple, actually. It's not surprising they have more than one place cleaning the money."

"How many are we talking?" Tyler asked.

"At least two. If I dug deeper, I could probably find more. Let's start with the smaller one. Héctor and Rodolfo are part owners of a car repair shop in Kingsville."

Tyler pounded his fist into his palm. "Alice told me they usually took their cars to one place for service. I never thought they'd have a piece of it."

"Makes sense," Rollins said. "You'll have some people paying in cash, and you're constantly buying supplies, gas, and all sorts of things."

"Right," C.T. said. "The bigger one was right under our noses. Héctor's tied into the community where he lives. His business partner is a guy named Todd Windholm. I've never been a fan of guys named Todd."

Tyler grinned. "The Carlin bit. I've met Windholm. He's an asshole and a toady."

"But not an idiot. He owns a couple companies by himself, so they're not traceable to Héctor or any of the cartel's interests. One of them is a construction supplier. Guess who provides all the equipment for Talbot Lakes?"

"Windolm's company," Tyler said even though the answer was obvious.

"You've played this game before, I see. A business like this allows him to make a lot of purchases of various sizes. It's a great way to clean a bunch of dirty money." C.T. paused. "It's local. My guess is they don't want to keep most of the cash with Héctor, so it's probably stashed somewhere at Windholm's. If you . . . want to break in and look around, for instance, I could probably help with the alarm there, too."

Aguilar and Rollins both nodded. "Yeah," Tyler said. "We definitely want to. In fact, we want to hit it tonight."

36

Héctor paced back and forth in his living room. His right hand held a Glock 17, and his left ran through his hair every few steps. He'd heard nothing about the shipment for far too long. The cartel sent a bunch of men to move and process everything. They were supposed to go back to Mexico, but Héctor was counting on Orlan to convince a few to come north. Even Orlan had been silent since last night. Héctor had called him a dozen times, and they all went to voicemail right away.

The American mentioned something about Texas. Did he find out about the shipment? How could he know? Raul and Nataniel were dead. Maybe he learned from them. It would be just like a former soldier to torture someone for information. Still, he would have been cut to pieces against Orlan and the men from Mexico. The idea of him breaching the Iron Tower was laughable.

Héctor, however, found nothing worth laughing about.

"It could all be fine," Rodolfo said from the couch.

"Shut up."

"We don't know why they're not answering. Service could be bad down there."

"I said shut up!" Héctor stopped pacing and pointed the pistol at Rodolfo. "This is all your fault!" His cousin shrank back as much as the sofa would allow. "First, you can't keep your girl in line, and then you go and kill her over some bullshit. If you handled your business, we'd be moving product and raking in the money right now."

"I told you—"

"Don't you dare tell me you're sorry," Héctor said. "Not again." His hand shook as he held the gun on Rodolfo. "Your father was always my favorite uncle. It's why you're still alive right now."

Rodolfo frowned and turned away. Héctor lowered the gun and resumed pacing. Hunger gnawed at his stomach, and he realized he'd neglected to eat since dinner last night . . . almost a full day ago. At some point, he'd need to put his nerves aside for a moment and get some food. No wonder he felt weak holding the Glock. Héctor's phone ringing snapped him from his thoughts. He looked eagerly at the screen and then scowled when he saw the call originated in Mexico. He declined it, which only worked briefly. Five minutes later, he picked up. "Héctor, how are things?" Tomás said.

Héctor cleared his throat and tried to inject some confidence into his voice. "Fine." He sounded good to his own ears.

"Why didn't you answer when I called the first time?"

"I was in the bathroom," Héctor said.

Tomás changed the subject. "Did the shipment arrive?"

"It's been processed. It'll be in Maryland soon."

"It's not there yet?"

"Orlan is being cautious," Héctor said. He took a chance Tomás didn't know much about the shipment yet. The cartel sent a bunch of men. As far as Héctor knew, none of them would be making their return trips. Did the cartel try to reach any of them? Was Tomás calling because he had many of the same concerns?

Héctor wiped sweat from his brow despite the house being pleasantly cool.

"I hope so," Tomás said, and Héctor winced at the skepticism he heard. If they caught on to what really happened, he was screwed. The cartel couldn't get into the Iron Tower, however. Their ability to gather intelligence would be limited. The security footage last night all looked normal. "Let me know when you have everything."

"I will." Tomás hung up. Héctor sighed and slipped his phone back into his pocket. Despite knowing it was futile, he dialed Orlan again.

It went right to voicemail.

UNDER COVER OF DARKNESS, Tyler, Rollins, and Aguilar drove to Windholm Construction Supply in Aguilar's SUV. It sat on a large lot off Route 7 near White Marsh. If the cartel kept money or drugs here, getting them to Bel Air would only take about twenty minutes. Windholm owned a large property encircled by a tall chain-link fence. The barrier lacked a gate, however, and anyone who wanted to could approach. Locked buildings and good security would deter anything more. Most of the time. Aguilar steered down the driveway. A long main structure was on the right, and a bunch of freestanding garages surrounded it on all sides.

Rollins dialed C.T. Ferguson. "We're in," he said when his friend picked up.

"Good. I've looked into this Windholm. He's pretty impressed with himself on social media. When he opened the company, he posted a picture outside the main office. A sticker in the window identified his alarm company."

"Nice work."

"Thanks," C.T. said, "but it's incomplete. What I don't know is which model he uses."

"Why does it matter?" Tyler asked.

"There are default credentials for all of them. None are the same. Most places never disable those built-in accounts, so I'm counting on them to work. The challenge is I'll need you to get inside and tell me the model on the control box. Then, I can give you a code which should disarm it."

"Should?"

"I think we're looking at a ninety percent chance of success," C.T. said. "The more you all stand around and dilly-dally, though, it drops."

"Yeah, yeah," Rollins said. "We can get into the main office."

"I have a snap gun," Tyler offered. He dug it out of the small bag he brought. "Let's go." The three got out of the vehicle and approached. "Any cameras we should worry about?"

"Yes," C.T. said. "Once I know what model the system is, I can help you with them. Considering what they might store here, I doubt Windholm has someone watching. He doesn't want a backhoe guy finding a bunch of coke."

"I hope you're right." The main building looked like a long trailer. Its beige siding was still in good repair. A prominent sign displaying the company name hung to the left of the door. There were only a few windows and none more than ten feet from the entrance. Most of the square footage must have been for storage. Tyler walked up three steps. He opened the lock with the snap gun in short order. As he entered, an alarm blared.

Tyler grimaced and searched the interior walls. He found the alarm control panel to the right of the door. "It's a model three thousand," he shouted over the shrill siren.

Rollins took a few steps back and relayed the information. Tyler put his hands over his ears. A few seconds later, the alarm fell silent. Tyler took a deep breath. "System's off," Rollins said, "and this one doesn't have a timer on it."

"One thing to note," C.T. said. "I can clear the camera footage, but everything I do gets logged."

"Can't you erase the records?" Tyler asked.

"Sure. And then there's an entry in a brand new log showing what I just did. I could get rid of the new one, too, but then we're in an infinite loop."

"You think anyone's gonna look?" Tyler flicked the lights on. Two desks and chairs occupied most of the space. Neither even had a computer on top. A closed office displayed Windholm's nameplate beside it. Past the reception area, a large door led to the rest of the building.

"Maybe," C.T. said. "It won't tell them much. I'm using the default account, so it's not attributable. They won't know any of us are involved."

Rollins walked inside. "I think we're good from here. We'll call back if something goes pear-shaped."

"I'll await your call, then."

"Very funny," Rollins said, and he hung up.

Aguilar slipped inside and closed the door behind him. "I didn't see anyone around, but lots of little buildings to check will take time."

"They're the right size for construction vehicles," Tyler said.

"Sure. Or a pallet or two of cash."

"Let's look here first." Tyler approached the large black door. The snap gun bypassed it quickly. Rollins and Aguilar stood nearby with their pistols ready. Tyler glanced at them, and both men nodded. He pulled the door open and stepped to the side. Rollins walked in and stepped to the left. Aguilar went right. Tyler drew his Sig and entered behind them. This area was one large room. Light from the main area illuminated the first few feet. The rest remained bathed in darkness. "I'm going to hit the lights," Tyler whispered.

"Roger," came two replies in stereo.

The blackness parted. A row of bulldozers lined the left side.

The three men cleared the area. Two large metal cabinets were the only other things in the area. Tyler popped the first with his snap gun. It held an impressive arsenal of weapons. "Nice. Anyone need to go gun shopping while we're here?"

"I've always wanted a MAC-10," Aguilar said as he grabbed one and a pouch of magazines loaded with 9MM ammo. "I guess they need to be prepared in case someone hits this place."

"I guess." Tyler opened the remaining case. Shrink-wrapped stacks of cash covered every available square inch of the interior. "Could be a few million in here. Let's load it up." Tyler and Rollins carried the money while Aguilar guarded them with his new automatic weapon. Five minutes later, they'd emptied the cabinet and filled up the rear of Aguilar's SUV.

"We burning this place?" Rollins said.

Tyler shook his head. "They'll know about it soon enough. Let's get out of here." They climbed back into the Durango and left.

AFTER PILING up the money in Tyler's basement, the trio retired to the kitchen. Despite the late hour, Tyler put a pot of coffee on. No one objected. At this point, he could drink it any time and still sleep at night. Once it finished and everyone had a full mug, Tyler dug a burner phone out of a kitchen drawer. "I'm going to call Héctor."

"Why not make him sweat a little longer?" Aguilar said. "He's gotta be feeling the heat from Mexico right now."

"I don't want them to take him out. If anyone kills the son of a bitch, it's gonna be me." He found the video of the burning drugs and sent it to the cheap mobile. Once Tyler saved the file, he dialed Héctor's number from memory.

"Who is this?"

"You know very well who it is, Héctor."

The line went silent for a few seconds. Then, Héctor said, "I should have known. You are a big pain in my ass, Mister Tyler."

"I won't be much longer. You're going to be dead."

"Am I?"

"Sure," Tyler said. "Even if I don't do it, I imagine your overlords in Mexico have a few questions about the shipment." He set the phone down long enough to text Héctor the video. "You can see what happened to a lot of it right there."

The connection went quiet again. "Those are my drugs!" Héctor yelled several seconds later.

"They were," Tyler said.

"*¡Eres hombre muerto!*"

"Not even original, Héctor. Besides, you've had a few chances to take me out, and all you've gotten for your efforts is a bunch of *hombres muertos* of your own. Orlan was your best chance against me. It was nice of you to send him to Houston, by the way. I beat him down and killed him with his own grenade. I only wish I would've had a chance to cram it down his throat first."

"What do you want, Tyler?" Héctor growled.

"Glad you asked. I have the rest of your drugs from Houston. I also have the cash you kept at your buddy Windholm's."

"I'll—"

"You'll shut up and listen," Tyler said. "They're in a safe place, and I don't think you have enough men left to come after me. Unless you want your Mexican friends to torture you for a week, you'll consider what I'm about to offer you."

Héctor's sigh hissed in Tyler's ear. "I'm listening."

"Good. Here are the terms, and they're not negotiable. I'll give you back all the drugs and most of the money. I'm going to keep a little for all the trouble you've put me through."

"Let me guess," Héctor said, "you want me to leave Maryland in exchange."

"Yes," Tyler said, "but it's not all. I want safe passage in and out of your complex, you and your asshole friends out of the state, and a guarantee you and the cartel won't come after me or anyone I know."

Héctor laughed. "You expect me to say yes? I think you over-estimate yourself, Mister Tyler."

"Fine. Take your chances with the cartel, then. I'm sure they'll be very understanding." Tyler hung up.

"What are you doing?" Rollins asked.

"We have him by the short hairs." Tyler shrugged. "He'll call back. He needs to take this deal to save his own ass no matter how much he hates it." The phone remained silent. "My guess is he'll wait a few minutes to try and save face, but we'll hear from him again." Tyler heated his coffee in the microwave and took a sip. He set a box of protein bars on the table, and everyone snagged one.

Five minutes after Tyler hung up on him, Héctor called back. "All right," he said, "I don't like your deal, but I've given it some thought."

"I figured you would."

"I agree to your terms. Come to my house tomorrow night at nine. You give me the drugs and money, and I'll uphold my end of the bargain."

"Great," Tyler said. "See you then." He broke the connection again.

"You know it's gonna be a trap, right?" Rollins confirmed.

"Sure." Tyler grinned. "I have a plan." He removed two short stacks of cash from his pockets. He set them down in front of Aguilar. "You've been a great help, and I can't thank you enough. We probably couldn't have done this without you. I got it from here, though."

Aguilar picked up the bills. "It's drug money."

"Go do something good with it, then. Redeem it."

He nodded and stood. "I suppose I can." Aguilar held out his hand, and Tyler shook it. "It's been great working with you. I think we put a big dent in the cartel."

"And I'm going to turn it into a big smoking hole from here," Tyler said. He glanced at Rollins. "Maybe with one more bit of help."

"You need something like this again," Aguilar said, "you call me."

"Likewise."

Aguilar shook hands with Rollins and left. The Durango fired up and drove away. "One more bit of help?" Rollins repeated.

Tyler nodded. "I'm going to Héctor's alone. I know you're not feeling a hundred percent right now, and I'll be able to handle it . . . if you do one part of the plan with me first."

37

Zeke stared at Lexi as she poured herself a cup of coffee. She'd put on new jeans, a black Maryland hoodie, and wore her hair in a ponytail. "You're going somewhere," the old man said.

She went to classes in yoga pants or sweats. Her grandfather caught on. "I sure am." Lexi rummaged through the fridge. With two people eating Zeke's food, his supplies grew strained. Lexi hoped she wouldn't need to be here much longer. Spending time with her grandfather was nice, but she lived with her dad. She pulled a half-gallon of milk from the top shelf and poured it into a bowl. She found and added the cereal afterward.

"Most people do it in the opposite order," Zeke said.

"I'm my father's daughter," Lexi said. "I'm not most people."

"You got that right." He paused. "Why do I get the feeling you're going to see your mother again?"

"Because I am." Lexi ate her cereal. It didn't live up to the mega crunch advertised on the package. Considering how long it might have been in her grandpa's pantry, she couldn't complain. "You were right. They're both shady, and I'm onto them. It's going to blow up in their faces."

"I'm sorry you had to find out about your mother this way."

Lexi shrugged. "I'd suspected something for a while. You never really want to believe the worst about your parents, though." She took another bite. "At least I ended up with one good one." Lexi finished her breakfast and took her gun with her to the car. She didn't notice anyone unusual hanging around. By now, she knew her dad was back from Texas. He'd been cagey about everything else, but she knew he'd devise a plan to finish the cartel's presence in Maryland.

Before reaching the correctional facility, Lexi stashed the pistol in the locked glove compartment. She went through the mantrap and signed in like the first time. The same guard led Lexi to the waiting room. Every eye flicked to her as she walked in, and for a second, she felt like she intruded on several private conversations. No one paid her any mind, however, and she slid onto a seat. Another guard brought her mother in a moment later.

"Alexis, it's so great to see you again." Rachel smiled, and she possessed the nerve to make it look sincere.

Be strong, Lexi chided herself. *These two are after your dad.* "You too, Mom. I thought Uncle George was coming today."

"He is." Her mother glanced at the clock. "Looks like he's running a few minutes late . . . as usual. I'm sure he'll be glad to see you again, too."

Lexi bit down a snide remark and plastered a grin on her face. "I hadn't seen him in a while."

"Your father should make sure you keep in touch with people," Rachel said.

"Uncle George is an adult, Mom. Besides, I'm in school. What's his excuse?"

"I'm sure he's a busy man. You'll find out how it is when you're older."

Again, Lexi swallowed what she really wanted to say. This time, she opted for silence. The door opened a minute later, and

Uncle George walked in. "There they are," he said loudly enough to earn a few glares from people talking nearby.

After a round of quick hugs, everyone took their seats. "I'm surprised you're both here again so soon," Rachel said.

Uncle George jerked his thumb toward Lexi. "She wanted to see us both. I guess we're kinda like a two-for-one deal."

Lexi spread her hands. She didn't want to drop the hammer on them so soon. "It's been a while since we were all in the same room before last week is all."

"A girl can miss her mother and her favorite uncle," George said, chuckling at his own observation. He was her mother's only sibling. Her dad had a brother, too, but James lived most of the way across the country and never seemed interested in coming back east. Still, James was merely aloof, not a grifter and a thief, so he earned the title of favorite by default.

"How often do you visit, Uncle George?"

He shrugged. "I guess once a week or so."

"You two email back and forth a lot?" Lexi asked.

Rachel looked from her brother to her daughter. "What's going on? Alexis, why do you want to know how often we talk?"

"I'm just wondering when you two hatched your plan to go after my dad's pension." To their credit, both remained silent, even when Rachel's wide eyes betrayed her. She'd never been great at hiding what she felt. It was probably why she ended up in prison while her brother remained free to cook up another scheme. "Don't sit there and act dumb. I mean . . . you are for thinking you'd get away with it, but give me a little credit."

"What are you talking about, kiddo?" Uncle George asked with smooth innocence. He'd probably enjoyed lots of practice with the question.

Lexi glared at him. "Don't 'kiddo' me, you prick. I saw your record. You've got a nice string of arrests for attempting to defraud people out of their pensions." She turned to her mother, who couldn't meet her gaze. "I actually thought better of you,

Mom. I know it didn't work out with you and Dad, but he was always good to us, and he gladly took me in when shit went south with you. He shielded his retirement from you for a damn good reason. Why would you make a play for it now?" George tried to get a word in, but Lexi cut him off with an upraised hand. "I'll bet if I look at your search history, you've contacted a bunch of shady lawyers."

"I'm going to need money when I get out," Rachel said in a small voice.

"Get a job," Lexi said. She glowered at someone gaping at her from a nearby table, and the mousy man quickly looked away. "Dad's leaving his benefits to me. You never considered that, did you?" They both remained silent. "Or maybe you did, and you just didn't care. Whatever. I don't give a shit anymore." She stood. "You two deserve each other." Lexi stormed out of the door opened by a watchful guard, ignoring her mother calling after her as she left. She got back into her Accord, pounded the steering wheel a few times, and sped away from the jail.

TYLER KNEW he'd asked a lot of Rollins already. When their comms went dead in Houston, he'd feared the worst. It nearly happened, and Rollins still wasn't fully recovered. This last request would be easy. "What do you need?" Rollins asked.

"Your sewing skills."

Rollins cocked his head to the side. "Really?"

"It'll all make sense once I explain what I have in mind." Tyler laid the idea out for him, and Rollins bobbed his head as he listened. At the end, Tyler asked, "What do you think?"

"It's got a little risk," Rollins said, "but so does every plan. I think it'll work."

"Great. You just need a needle and thread."

"I like how you assume the gay guy knows how to sew."

"You've gotta be better than me," Tyler said.

Rollins grinned. "I am. Even have a machine, but I think doing this one by hand is the way to go. You get your stuff set up. I'll be back soon." His large pickup rumbled to life as he drove away. Tyler walked back downstairs and unlocked his secret room. The claymore mine had long been a part of the US military arsenal before Tyler signed up. Special Operations Command developed a smaller version only about three inches tall. With less C4 inside, its lethality covered a shorter distance, but it would still be plenty adequate for Tyler's purposes. Best of all, they could be detonated wirelessly. SOCOM thought of everything in this case.

Rollins returned about a half-hour later. Tyler set a large gym bag on his table. It was about twenty inches long and a foot deep. Unmodified, it would hold most of the money. With the alterations Tyler planned, all the cash he planned to give to Héctor should fit. "I'll need some materials to make the new bottom," Rollins said. "Something like a gym shirt's probably good."

"Can do."

"We need to support it somehow, too. I guess you're planning to glue the claymores in?"

"Yeah," Tyler said. "I think I have something for the rest, too." He walked upstairs and returned a minute later with a black gym shirt and a foam roller. "It's long enough to cut into pieces for the false bottom."

"Hope you have a lot of glue," Rollins said.

"You just make it look good and convincing." Tyler held the remote detonator. "I'll work on making it go boom."

38

Tyler checked the bag one more time. Rollins did a hell of a job. Héctor and his lackeys would be too busy gawking at the stacks of cash to notice they didn't quite go all the way to the bottom. The drugs took up another two bags Tyler didn't care about. He expected everything to either explode or burn. The detonator—the same model he'd used in Afghanistan—was clipped onto Tyler's belt. He brought the Sig even though he expected someone would disarm him. A vest, however, would be pushing it. They wouldn't let him in dressed for war. As it was, Tyler wore all black, including the thin gloves covering his hands.

He drove the 442 north to Bel Air. Evening traffic was light, and Tyler hit the neighborhood ten minutes early. It gave him a chance to poke around. He didn't see any guys stashed at Windholm's model house. A search with night vision binoculars showed no one lurking in the trees behind Héctor's property. He probably didn't have enough men left to get cute in how he deployed them. At the appointed hour, Tyler guided his car up Héctor's driveway and stopped at the gate.

A Spanish-accented voice came over the intercom. "What do you want?"

"Héctor's expecting me."

"What's your name?"

"If he doesn't want his stuff back," Tyler said, "I'm happy to leave. I'm not going to sit here and play your little games."

No reply came. The gate swung open a moment later, and Tyler drove up the rest of the driveway and stopped alongside the house. He watched the barricade close in the rearview mirror. He was committed to this plan now. No early escape. No easy way out.

Exactly like he wanted it.

Two slender Latinos emerged from the side door, both of them training their guns on Tyler. "Out of the car," one of them said.

Tyler got out and turned so he presented his side to the duo. "Stuff's in the trunk."

The one who spoke took a few steps forward. His pistol was about three feet from Tyler's face now. "Maybe we kill you and take it."

"Héctor and I had an arrangement," Tyler said. "I expect him to live up to it." There had always been a possibility he wouldn't, of course. Tyler readied himself to make a grab for the gun. One step to the left would allow him to use one man to screen the other. He didn't want to do this outside, but if Héctor and his paid idiots forced Tyler's hand, he would. After another few seconds of staring and posturing, both men lowered their weapons.

"We gotta search you," the pair's apparent spokesman said.

"I figured you would." The guy patted Tyler down. He found the M11 right away. "You can just toss it in the car." Like a good lackey, he threw the gun through the 442's open driver's side window.

"What the hell is this?" The man said as he felt the outline of the detonator.

"I'm diabetic," Tyler said.

"Fine." He finished the mediocre patdown and stood. "Let's get the stuff inside."

Tyler opened the trunk, set the two bags of coke down, and picked up the one with the cash. He pushed the lid closed again. "I'm carrying the money," he said. "You two can bring the other stuff."

"I ain't here to carry your shit," the second man said.

Tyler shrugged. "Leave it here, then. See what your boss thinks of your decision. We going in?"

The two looked at each other and turned up their hands. They held a short conversation in Spanish before each stuffed a pistol into their waistbands and hoisted a bag. Tyler followed them inside. Héctor's massive kitchen could hold the first floor of most Baltimore houses. White granite countertops gleamed in soft overhead light. All the appliances were stainless steel. The rest of the first floor looked like it came from a luxury furnishings catalog. Two more Latinos stared at Tyler from a sofa.

They walked through the kitchen, and the guy in front of Tyler opened a door in the main hallway. He gestured for Tyler to walk down the stairs. He did, and both men followed him. The main area of the basement held another couch, TV, and a foosball table where two more guys played a game. Another door was open to a large room. Tyler's escorts led him inside. A well-dressed man sat behind a huge wooden desk. Most of the floor space was empty save a smaller desk and chair on the opposite wall. "You must be Héctor."

He didn't smile. Someone in Héctor's position couldn't afford to. He'd taken a bad deal because the alternative was even worse. "Mister Tyler. You're carrying the money, I presume?"

"I am." He set the bag in front of Héctor, making sure to point the business side—the one with the logo—toward him. "Your guys have the drugs."

Héctor nodded. His workers set their bags down nearby and

flanked their boss. "I know how much money Windholm had at his company," Héctor said. "How much will I find here?"

"I honestly don't know," Tyler said. "I never counted it. I just kept a little to compensate me for my annoyance."

"We're going to see how much is here." One of the two guys who had been playing foosball approached Héctor and whispered something in Spanish. He repeated himself louder when the main man didn't respond. "I heard you, Rodolfo. If I need you, I'll call you."

Rodolfo turned away and glared at Tyler. "Hi, Rodolfo. How's it feel to be the one who screwed your cousin?"

"Ignore him," Héctor said as Rodolfo seethed. One of the other guys led him from the room and closed the door. "You don't mind staying while we count, do you?"

Tyler felt he didn't really have a choice in the matter, but he was happy to stick around. "Sure. Can I sit at the other station?"

Héctor turned up his hand, and Tyler crossed the room and sat behind the smaller desk. Maybe Héctor employed a secretary in the past. Perhaps this was the room where the men counted the money in one spot and divided up the drugs in the other. One of the lackeys opened the bag and whistled. It was the reaction Tyler hoped for. He reached toward the contents, but Héctor slapped his wrist. "We'll take our time and see how much is here. This isn't a race."

Both guys removed some stacks from the bag and counted. A lot still remained. Tyler wanted them to pull a few more out before he got on with the plan. The less weight on top of the claymores, the better. A few minutes later, they grabbed several more piles each. Tyler put his left hand under the desk, grabbed the detonator with his right, and scooted back an inch in the chair. His thumb popped the hinged cover up, exposing the circular button. A tiny red light pulsed to indicate a connection to the explosives.

With everyone distracted by the money, Tyler flipped the

secretary table forward. When the three men looked up at him, he hit the button.

39

Tyler ducked behind the desk when the blast went off. Claymores used C4 to propel small metal balls at high speeds in about a sixty-degree arc. Anyone caught in the radius would likely die a gruesome death. A hard enough surface could deflect some of the balls, especially if they had to cover yards of distance. Drywall at six to ten feet would take it all. The room shook like an earthquake rocked the area. The lone painting on the walls crashed to the floor. Tyler's ears rang, but he was unhurt. A white cloud of cocaine covered the front part of the room, and smoke billowed from the rear of the ruined gym bag. Tyler left the desk in place and moved around it toward the carnage. He locked the door on his way. Héctor and his two stooges got shredded in the explosion. Tyler held his breath while he searched the bodies for a gun and found a Glock in good working order.

Someone pounded on the door and hollered in Spanish. Tyler unlocked it again as he moved past. A man pushed in and gaped at the scene. Tyler shot him in the head. The gun worked. He backed toward the far wall and kept an eye on the door. Tyler crouched behind the desk. Rodolfo ran in unarmed. "Héctor!" he yelled. He turned toward Tyler. "¡Puta! You're dead."

"Still think you should've killed Alice?" Tyler asked.

"The hell with her."

"Wrong answer." Tyler shot Rodolfo once in the chest and a second time in the head. He collapsed in the doorway. Tyler heard more footsteps running their way. Some of the charred remains of the money on the floor smoldered. It would make the second part of Tyler's plan easier. Another ran in, nearly tripped over Rodolfo's body, and stared at the grisly spectacle at the main desk. When his head turned, Tyler put a bullet directly above his right eye. Counting the two killed in the explosion, it made five lackeys down.

No one else advanced on his position. Tyler inspected the money for any which remained intact. A few stacks did, and he tucked them away. He piled up more scraps near the smoldering pile, took a lighter from his pocket, and set the whole thing ablaze. Tyler swatted some airborne powder away from his face as he knelt at the bodies. He touched the lighter's flame to Héctor's tattered shirt. It caught, and a small blaze crawled up his mangled body.

Tyler left the room with the stolen Glock leading the way. As he crossed the basement, someone came running down the stairs shouting curses in Spanish. Before the man got a chance to lift the large automatic weapon he carried, Tyler shot him in the neck. He fell and sprayed the ceiling with a hail of gunfire as he died.

He was probably the last guy, but Tyler didn't rush up the stairs. He cleared the living room and kitchen on his way out and didn't see anyone else. With the coast clear, Tyler tossed the gun into the trees past Héctor's yard. He climbed into the 442 and approached the gate, which withdrew automatically as the car tripped its sensors. The neighbors might be used to certain activities at Héctor's, but if any of them heard or felt the explosion, the police could be en route.

Tyler hit the street and got on the gas but not enough to draw attention by speeding out of the neighborhood. At the end of the main drag, he turned onto Route 543 headed toward the highway. About a mile down the road, three Harford County Sheriff's Office cars zoomed toward Talbot Lakes. Once they were in the rearview, Tyler sent a text to Lexi. *Everything is done. Come home anytime. Love you.*

Before he merged onto I-95, his phone buzzed with a reply. *See you tomorrow, Dad. Love you, too.*

TOMÁS QUINTERO FROWNED at his phone. All his calls to Héctor still went straight to voicemail. It would be about ten in the evening in Maryland, and Héctor kept whatever hours the cartel demanded of him. He should pick up. Tomás tried again and got the same result. To make things a little bit worse, Bernardo Espinoza stepped into the office. He'd demand an update, and Tomás would need to provide one. Héctor wasn't worth lying to the man in charge.

"Any word from Héctor?" Bernardo asked. He sat on the edge of Tomás' desk rather than use any of the three chairs set in front of it. It allowed him to look down at his subordinate, and Tomás swallowed hard before he answered.

"Five times now . . . right to voicemail."

"You think he's ignoring us?"

"He knows better," Tomás said.

Bernardo nodded absently as he looked out the window. "He does. Héctor's been having problems recently. I wonder if you've told me everything?" Bernardo's eyes turned from whatever he looked at outside and bored into Tomás's.

"I've told you whatever Héctor has told me."

"Ah," Bernardo said. "Easy to cover a lie of omission, then."

"I'm not—"

Bernardo cut him off by waving his hand. "I think you've been telling me the truth. It's Héctor I wonder about. He's family, but he's always had some . . . interesting ideas. The past week has made me wonder if I was wrong to buy into his expansion plan."

"Maryland is quite a bit farther north than anywhere else we've gone," Tomás offered.

"Yes, I know. I, too, can look at a map." Bernardo rolled his eyes. "Did Héctor get the shipment?"

Tomás sighed. "I don't think so. He told me it was coming, but he sounded a little evasive. None of the men we sent with it have come back, either."

"I saw your message earlier," Bernardo said. "What happened to Héctor?"

"My understanding is his cousin killed his girlfriend, and it pissed someone off."

"Someone very dangerous, it would seem."

"Yes," Tomás said. "We could try the house's cameras."

"Do it." Bernardo moved off the desk and stood beside Tomás, who fired up his laptop. He opened an app, and a moment later, security images from Héctor's house filled the window. "Do we have footage of what happened earlier?"

"No. Only live. It's how Héctor set it up."

"Did you try—"

"I had a few people try," Tomás said. "We can only get the live feed."

Bernardo grunted. Tomás knew his boss wasn't used to hearing no. "Let's look at some other cameras, then." It took a moment, but Tomás found one for the basement. It showed the large common area. A man lay dead near the stairs. "Shit," the boss muttered. It got worse when Tomás switched to another device. It depicted Héctor's large downstairs office where money came in and drugs went out. The disarray made it look like a bomb went off in there. Mutilated bodies burned near the desk, and more flames lapped at piles of money and drugs. Others lay dead from gunshot wounds near the door.

"*Madre de Dios*," Tomás whispered as he viewed the carnage.

Bernardo paced the area behind Tomás' chair. "What kind of problem was Héctor having?"

"He didn't get into specifics about who it was if that's what you mean."

"Of course it's what I mean." Bernardo pounded the desktop. "It must be another cartel. They learned we were moving north, and they took action against us."

"Héctor didn't tell me—"

"He obviously didn't know," Bernardo said. "Whoever he and Rodolfo pissed off sold him out to our rivals."

"But which one?" Tomás asked.

"We need to know." Bernardo waved his hand at the monitor. "Maryland is a loss. Let's forget about it and move on. We need to focus on what's in front of us. A bunch of men attacked Héctor's house and killed everyone. They burned bodies. Héctor could have been tortured." Tomás thought he heard his boss' voice crack when mentioning his cousin. If so, it would be a rare display of emotion. "We have to assume another cartel is going to keep the pressure on us."

Tomás knew the answer he would get, but he felt compelled to pose the question, anyway. "We're going to take it to them?"

"Yes!" Bernardo said. "We're going to figure out which one tried to screw us, and then we're going to burn them down. Héctor might have helped us after all. Once we take out a rival, we'll be the biggest cartel in Mexico.

And a bigger target, Tomás thought, but he'd gotten good over the years at keeping his musings to himself.

40

T yler slept well for the first night in a while. He still got up early the next morning thanks to years of making it a habit. After swigging a couple cups of coffee and eating a bowl of cereal, he retreated to his basement. His hidden room now held a bunch of cartel cash in addition to the normal supply of guns and ammo. He moved several stacks into a paper bag, closed up shop, and left the house.

About a half-hour later, Tyler drove past the charred remains of Smitty and Son's. The building itself still stood, but the gutted interior was obvious even from a quick drive by. Tyler made a right at Fullerton Avenue and followed the GPS on his phone. He ended up on a network of streets packed mostly with duplexes. Tom Smith lived in a small single house at the terminus of a dead-end street.

Tyler parked the 442 and took his bag to the front door. He rang the bell and waited. Smitty opened a moment later but only wide enough to stand in the doorway and look out to see who it was. "What do you want?"

"I brought a peace offering." Tyler held up the bag.

"Don't feel much like drinking," Smitty said, "especially not with you."

"This isn't booze," Tyler said. "I know you're pissed at me. Don't blame you."

Smitty crossed his arms. "I don't think we have much to say to one another."

"Hear me out. Do it in exchange for me getting Jake out from under with Braxton." Smitty glared, but Tyler continued. "I won't make a habit of holding it over your head, but I just want a few minutes of your time."

For several seconds, Smitty stood still. Finally, he sighed, opened the door wider, and moved aside. "Fine. A few minutes."

"Thanks." Tyler entered, and the two adjourned to the nearby living room. The place looked like Smitty hadn't refreshed it in a decade. Tyler never asked, but he presumed there hadn't been a Missus Smith for a while, and the look of the house confirmed it. He sat in a recliner. Smitty took a spot on the couch.

"I guess I gotta ask . . . what's in the bag?"

Tyler tossed it toward him. Smitty leaned down, unrolled the top, and gaped at the contents. "Héctor sends his regards," Tyler said.

"Did you . . . are they . . . dead?"

"Yeah. Their operation is done. Héctor, Rodolfo, all their men."

"Jesus." Smitty looked from Tyler to the brown paper sack. "This is drug money, though."

Tyler shrugged. "Who cares? Put it to good use. I'm giving it to you because I don't know what your insurance will cover. Your place never should've been burned down. I admit I had a vendetta going, but Héctor didn't need to involve anyone else." He paused. "I have no idea if it's enough to rebuild or if you even want to. Whatever. Take it and use it for something good."

"Insurance is still doing their thing," Smitty said after a

moment. "I'm not sure what they're gonna tell me." He sighed. "I reduced my coverage a few years ago after I made some upgrades. Cash was tight, and the risk of equipment starting a fire was close to zero. I never thought some asshole would light up my shop."

"I know," Tyler said. "I'm sorry it happened."

Smitty's head bobbed a fraction. "It was pretty much your fault." Tyler knew it, but he still felt the comment like a punch to the gut. Smitty picked up the bag and set it beside him on the couch. "I haven't thought much about what I want to do. You expecting me to hire you back if I can reopen?"

"Do what you want. Rehire me or not. I just don't want you to lose your livelihood."

"I appreciate it." Smitty puffed his cheeks and blew out a long breath. "Still not sure about this drug money, though."

"It's clean," Tyler said. He stood. "I took it from one of their stashes. I have a kid in college, so I'm keeping some for her education, too. I burned the rest with the cartel."

"I'll always be grateful for what you did for Jake," Smitty said, "but I don't need to hear the war stories."

"Fair enough. Good luck with the insurance company." Tyler moved toward the door.

"Hey," Smitty called. "I'm glad you were able to get revenge for your new girlfriend."

Tyler grinned. The comment made him wonder if his current girlfriend would still be talking to him, but he didn't want to dampen Smitty's sudden display of good spirits. "Yeah, me, too." He left the house.

THE SOUND of Lexi's V6 approached the house a couple hours after Tyler returned from Smitty's. Lexi walked in with her bags a minute later, and she set them down right away to hug her dad. "Good to see you, kiddo. How's the old man?"

"The usual," Lexi said.

"Ornery and oddly endearing?"

"You two are a lot alike." She picked up her stuff. "I'm gonna run this upstairs. Is there any coffee?"

"There will be in a few minutes," Tyler said. He brewed a half pot, and the machine beeped its completion as Lexi came back into the kitchen. She grabbed a mug and poured the first cup.

"You want any?"

Tyler shook his head. "Later. I've been up and at it for hours already." They walked into the living room. Lexi sprawled out on the couch, so Tyler took one of the recliners. "Did you see any cartel assholes?"

"No," Lexi said. "I know you were being careful, but I didn't think we would. Grandpa picked his condo for a reason. I guess they might have driven by and thought it would be too risky." She sipped her hot drink. "Enough about me. What happened with the cartel? You weren't exactly voluminous in your updates."

"Rollins helped me," Tyler said. "Through Sara, I met a guy who worked in counterintelligence. He had some good knowledge about how the organizations work. The three of us went down to Texas and hit a facility where they process their shipments."

"Did you take their drugs?"

"Some . . . for a little while?"

Lexi grinned. "My dad the cocaine lord."

"Nothing quite so Netflix-worthy," Tyler said with a chuckle. "We burned most of the product. Then, we came back to Maryland and raided the place where they keep the money they've laundered. I offered the powder and cash back to Héctor in exchange for certain things."

"He took the deal?" Lexi asked.

"He didn't have much choice. His bosses in Mexico would have flayed him for a week if he lost a ton of drugs and money."

"Gross, Dad." Lexi shuddered. "I guess you took out the giant, too?"

"The third time was the charm, after all," Tyler said.

"I have some news, too." Lexi sat upright and tucked her feet under her knees. "Remember I told you Mom wanted me to visit her in prison?"

Tyler bobbed his head. "I hope you did."

"I did. Uncle George showed up, as well." Tyler frowned. His former brother-in-law was involved, after all. "I was surprised. It all seemed a little too convenient."

"A lot of things were too convenient where they were concerned."

"It gets better. I talked to Grandpa about the situation with Mom. He said I should ignore her and move on. I didn't listen. I . . . took out your laptop and did a little digging."

Tyler crossed his arms. George had always been a pain in the ass. Rachel was no saint, but her brother's poisonous influence usually pushed her over the edge when it looked like she might be willing to move on. "He's a grifter, Lexi. He probably knows some dangerous people. I hope you were careful."

"I was," she said. "You should be happy I didn't take Grandpa's advice. Uncle George has a pretty long arrest record. Guess what he got popped for the last three times?"

"I don't know. The police can't charge someone with being an asshole."

"Attempted pension fraud."

It took a second for the words to sink in. When they did, Tyler pounded the arm of the chair. "Son of a bitch. I figured your mother was bitter about it, but on some level, she understood. She did it to herself. Your uncle probably knows a few shady lawyers who whispered in his ear at the bar one night." Tyler stood and paced from the living room to the kitchen and back.

"Don't go and do something crazy," Lexi said. "I just wanted you to be aware of what I found out."

Tyler stopped walking. His daughter was a smart and tenacious young woman. He didn't know how much he'd contributed to either over the years—she would probably put the estimate higher than he would. Tyler smiled. "I know. You did a great job, Lexi. Thanks for looking out for me."

"What are you going to do?"

"I'm going to wait until the bars close tonight," Tyler said. "Then, your uncle George and I are going to have a conversation, and I don't think he'll like it."

GEORGE HAD ALWAYS BEEN A DRINKER. At one point in his younger days, Tyler admired the man's tolerance for alcohol. He never quite got to falling-down drunk, but George's questionable ethics and judgment grew even more compromised with a few beers in his belly. He needed income in part to pay his bar tab. Tyler learned his address from Lexi and drove there in the Accord coupe—the least conspicuous car he had access to—at about ten-thirty. George's driveway sat empty.

Tyler checked the surroundings. The street was quiet. No one milled about. Lights on poles provided some illumination, but it didn't reach much past the sidewalk. Tyler closed the Honda's door quietly and walked up to George's front door. He didn't see any people, but he wanted to maintain the illusion for a potential nosy neighbor. Of course, no answer came. George's small porch featured a low wall painted the same color as the home's exterior. Tyler crawled to the far end, lifted himself over, and dropped onto the grass.

He stayed low and moved to the rear of the house. Darkness was his ally here, and his black clothes and gloves would allow him to fit right in. Three steps took him to the back door, and Tyler popped it in short order with the snap gun. No alarm went off as he opened it and crept inside. George's kitchen was a mess.

Dishes filled the sink, and empty beer bottles lined the counter near the trash can. Tyler moved into the living room.

A shopworn couch sat against the wall under a large window. Two matching recliners provided seating on the opposite side. Tyler nosed around in cabinets and a freestanding buffet in the dining room, eventually finding a .357 Magnum revolver hiding there. He figured there was zero chance George owned it legally —a suspicion he confirmed when he saw the serial number ground away. Removing the cartridges only took a second. Tyler slipped them into his pocket and replaced the gun. There was no other ammo stored with it.

Then, he sat in a recliner and waited. He was good at waiting. The army provided plenty of practice to "hurry up—and wait" over the years. Younger soldiers rarely learned the value of patience without some form of hardship. Tyler watched occasional headlights approach, but they all veered away before reaching the house. Finally, just after midnight, George returned. His beams lit up the front window as he pulled into the driveway. The engine cut out a moment later, and a key soon turned in the lock.

The front door swung open. George's head was down to look at his keys, but Tyler recognized him. Other than gaining about ten pounds and adding some gray hair, he hadn't changed. George turned to close and lock his front door. When he came back around, he froze as his eyes landed on Tyler. "Hello, George."

"For Christ's sake," he said as he slowly moved toward the window and snapped on a lamp. "What the hell are you doing in my house?"

"I thought we should have a conversation," Tyler said, "in light of recent events."

George stuffed his keys in his pocket and crossed his arms. "Tell me why I shouldn't call the cops."

"No one with your record will. Besides, how many drinks did

you have before you drove home? I'm almost surprised you left so soon after last call."

"Screw you, John." George sank onto the couch. "What do you want?"

"It's what you want . . . you and Rachel, though I think you're the one who came up with the idea."

He scoffed. "Lexi told you. She's young. She don't know better yet."

"She's smart," Tyler said. "Smarter than you and probably me, too. I believe her, especially considering your history."

"Here we go." George jabbed a finger in Tyler's direction. "You always thought you were better than me."

"I always have been." George scowled, but Tyler continued. "I knew you never liked me. At first, I thought it was because you felt a guy in the army wasn't good enough for your sister. It took a while, but I figured out I was wrong. You were worried I'd catch on to you and Rachel and your schemes."

"Well, you didn't." George smiled and spread his arms behind him on the sofa. "You didn't. You never knew."

"I know now," Tyler said. "You're after my pension."

"Half of it should be Rachel's!"

"If she weren't a criminal, it would've been. I'm sure you want a piece of it. Blame yourself, George. You led her down the path. But I'll be damned if I let you take something which will be Lexi's one day."

"Maybe we'll still come for your money," George said.

Tyler reached into the interior pocket of his jacket. George recoiled on the couch. "Relax. If I wanted to kill you, I wouldn't use something as noisy as a gun in a residential neighborhood." He tossed three stacks of bills onto the coffee table.

George's eyes narrowed. "What's this?"

"Thirty thousand dollars," Tyler said. "It's yours, but it comes with a heavy string attached."

"What?"

"You get out of here and leave everyone alone. Me, Lexi, the pension, everything. Including Rachel. She deserves a chance to live a real life when she gets out . You've always been the devil on her shoulder. Now, take this money and go to hell."

The cash remained on the table. "You're offering me a bribe? Where's your moral superiority, now?"

"Call it what you want," Tyler said. "If you take it, you go. Start over somewhere else. Run some new scams on a fresh set of rubes." Tyler shrugged. "I really don't give a shit. I just want you out of here."

"And if I don't take it?"

"I'll bury you so deep a bloodhound would piss on your grave before he ever howls over it."

George swallowed hard. He couldn't meet Tyler's stare. "Not much of a choice, is it?"

"You're not negotiating from a position of strength here, George."

"Here you go again. You think you're better than me. You think you can break into my house, flash some cash, and get your way."

"I came here and gave you a choice," Tyler said. "I don't care which option you pick."

George stood. "I shoulda done this a long time ago." He walked into the dining room. Tyler searched the first floor thoroughly when he arrived. The only gun George would find currently held no bullets. Still, he turned to follow the other man's movements and shifted his feet to leap to the ready if need be. Sure enough, George flicked on a light and pulled the revolver out of a drawer in the buffet.

It was a classic Colt model. Brown grip. Black barrel and cylinders. It was also empty, and George pointed it at Tyler like he thought it held six rounds. "You can't come into a man's house and make demands. You can't just buy me off."

"Everyone has a price, George. Why don't you put the gun down?"

"Now who's not negotiating from a position of strength?" George said. He ran his left hand through his graying hair. "There's thirty thousand on the table. You tried to rob me, and I stopped you."

"With a stolen gun you can't legally own as a convicted felon? I thought you were supposed to be good at scheming."

"Shut up!" George jabbed the gun in Tyler's direction. "Just shut up. I'm tired of you. Rachel and I had a good thing going until you came along." He pulled the hammer back even though it was a double-action revolver. The sound filled the house. "I'll let Lexi collect at least a little of your pension before I come after it."

George pulled the trigger. Steel on steel simply gave a disappointing click.

He did it again and got the same result. Tyler stood. "I found the gun before you got here." He patted the left pocket of his jeans. "If you want the cartridges back, come and get them." George stared ahead silently. "The weight of the gun should've tipped you off." Tyler moved closer to George and snatched the Colt from his hand. He took a deep breath to calm himself and drive down the temptation to reload it and shoot George on the spot. "Same offer as before, George. You take the thirty grand and agree to leave Maryland. Now, there's some immediacy attached."

"What do you mean?"

Tyler gripped the barrel of the Colt and shook the weapon. "If you say no, I'll beat you to death in your own dining room."

"But you'll—"

"Please. With as many crooks and ex-cons as you know, the cops will have a Rolodex of people to sift through before they ever get to me. Besides, do you think anyone saw me come here tonight?"

"Fine," George said through clenched teeth. "I'll take your damn blood money."

"Good decision." Tyler tossed the gun into the far corner of the room. "Remember—I'll be checking on you in thirty days." He walked toward the front door.

"What about my bullets?" George asked.

"You have thirty thousand dollars," Tyler said. "Buy more."

41

Tyler was drinking his second cup of coffee the next morning when his phone rang. The display showed a Maryland number he didn't recognize, but he answered it anyway. "This is Deputy Parker from Harford County," a semi-familiar voice said.

"Good morning, Deputy. What can I do for you?"

"I remember you came to me about Alice Simard. We've been investigating. Looks like a lot of the people we wanted to arrest are dead. Do you know what happened to Rodolfo and Héctor Espinoza?"

"I have no idea," Tyler said.

"Someone killed them," Parker said. "Looks like a bomb went off in the basement, plus the usual gunfire. A lot of dead men in the house."

"I don't mean to sound insensitive, but Héctor was a drug dealer. It's a fairly hazardous line of work from what I hear."

"It is." Parker paused. "We also uncovered some other evidence, and we've arrested a man named Todd Windholm."

"Don't know him," Tyler said.

"Of course you don't. Look, you brought this to my attention, and I recall you telling me you're resourceful."

Tyler took a large sip of coffee. "Where are you going with this, Deputy?"

"Do you have an alibi for two nights ago?" Parker asked.

"Sure," Tyler said. "I was home. My daughter can confirm. She stays up later than I do."

Sounds of a pen scratching over paper came through the connection. "All right. Good to know. I think I have everything I needed. Enjoy your day, Mister Tyler."

Tyler hung up. Someone was bound to discover the Espinoza house eventually. Probably Windholm or a service provider like a maid. The latter seemed more likely. Héctor treated Windholm like a lackey rather than a partner. He wouldn't give the man a key to his house. With the money man arrested, the cartel's presence in Maryland was officially over. Considering the distance from Mexico, the trouble they went through with Héctor, and the constant battles back home, Tyler didn't think they'd try again.

He chalked it up as a win for everyone.

TYLER MET Sara at her house after her day at work. They planned to go to dinner at Clyde's, but a happy reunion kiss turned into quite a bit more. Sara ordered Chinese for delivery and then pounced on Tyler for another round. They both ignored the doorbell when it rang. Later, Sara threw on a T-shirt, and Tyler walked downstairs in his shirt and boxers. He collected the bag from outside, and after a quick reheat, they ate dinner at Sara's table.

"You haven't talked much about the cartel," she said after finishing her soup.

"I figured you didn't need too many tales of me being a knight-errant." Tyler unwrapped a bag of egg rolls and plopped one on each of their plates. "Thanks for sending Aguilar my way. We couldn't have done it without him."

"I guess you got your revenge, then."

"Someone had to." Tyler shrugged. "The state and the world are better off for Héctor and his men being dead. I have no regrets."

"I wouldn't expect you to." Sara ripped open a packet of sauce and added it to her small plate. She picked up her egg roll, put it back down, and sighed. "I like you, Tyler. We're both old enough not to play games. I appreciate the code you live by, but I wish you wouldn't put yourself in danger for people you barely know." She held up a hand when he started to talk. "Yes, I realize you did the same for me, and I'll obviously be grateful forever. But I'm forty-six. I need some stability."

Tyler bobbed his head. He understood. He needed the same thing. Sara was a dependable professional woman. By contrast, he was an out-of-work mechanic who recently flew to Texas to kill members of a drug cartel. "I'm working on it. Smitty's shop was a casualty of Héctor's war. We're hoping his insurance comes through and lets him rebuild."

"What if it doesn't?"

"I have an idea if the worst happens," Tyler said.

"I've thought a lot about this." Sara finally took a bite of her egg roll.

While she chewed, Tyler upended the rice container to put a pile on his plate. "If you want to break things off, I get it. I'm not exactly the picture of stability right now." He added several chunks of sesame chicken to it. The sweet and tangy smell of the sauce filled his nostrils. "Hell, I might never be."

Sara smiled. "Would I have spent the last two and a half hours ravaging you if I wanted to kick you to the curb?"

"It'd be a damn fine send-off," Tyler offered.

"It would," she said. "I admit I thought about it around the beginning of this whole mess. Especially when you asked me to find you someone to help. It was like you were crossing a line from personal to professional, and I didn't know how to handle it. I probably still don't. It's good to have some separation." She spread her hands. "In the end, I realized you did something good in your own way. It's who you are . . . and I'm the last person who shouldn't appreciate how you do things."

"As my daughter might say . . . those are certainly some words."

"Go to hell," Sara said with a small laugh. "I appreciate you for who you are, Tyler. Even if you're not the most stable person in the world. I know you're dependable even if it's not the same way everyone else is."

Tyler winked. "You're lucky to have so unique a boyfriend."

"You're pretty lucky, too, you know."

"I do," he said. "I'm glad you'll be keeping me around."

Sara helped herself to some rice and beef with broccoli. "Just don't go flying off to Texas again anytime soon."

"Deal," Tyler said.

TYLER TOOK some Chinese food home for Lexi. She filled her plate with all the leftovers and ate at the table before disappearing upstairs to do homework. A short while later, someone knocked on the door. Tyler didn't expect anyone, so he carried his MII with him. A look through the peephole showed Smitty standing on the stoop with a paper bag in his hands. Tyler stuffed the Sig into his waistband and opened up.

"Expecting someone else?" Smitty said, glancing at the gun.

"Considering who I've tangled with recently, you never know."

Smitty walked into the kitchen, put the bag into the fridge, and took two longnecks from it. "Want a beer?"

"Sure."

"Got time to chat?"

"You see anyone else beating down my door?" Tyler asked.

Smitty jutted his chin toward the back of the house. "It's a nice evening. Got a place to sit outside?"

A moment later, they sat in outdoor chairs on Tyler's patio. Like most people in Baltimore, his house didn't feature a big yard. The vagaries of property lines meant it was fairly deep but not wide. The patio, grill, and furnishings took up about a fifth of it. Smitty enjoyed a long pull of his beer. "Did I tell you I dialed back my insurance a while ago?"

"Yeah." Tyler dreaded where the conversation was going.

"They're screwing me," Smitty said. "Bastards. Something about accidental fires being covered but not arson."

"Sounds like bullshit to me," Tyler said.

"Of course it is." Smitty snorted. "Oh, well. It was just a shop."

Tyler shook his head. "No. It was *your* shop. It was *your* dream, and I was happy to get to share in it."

"I won't be needing your money," Smitty said. "Look in the bag. Most of it's back in there."

"Most of it?"

"You've seen my house." Smitty smirked. "It could stand a few updates."

"I've been thinking." Tyler drank some beer and swirled it around in the glass.

"No good can come from it," Smitty said.

"You're probably right. What if I take the money in the bag and open my own shop?"

"Good for you, then."

"Let me finish," Tyler said. "I was thinking of opening my own place and asking you to run it."

Smitty frowned. "Me?"

"Sure. You're much better at dealing with people than I am." Tyler clinked Smitty's beer bottle. "And you're a half-decent mechanic to boot."

"Where would this shop be?"

"Hell, I don't know," Tyler said. "I just started thinking about it. I was in the army . . . it takes us a while to figure things out."

"All right," Smitty said. He drained the rest of his lager. "You let me know when you've got a line on something. I still own the place on Belair Road. Moving some of the equipment might suck, but I'd be happy to provide it."

Tyler nodded. "Thanks. I'll keep you in the loop."

Smitty left a few minutes later, right after Lexi rejoined Tyler on the first floor. "Your boss seems happy all things considered," she said once he drove away.

"He's not my boss anymore. I might end up being his."

"What's going on, Dad?"

Tyler explained his nascent plan to look for a place to open a classic car repair shop. Between the cash in his fridge and money he'd squirreled away, he should be able to find a decent building. He had no idea how long the process would take. Buying this house several years ago proved to be enough of a chore. He suspected opening a business would be even worse. "I like the idea of being my own boss," he said. "Working for Smitty was good, but at the end of the day, I've spent a long time taking orders from people. I don't need to do it anymore."

"Good thinking." She smiled. "I'm proud of you."

"You're stealing my lines."

"Can I have a job over the summer?" Lexi asked.

"Maybe," Tyler said. "I'll put in a good word with the manager."

END of Novel #2

HI THERE,

I hope you enjoyed *White Lines*. This isn't the end of Tyler's adventures, though. What's supposed to be a favor to a friend leads to our hero taking on a band of international traffickers in *Lost Highway*. You can order it now at https://books2read.com/losthighway.

THE END

AFTERWORD

Thanks for checking out this novel! I hope you enjoyed reading the book as much as I enjoyed writing it.

I write mysteries and thrillers with snark and flawed heroes. If this sounds like something you like, you can check out my catalog below.

The John Tyler Thrillers

1. The Mechanic
2. White Lines
3. Lost Highway (October 2021)

The C.T. Ferguson Crime Novels:

1. The Reluctant Detective
2. The Unknown Devil
3. The Workers of Iniquity
4. Already Guilty
5. Daughters and Sons

6. A March from Innocence
7. Inside Cut
8. The Next Girl
9. In the Blood
10. Right as Rain
11. Dead Cat Bounce (December 2021)

While these are the suggested reading sequences, each novel is a standalone thriller or mystery, and the books can be enjoyed in whatever order you happen upon them.

Connect with me:

For the many ways of finding and reaching me online, please visit https://tomfowlerwrites.com/contact. I'm always happy to talk to readers.

This is a work of fiction. Characters and places are either fictitious or used in a fictitious manner.

"Self-publishing" is something of a misnomer. This book would not have been possible without the contributions of many people.

- The great cover design team at 100 Covers.
- My editor extraordinaire, Chase Nottingham.
- My wonderful advance reader team, the Fell Street Irregulars.